ELIZA NEVIUS

The Jaded Knight

Book One in the Lux Bellator Series

To the ones who never fit the mold—
You were never too much. You were always magic.

Contents

1

Survivor: Indiana Edition

"Oh my God, slow down!" I holler, gripping the "oh shit" handle above my door like it's a lifeline. Every time Kat gets behind the wheel, I'm convinced we'll end up in the fetal position in a ditch. Why I continue to get in the car with her is a mystery on par with Bigfoot. You'd think we were fleeing a pack of man-eating squirrels the way she sprays the speedometer with dopamine, but nope—just off to torture our glutes at the gym.

With Kat behind the wheel, it feels like a two-hour special of Survivor: Indiana Edition. We're part of Lux Bellator, the world's premier squad of supernatural monster-bashers. While the human population knows us supes exist, we try to keep the supernatural exposure to a minimum.

The old square's shops and cafes blur past like a bad Instagram filter. Every brick and rusty awning screams "ho-hum," doing nothing to calm my frayed nerves as Kat drifts into a turn hard enough to grind our teeth into paste.

"We're gonna be late if we don't hurry," Kat growls, eyes fixed on the road, a predatory glint promising a rear-end demolition derby if we don't hustle. I can sense her excitement, the predator within her yearning for the challenge that awaits us at the gym.

"Better late than dead," I mutter, closing my eyes and focusing on steadying my breathing. I can feel the magic thrumming beneath my skin, responding to my heightened emotions. With a deep exhale, I open my eyes and watch as small sparks dance across my fingertips.

"You need to relax, Sadie," Kat says. "I know you're worried about where we'll be assigned, but we'll just have to make the best of it."

I need to relax? Am I the one who just took a turn on two wheels? I didn't even know that was possible outside of Hollywood.

"Me, relaxed?" I snort. "Compared to you, I'm a Zen Buddha on Xanax. And it's not just the assignment. It's—"

Before I can finish, Kat slams the brakes so hard I briefly float out of my seat. My seat belt chews into my ribs.

"What the actual hell?" I gasp, my heart auditioning for a horror-flick soundtrack.

"The idiot in front of us slammed on their breaks. Hey asshole," she yells, rolling down her window.

"Kat, there's a red light. We stop at those" I say, cutting her off before she can square up for yet another brawl this week.

Kat grumbles under her breath, her fingers drumming impatiently on the steering wheel. I can almost feel the energy radiating off her, the lion within itching to break free. Sometimes I wonder if her reckless driving is just another outlet for her wild nature.

As we wait for the light to change, I notice something odd across the street. A robbed figure stands motionless on the corner, their face obscured in shadow. Despite the warm spring temperature, they're wrapped in a long, dark cloak. A chill runs down my spine as I sense a faint pulse of otherworldly energy.

Before I can think too much about it, the light flips green, and we jerk forward so fast my skull bangs the headrest. When I finally swivel around, the figure's gone. "Kat, did you see that person on the corner?" I ask, twisting in my seat to look back.

"What person?" Kat replies, her eyes darting to the rearview mirror. "I didn't see anyone." I frown, stomach doing that uneasy-guts thing. "Never mind," I mutter. "Probably just my imagination."

As we screech into the parking lot of an abandoned warehouse on the outskirts of town, I breathe a sigh of relief. The gym may look like a dilapidated mess from the outside, but inside...it's still a piece of shit. There are a couple of half-functioning weight benches that rattle like an old tin can, a padded floor that's seen more fistfights than a biker bar, and a handful of training dummies we slice into for target practice. No sauna, no smoothie bar, hell, sometimes the lights flicker off mid-sparring—but hey, it's all part of the experience.

The Lux Bellator operates much like human law enforcement, tracking down leads, solving paranormal crimes, fighting the bad guys. Think cops—but instead of busting speeders, we chase vampires, poltergeists, and whatever else slipped through the cosmic cracks. If you're dumb enough to sign up at 15, you slog through six years of bullshit drills and awkward torque therapy until you're 21 and can finally get your own badge and maybe a decent dental plan.

Since we were teens, Kat and I have been joined at the hip, our days filled with rigorous training and preparation. But now, as we both turn 21, we stand on the cusp of a new chapter in our lives: becoming official agents.

Kat's a lion shifter, extremely vicious when her claws are out. In her human form, she's a 5 foot 3 inch bundle of sass. Her layered honey blonde hair frames a perfectly heart-shaped face and deep blue eyes that has tempted probably every male in this town.

As for me, I'm a witch. I'm told I'm one of the most powerful witches of my time by my mentor Michael, a half angel known as a Nephilim. He's served the Lux Bellator since he was young, here in the Midwest. I was taken under his wing early on when he saw my potential with magic at a young age.

Most witches can do potions (I can't), and maybe a few parlor tricks, but not me. I can conjure items out of thin air, create memory orbs, manipulate certain forces, I can even move objects with my magic which is how Michael was able to discover me.

It was an unfortunate experience, embarrassing really. I was with my parents at the local grocery store when a tantrum overtook me. I wanted sweets, my parents said no and that turned into an accidental magical outburst. Every piece of candy in the store suddenly flew off the shelves and pelted the other shoppers. People screamed and some cried, it was all very dramatic.

Michael happened to be there and quickly contained the situation, erasing memories and cleaning up the mess with my mom (also a witch, but let's be real, she's more "skim-latte dabbling" than "arcane badass"). From that day on, he took me under his wing, teaching me to control and harness my powers.

He is tough as nails, but he has a good heart. I couldn't ask for a better mentor.

We rush inside, our senses immediately assaulted by the familiar scent of sweat and magic that permeates the air. The heavy steel doors creak and groan as we push through, the cold metal sending shivers down our spines.

Michael is already waiting for us, his arms crossed and a stern expression on his face. His wings, usually hidden, are partially visible, shimmering with an otherworldly light. Not all Nephilim have wings, most don't in fact. But the more angel blood in them, the more angelic features they have.

"You're late," he says, his deep voice echoing in the cavernous space.

"Sorry, Michael," I start to explain, but he holds up a hand, silencing me.

"No excuses. Time is of the essence today." His eyes, a striking silver, scan over us both. "The Council has made their decision regarding your assignments."

My heart kicks into overdrive, and I can feel Kat stiffen beside me. This is the moment we've been anticipating, training for, our entire lives. Michael's expression softens just a tad. "You've both demonstrated exceptional skill and dedication. The Council has decided to keep you together as a team."

Relief washes over me, and I hear Kat let out a triumphant sigh, like someone finally undoing a too-tight bra at the end of a long day. "But," he continues, "you're being assigned to a new region, at least for now. New York City will be your new home for the foreseeable future."

My heart plummets like a lead balloon. I have a sneaking suspicion I know exactly whose team we'll be shadowing— Nathan Blackwood's team. He's a few years older than me and notorious in the Lux community for his accomplishments. He leads a team of four: a fae, a vampire, and a shifter (though I can't recall what kind). Rumor has it the shifter has an attitude that makes you want to slap the smirk right off her face. As for Nathan, he's another Nephilim, strong and nimble. Also, insufferably arrogant, like the kind of guy who'd flex in the mirror and wink at himself.

"You'll be working with Nathan Blackwood's team," Michael confirms my fears, his silver eyes studying my reaction. "I know you have your... reservations about them, Sadie, but this is an opportunity to learn from some of the best in the field."

I bite back a groan, forcing a neutral expression onto my face. Kat, ever the optimist, bumps her shoulder against mine. "Hey, at least we'll be in the Big Apple. Think of all the trouble we can get into there!"

Michael raises an eyebrow at her enthusiasm. "This isn't a vacation, Katerina. New York City is a hotbed of supernatural activity. You'll need to be on your guard at all times."

"When do we leave?" I ask, trying to keep the dread from my voice.

"Friday morning," Michael replies. "You have the next couple of days to pack and say your goodbyes. I nod, my mind already racing with all the preparations we'll need to make. Leaving Indiana, the only home we've ever known, is daunting enough. But the thought of working with Nathan's team makes my stomach churn.

"Now," Michael says, clapping his hands together, "let's make the most of our last training session together. I want to see you both push yourselves to your limits."

For the next two hours, we train relentlessly. Kat shifts

between her human and lion forms, her movements becoming more fluid and powerful with each transition. I focus on honing my magical abilities, conjuring shields, casting illusions, and manipulating the elements around me.

By the time we finish, we're both drenched in sweat and gasping for breath. Michael looks on with a mixture of pride and sadness in his eyes. "You've both come so far, I could not be prouder."

Kat, never one for sappy moments, "We need to celebrate and give this town a proper goodbye. Let's party tonight!"

Michael sighs, but I catch a hint of amusement in his eyes. "Just remember, you're representing the Lux Bellator now. Try not to cause too much chaos before you leave."

As we turn to head out, Michael calls out, "Oh, and Sadie?" I pause, looking back at him. "Don't let your preconceptions about Nathan cloud your judgment. He may surprise you."

I force a smile and nod, but inwardly, I'm skeptical.

2

Witch, Interrupted

I stand in front of my mirror, my mind a cocktail of thoughts and emotions, shaken but not stirred. Today is the beginning of a new chapter in my life—like when you finally decide to switch from box wine to the good stuff. I take a moment to scrutinize my reflection, noting every detail with the precision of a detective in a noir film. At 5'8", I've always been tall and slender, but confidence in my appearance? About as elusive as a low-calorie chocolate cake. Yet today, I find myself appreciating the unique quirks that make me, well, me. My hazel eyes, sometimes flecked with green or brown, are like a kaleidoscope of confusion that never fails to captivate me. They're my favorite feature, giving me a sense of depth and mystery—like the mysterious allure of a locked minibar in a hotel room.

My skin, tanned from long days spent under the warm summer sun, has a golden glow to it that makes me feel alive.

And then there's my hair—we have a love-hate relationship akin to that of a rom-com couple. Its medium brown hue seems to change with the lighting, sometimes casting hints of red throughout its waves that fall gracefully down my back. Despite our tumultuous affair, I can't help but admire its natural beauty.

Well - okay so, it isn't exactly natural, per se. It's more uh—alright, here's the story. I was messing around with an old witch's grimoire that I "found" when I came across this spell entitled alluring locks. Naturally, I was intrigued because my brown locks were about as alluring as a wet mop. Flat and boring.

I went online, the Magic Google if you will, to dig up information on this spell before doing something I'd regret. The consensus was mixed about whether these spells should be used. Apparently, a couple of decades ago, some witches tribunal decided that "glam" spells were as unethical as pineapple on pizza.

I pondered it deeply, weighing the implications, and examining my ethics before I ruled that it was, in fact, not against my personal code of conduct. So, I did the spell. I have not been disappointed with the results—nor with my decision.

Needing a distraction from my disarray of thoughts, I glance around the room looking for something to do.

My eyes land on my spell book. No time like the present to get some practice in.

As I flicked my wrist, a cascade of books levitated off the shelf, dancing in mid-air like leaves caught in an autumn breeze. "I'm starting to think you're just making me do your bidding for entertainment," I mused aloud, watching as Orion, that sneaky furball of mine, perched atop my floating pillow, his green eyes following every move with feline amusement.

"Meow," he replied, which I took to mean, "Obviously."

"Lazy cat," I chided, but the grin on my face betrayed my

mock annoyance. Books orbited around us in a literary solar system; I was the sun, and they were my planets. Sometimes I imagined myself a conductor, each flick and flourish of my fingers summoning a symphony of objects. It was a quirky way to practice telekinesis, sure, but if you can't have fun with magic, what's the point?

"Alright, Orion, time for your grand entrance." With a gentle push of my power, the pillow began to rise higher, elevating His Majesty to new heights. "Don't get airsick now."

Orion retorts with a sneeze, clinging to his makeshift magic carpet. I took it as his stoic acceptance of the challenge.

"Such bravery," I teased. "You know, some cats chase mice, climb trees, maybe cough up the occasional hairball. But you? You fly on pillows and judge my book-sorting skills."

A soft purr came the dry response, which I interpreted as, "Keep the compliments coming."

"Ah, the life of a witch's familiar," I sighed dramatically, twirling in place as the books lined themselves back onto the shelf in perfect alphabetical order. "You could be out there, living wild, but instead, you choose domestic flight."

Giving him a conspiratorial wink. "Who needs the great outdoors when you've got a room that defies gravity?"

He agreed with another soft purr, or at least that's what I decided he meant. It was either that or a request for more treats.

"Your wish is my command," I said, snapping my fingers. A small bag of gourmet cat treats sailed through the air, landing neatly beside him on the pillow. "But don't think for a second that this means you're getting a raise in your allowance."

Orion nudged the bag open with his paw and looked at me with those eyes that said, "We'll negotiate terms later."

"Fine, fine," I laughed, plucking a treat from the bag and tossing it into the air where he skillfully caught it between his teeth. "For a nonchalant kitty, you sure do drive a hard bargain."

He purred contentedly, settling down to enjoy his spoils.

"Alright, back to work," I said, rolling up my sleeves before remembering they were already rolled—habit, I guess. "These spells aren't going to cast themselves, and we both know potion-making is off the table after last week's... incident."

With a hiss he reminds me, and I groan.

"Never let a witch live down her potion blunders, huh? You're lucky you're cute."

Orion stretched out on the levitating pillow as I reached for my grimoire, ready to tackle the next enchantment with my trusty sidekick by my side—or rather, above me.

As I work through my spell, my mind drifts back to the one and only time I met Nathaniel Blackwood. I was sixteen at the time, he was nineteen. We were at a Lux Bellator training retreat for future agents. Everyone wanted to meet him, he was already making a name for himself as a badass. I couldn't show off my witchy skills, Michael to this day wants me to conceal just how powerful I am, afraid that the wrong person will use that to their advantage.

Anyway, since I didn't stand out much, I wasn't good enough to talk to Nathan. I think our eyes met a few times, disdain dripping from his cold glare.

Suddenly the memory solidifies. My first meeting with Nathan, if you could call it that.

Five Years Earlier

The training retreat unfolded in a secluded mountain lodge, nestled amidst towering, ancient trees, their leaves a vibrant tapestry of green, and embraced by the crisp, invigorating mountain air that seemed to purify the soul with every breath. I remember feeling like an outsider among the other young Lux Bellator trainees, many of whom effortlessly displayed awe-inspiring supernatural abilities, their talents shimmering like stars in the night sky. I had to restrain myself; Micheal, with his penchant for the dramatic, believed my power was a volatile force, one errant spell away from obliterating a generation of Lux recruits.

Out on a creaky wooden bench that felt like it belonged in a haunted pension, I sat alone, fingertips grazing the weathered planks while I practised tiny, innocuous charms. Nothing fancy—just enough sparkles and puffs of smoke to keep my secret intact. A cluster of trainees swaggered past, their laughter ricocheting off the lodge walls like drunken elves in a tavern. At their center stood Nathan Blackwood— nineteen, impossibly photogenic, and radiating power like a neon billboard in Times Square. His chiseled jaw could've sliced cheese, and his gaze apparently had its own gravitational pull. The girls practically tripped over each other trying to catch his eye; a few of the guys even sniffed the air for his cologne.

I was so smitten I nearly choked on a gust of pine-scented wind. Here I was, a reluctant "little witch," desperately trying not to hyperventilate in full view of Mount Olympus in jeans. Of course he didn't know I existed—why would the top-tier hottie care about someone who practiced stealth spells like they were minor party tricks?

Then, like a spotlight striking at dusk, I felt it: his gaze drilling into me. I looked up to find those piercing blue eyes fixed on my bench-session. Hope flared. Maybe he'd finally noticed my stellar magical résumé? Instead, he arched a brow, lips curling into a smug smirk. "Careful with those parlor tricks, little witch," he drawled, voice thick with condescension—and maybe a hint of amusement. "Wouldn't wanna strain yourself."

I had this glorious urge to unleash my full power: turn his hair into a flock of angry sparrows, or at least singe off that too-perfect mane. But Michael's voice echoed in my head: "Restraint, dear fledgling. Don't nuke the newbies." So I settled for shooting him my most venomous glare—and a very classy middle finger—before returning to my modest spellwork, trying to pretend he was yesterday's stale doughnut.

His laugh bounced around the clearing, low and reckless, like a man who knew exactly what effect he had on people. My cheeks turned a sexy shade of beetroot reed. It was the kind of laugh you'd expect when the universe is in on a joke—just not one I was invited to.

That was our one and only exchange. Yet from that moment on, Nathan Blackwood's shadow draped itself over every lofty goal I dared to set. And I knew, with a deliciously wicked certainty, that our paths would cross again.

As the memory fades, I find myself back in my room, surrounded by floating books and a slightly concerned-looking Orion. I realize I've been gripping my grimoire so tightly my knuckles have turned white.

Orion watches me closely, his tail twitching with curiosity, clearly, he wants to know where my head went.

"Just remembering why I can't stand Nathan Blackwood," I mutter, setting the grimoire down with a sigh. "And now we have to work with him. Great."

I flop onto my bed, causing a few nearby objects to wobble in the air. Orion gracefully leaps from his pillow perch to land beside me, nuzzling my hand in a rare show of comfort.

"Thanks, buddy," I scratch behind his ears. "At least I'll have you and Kat with me in New York."

I spent the rest of the evening bouncing a ball of light between my hands, the luminescent sphere casting shadows that danced around my room like spirits at a séance. Orion, sprawled on the windowsill, watched with an air of feline indifference.

"Come on, whiskered wonder," I teased, flicking the ball of light in his direction. "No cat-like reflexes to show off?" The ball bounced off his nose, and he responded with a lazy swat, nearly toppling a vase in the process.

"Careful!" I scolded, catching the vase mid-fall with a flick of my wrist. "That's a genuine fake antique."

Orion yawned, clearly unimpressed by my telekinesis or my taste in décor.

As I continued to practice, my phone buzzed with a text from Kat. "Hey witch bitch, you ready to paint the town red tonight? Or should I say, paint it with magic?"

I chuckled, typing back, "As long as you promise not to literally paint anything. Remember the mural incident?"

"That was ONE time," came the swift reply. "Besides, I'm sure they've almost finished scrubbing the lion paw prints off City Hall by now."

Rolling my eyes, I sent back, "Meet you at Moonbeam's in an hour. Try not to maul anyone on the way."

Orion gives a pained meow, along with a look that clearly said, "You're really leaving me for her?"

"Oh, don't be jealous," I cooed, scratching behind his ears. "You know you're my number one familiar."

The bitterness of that encounter with Nathan still lingers in my mind, mingling with the anxiety of our impending move to New York.

Orion interrupts my brooding with a swipe of his paw to my cheek. Such a doll.

"You're right," I sigh, interpreting his aggression as a reminder to focus on the present. "No use dwelling on the past. We've got packing to do."

I wave my hand, and the books settle back onto their shelves. Orion stretches lazily on his side, then fixes me with his knowing green eyes.

"Don't give me that look," I tell him, hands on my hips. "I know what you're thinking. 'Sadie, you're not that awkward sixteen year old anymore. You're a powerful witch now.' And you're right, as usual."

I start pacing the room, my thoughts racing. "But it's not just about Nathan. It's everything. Leaving home, starting a new life in New York City, working with a team we barely know. It's a lot to take in."

Orion watches me with his usual air of feline superiority, occasionally flicking his tail as if to punctuate my rambling.

"And what if I mess up? What if I can't control my powers and blow our cover? What if-"

My spiral of anxiety is interrupted by a loud knock at the door, followed by mom's voice. "Sadie! Are you talking to your cat again? Come on, we're going to be late for your going away dinner!"

I take a deep breath, centering myself. "Coming!" I call back effectively putting an end to Orion's and my conversation.

3

One Last Brew-Ha-Ha

I roll into Moonbeam before Kat, snagging a corner booth so far from the other three patrons it might as well be its own zip code. The Moonbeam's our favorite dive—equal-opportunity watering hole for humans and everything that bites, claws or sprouts wings. To a tourist it's just stale stools and warped floorboards, but if you know your glamours from your grimoires you can spot the shimmering wards at the door—and maybe the bartender's fae-ears if he's in a generous mood.

I flop into the cracked leather seat and trail my fingertips over the carved runes etched into the table. They pulse under my touch, like they've clocked my magical aura and are giving me a little nod of recognition. The air smells like skunky beer, half a pack of cigarettes, and something floral—probably fairy dust leftover from yesterday's improbable bender.

"Look who finally decided to adult," drawls Corey, sashaying up with that infuriating smirk plastered on his fae face. His glamour is off tonight, so his skin glows like a neon sign and his ears taper to points sharper than my ex's tongue.

"Don't remind me," I groan, flopping my head on the table like a keepsake hangover. "I'm still trying to process my impending transformation from small-town witch to big-city stressball."

Corey chuckles, plopping down a fizzing, radioactive-purple shot. "On the house," he says with a wink. "My farewell special. Guaranteed to be memorable." He leans in conspiratorially. "Probably more memorable than your last Tinder date."

I eye the glass like it's a suspicious ex. Corey's "special" potions are legendary for turning you into a giggling maniac—or worse, karaoke-starved. Last time I took one I spoke exclusively in interpretive dance for 48 hours.

"Thanks, Corey," I manage, sniffing the brew. It smells like lavender shampoo mixed with used engine oil. "Pretty sure this is safe."

The front door slams open, and Kat storms in, hair doing that "I may or may not have eaten live electric eels" look. Her eyes lock on me, and she practically cartwheels to the table, excitement radiating off her like cheap body spray.

"There's my favorite witch!" she hollers, flinging herself onto the bench opposite me. "Ready to get sloshed in our sad little burg one last time before we hit the big city?"

I crack a grin. "As ready as I'll ever be." I nudge the purple terror toward her. "Here—Corey's got us a 'farewell' drink. Consider yourself the guinea pig."

Kat's grin turns maniacal. "Hell yes," she cackles, hoisting the glass and downing half in a single gulp. I brace myself, half-expecting her to sprout wings or recite Proust in Elvish.

Silence. Then suddenly Kat's eyes go wide. She lets out a startled "RAWR!" that echoes off the walls like a drunken lioness.

I burst out laughing as she slaps a hand over her mouth. "Did I just… roar?" she stammers, her voice oddly feline, like someone forgot to add a filter.

"Looks like you're channeling your inner cougar," I tease, wiping tears from my eyes.

Kat narrows hers with a wicked smirk, sliding the half-full glass back to me. "Your turn, sad-sack. Let's see what it does to you."

I eyeball the neon sludge and swallow. Taste? Imagine bubblegum sex on a gasoline-slick trampoline. I don't know what that means either. For a beat, nothing happens. Then a tingle blossoms at my fingertips, racing up my arms like tiny lightning bolts.

"Uh, Sadie?" Kat peers at my hands. "You're… glowing."

Yep—my limbs are illuminating the booth like an impromptu disco ball. "Jesus … easy there, sun goddess," I grumble, willing the light to dim. No dice.

Kat erupts into purr-chuckles—like she's part cat, part hyena. "We're the world's worst agents: one meowing, the other beaming. Perfect cover."

I crack up anyway. God knows I needed to laugh before I get swallowed alive by Manhattan traffic.

"Well," I say, holding up my radiant hand, "at least we won't need flashlights on clandestine missions."

"And I can scare the bad guys with my sexy roar," Kat adds, flexing her claws and letting out another surprisingly melodic growl.

We switch to regular booze—none of Corey's experimental nightmares—and spend an hour trading war stories, tarnished glory days, and predictions for what New York's gonna do to our souls. By the end of it, my pre-move jitters are half-drowned and fading fast.

"You know," Kat says, voice dropping to a stage whisper, "I heard why they're really shipping us to New York."

I lean in. "Spill."

She glances around like she's about to talk espionage. "Someone noticed there's been a surge in freaky supernatural shit in the city. Stuff that usually lurks in the shadows is popping up like bad one-night-stands. Council's freaked, but they're playing it close to the vest."

My pulse spikes. "And they're sending us—rookies?"

Kat shrugs, lips twitching with a mix of excitement and gallows humor. "Either they think you and your purring sidekick can spot what the big shots missed, or they just want to see if we survive. Plus, new city, new bar crawls, am I right?"

A shiver runs down my spine—equal parts hype and terror. "Portals to hell? Rogue demons? This is gonna be one hell of a party."

Kat clinks her glass to mine. "Welcome to the big leagues, baby." Kat continues with a nod. "But here's the kicker - no one seems to know who or what is behind it all. It's like the whole supernatural population in New York is going haywire."

I lean back in my seat, my mind racing. "And they think we can help figure it out? Us?"

Kat shrugs, a grin spreading across her face. "Maybe they're counting on your witchy intuition and my feline instincts. Or maybe," she adds with a wink, "they just want some fresh meat to throw at the problem."

I can't help but laugh at that, though there's a nervous edge to it. "Great. So, we're either the chosen ones or the sacrificial lambs. Fantastic."

"Hey, look on the bright side," Kat says, reaching across the table to give my hand a squeeze. "Whatever's waiting for us in New York, at least it won't be boring. And who knows? Maybe you'll get to show off those fancy powers of yours without Michael breathing down your neck."

The thought is both thrilling and terrifying. I've spent so long holding back, keeping my true potential under wraps. The idea of finally letting loose is exhilarating, but also daunting. What if I can't control it? What if I mess up?

As if reading my thoughts, Kat adds softly, "You've got this, Sadie. You're not that scared little witch anymore. You're a badass, and it's about time the world saw it."

Her words bolster my confidence, and I feel a surge of determination. "You're right," I say, straightening up in my seat. "Whatever New York throws at us, we'll face it together. The city won't know what hit it."

Kat grins, raising her glass in a toast. "To new adventures, kicking supernatural ass, and showing Nathan Blackwood what real power looks like."

We spend the rest of the evening planning and speculating, our excitement growing with each passing minute. As last call approaches, we stumble to the exit of Moonbeam, arm in arm, giggling at our magical predicaments.

The cool night air hits us as we step outside, and I take a deep breath, savoring the familiar scents of our small town. "I'm going to miss this place," I admit, a sudden wave of nostalgia washing over me.

Kat squeezes my shoulder. "Me too. But think of all the adventures waiting for us in New York. The Big Apple won't know what hit it."

As we walk home, my skin still faintly glowing and Kat occasionally letting out a purr-like hiccup, I find myself excited about the challenges ahead.

4

Don't Feed the Phooka

I slid the zipper shut on my final suitcase and spun around, surveying the ghost of my old bedroom. Where vibrant posters of my favorite bands once cascaded down the pale blue walls, only faint outlines and tiny nail holes remained. The carpet—once hidden beneath a scatter of band T-shirts, journals, and stray socks—lay bare, its faded threads flattened by years of restless pacing. In that emptiness, I felt the weight of every memory I was packing away.

Perched on the windowsill, Orion regarded me with wide, amber eyes. His silver-striped fur rippled in the late-afternoon sunlight, and his tail flicked back and forth like the pendulum of a nervous clock. The window glass was streaked with dust and fingerprints—our shared vantage point of the world outside, soon to be left behind.

"I know, buddy," I murmured, kneeling to scratch between his ears. His purr rumbled through his chest, a small reassurance. "You're coming with us. No way I'd leave my familiar behind." He pressed his head into my palm, Orion vibrating, as if he understood the journey ahead.

A sharp rap sounded on the doorframe. Kat's blonde locks peeked around the edge, sunlight dancing through individual strands. "Sadie, you good? The car's all packed—roof rack's loaded, too." She stepped in, her blue eyes bright with excitement and a few strands of hair plastered to her forehead by sweat.

I swallowed, tasting the salt of unshed tears. "Just saying goodbye to the old place," I said, lifting my chin to steady my voice. My throat felt tight, the empty room echoing each word.

Kat's smile softened. She crossed the threshold and draped an arm around my shoulders. "I know it's hard. But New York's waiting—miles of skyscrapers, hidden alleys, supernatural secrets. We're going to kick some serious otherworldly butt." Her optimism was like a spark in the dim room.

Clipping Orion into his padded carrier, I hauled my suitcase and stepped onto the creaking stairwell. My parents stood at the bottom, dressed for a bright spring afternoon. The scent of fresh coffee and cinnamon rolls still hung in the air. My mother's green eyes shimmered with pride and sorrow, her dark brown hair catching the light as she drew me into a warm, lingering hug. Her perfume—jasmine and vanilla—felt like a balm against the ache in my chest. My father, sleeves rolled up from his weekend woodworking, simply pressed his calloused hand to my shoulder. In that single squeeze lay more emotion than words could ever express.

Buckling into the passenger seat, I watched our home recede in the rearview mirror: the chipped white porch rail, the swing swaying in a pale breeze, the maples lining our street still blossoms in bloom. The familiar streets of our small Indiana town blurred past—every mailbox, every cracked sidewalk tile a bittersweet punctuation.

Kat reached for the radio dial, cranked it high, and the opening chords of our favorite road-trip playlist spilled into the cab. The car smelled of old leather seats warmed by the sun, of lingering coffee, and of fresh spring air drifting through the cracked window. She belted out the lyrics with joyful abandon; I rolled my eyes but joined in, my voice faltering into the chorus. From his carrier in the backseat, Orion let out a disgruntled yowl, his protest echoing off the car's panels.

Soon we crossed the state line—the tall marker arching overhead like a silent promise. Behind us, flat fields of rippling corn and gently rolling hills gave way to clusters of homes, then denser suburbs, then the first hints of urban sprawl. The scent of exhaust intertwined with the earthy perfume of fresh-cut grass at every crossroads. Sunlight hammered down in sharp angles, casting long, shifting shadows across the asphalt.

Each mile carried me farther from the only life I'd ever known, and closer to whatever awaited us in the city beyond the horizon. My heart stuttered somewhere between fear and exhilaration, a tempest brewing in my stomach. Beside me, Kat nudged my elbow, grinning wide. "Come on, Sadie—this is our big adventure!"

I inhaled deeply, letting her excitement wash over me. Then I leaned into the next chorus, our voices entwining in imperfect harmony as the road stretched out, endless and inviting, before us.

The afternoon sun slanted in through the windshield, warming the dashboard and turning dust motes into drifting sparks. Kat's hands gripped the steering wheel, knuckles white, her dark curls brushing against her shoulders as she kept her eyes locked on the road ahead. "So, what's our game plan when we get there?" she asked, voice low and steady over the hum of the engine. "I mean, besides not strangling Nathan within the first five minutes."

I leaned back in my seat, the faux-leather cushions creaking under me, and let out a chuckle. "That's ambitious," I snorted, my words rattling against the roof of the car. I leaned forward and ran a hand through my tangled brown hair, scattering stray strands across my forehead. "I was thinking more like the first thirty seconds." My voice softened with a sigh. "Honestly? I don't know. I guess we just… try to learn as much as we can. Even if it means swallowing our pride."

Kat's lips curved into a crooked grin as she steered us around a bend. The late-spring fields beyond the guardrail blurred into rolling bands of green and gold. "And maybe showing off a little?" she teased, a mischievous light dancing in her dark eyes. "Come on, Sadie. You've been holding back for years."

I swallowed hard, fingers curling around the hem of my cotton T-shirt. Kat was right—I'd hidden the true breadth of my gift at Michael's insistence. She'd been by my side through every clandestine practice session, seen the way my power pulsed under my skin. But Michael had always warned me: don't let the world see what you can do.

I could still feel the electric hum of that warning in my veins, the way it tightened my chest. My gift was rare—a swirl of violet energy that resonated with the moon, unlike anything another witch could conjure—but Michael's fear had kept me in the dark. Maybe he thought someone would try to claim me. Or worse, that I'd lose control. Whatever his reasons, they only deepened my curiosity, stoked the quiet flame of rebellion in my heart.

Her words echoed in my head as I weighed the risks. The

thought of finally unleashing everything, of letting my power bloom like wildfire, sent a thrill racing along my spine. Yet I couldn't ignore the gnawing dread of what might happen if I overstepped—if I forced open a door I wasn't ready to face.

"I don't know, Kat," I murmured, my gaze dropping to my trembling fingers. "Michael always said—"

"Michael's in Indiana," Kat interrupted gently, her tone both compassionate and firm. She eased off the accelerator, the car slowing as the scenery shifted to rolling hills and ancient oaks. "We're on our own now, Sadie. Maybe it's time to show the world—and Nathan's team—what you're really capable of."

I bit my lip, watching a flock of birds wheel against the sky through the passenger window. Part of me ached to prove my strength, to shatter their assumptions about the "small-town witch." But another part trembled at the thought of unleashing a storm I'd held at bay for so long.

"Maybe you're right," I said at last, voice low as the trees slid past in muted greens. "But let's play it by ear, okay? We don't want to reveal our whole hand too soon."

Kat's lips quirked into a sly smile, sunlight sprinkling gold across her hair. She tapped the steering wheel twice. "Fair enough. But when you do decide to unleash that witchy wonder, I want front-row seats."

I must have nodded off somewhere between here and hell, because the next thing I know I'm staring at a beat-up gas station with two rusty pumps that look like they've never met a maintenance crew. I blinked hard, trying to kick my groggy brain back online. In the distance, I heard raised voices and the unmistakable clink of someone losing their temper.

I stumble out of the car just in time to catch Kat—five-foot-three of pure sass—flailing her arms at a dwarf who's barely to her waistline. His cheeks are turning a suspicious shade of red, and his beard is vibrating like he's got tremors.

"Look, buddy," Kat hisses, voice rising like she's headlining a MMA fight, "I just want to know if this dump's on the road to New York. Yes or no!"

The dwarf jabs a stubby finger at her sternum. "And I'm telling ye, lassie, ye humans have no business sniffing around our secret pathways! Now begone before I turn ye into a toadstool—or something even messier."

I sighed so hard I thought my lungs might empty. If Kat lost her shit and ate him—literally or metaphorically—that'd be on my tab. I stepped in, feeling the air get crackly like someone dropped a lightning bolt in a bucket of static. Definitely not your average roadside kerfuffle.

"Excuse me," I say, slipping between Kat and the dwarf. "Sorry about my friend's… affinity for overreactions. We're new around here and hopelessly lost. Mind if we start over?"

The dwarf's eyes narrow, sizing me up like a hungry dog. "Ah, a witch," he grumbles, although the growl in his voice loses some teeth. "At least you don't reek of frat-house regrets."

Kat opens her mouth—probably to unleash some scathing comeback—but I shoot her a look cold enough to freeze her spit midair.

"I'll be straight," I continue. "We're on our way to New York City—fresh recruits for Lux Bellator. Just making sure we're not barreling off a cliff."

At the words "Lux Bellator," the dwarf's bushy eyebrows shoot up so fast I half-expect them to launch into orbit. "You say Lux Bellator? Why didn't ye brandish that card sooner?"

He strokes his beard, then jerks his thumb at a dusty path

that definitely wasn't there five seconds ago. "Take that there shortcut. It'll shave hours off, and ye won't bleed your coin on human toll booths."

I stare. "A… magical shortcut?"

He winks. "Let's call it a friends-and-family discount for those who keep our world from going to hell. Now off with ye—before I sober up and change my mind!"

Back in the car, Kat's still muttering something about dwarf pheromones, but I'm buzzing with a mix of excitement and dread. We'd barely left the parking lot, and already we're elbow-deep in hidden magic roads. If this was just the teaser, I can't wait for the main event in New York.

Kat steered the rattling sedan onto the narrow dirt lane, and almost at once the world around us seemed to ripple like a heat haze. The towering oaks and birches on either side bent inward, their gnarled limbs weaving overhead into a vaulted arch so thick that no sliver of sky penetrated the gloom. Pale tendrils of mist curled around our tires, licking at the wheel wells as though eager to tug us further into the forest's depths. In the shifting shadows between trunks, I thought I glimpsed pale faces—eyes blinking in unison, lips parting in silent whispers.

"Uh, Sadie?" Kat's voice was taut as a bowstring. She kept her foot poised on the accelerator, though the world outside our windows begged us to stop. "Please tell me you're seeing this too."

"Oh, I'm seeing it," I muttered, heart hammering. My gaze flitted from one warped tree to the next as the undergrowth seemed to swallow the path behind us. "I think our dwarf guide neglected to mention a few key details about this 'shortcut.'"

From the backseat came Orion's low, rumbling growl—half warning, half plea. I reached back to stroke his bristling grey fur; his hackles rose under my fingers like steel bristles. "It's okay, buddy," I soothed him, though my own voice trembled. "We've got this."

A sudden flash of ebony tore across the road. Kat slammed on the brakes and the car fishtailed to a smoky halt, clutching at gravel as the mist curled through the wheel wells. My pulse thundered in my ears as I peered through the rain-spattered windshield.

There, bathed in the forest's ghostly half-light, stood a horse—slender, impossibly lithe, its coat a burnished black that seemed to drink in every stray beam of moonlight. Two embers of flame glowed in its eye sockets, brilliant and watchful. A phooka, a trickster spirit from old Irish tales, blocking our path.

"Holy shit," Kat breathed, knuckles whitening as she gripped the steering wheel. "Is that what I think it is?"

I swallowed, voice husky: "A phooka. Shapeshifter. Favors mischief and lost travelers." I cleared my throat. "We should probably—"

The engine cut off mid-sputter, plunging us into an eerie silence. The phooka tossed its midnight mane, and I caught the faintest arch of amusement flickering in its luminescent eyes.

"Great," Kat muttered, exhaling in frustration. "Stranded in a haunted forest with a mythical horse for a gatekeeper. This is not what I had in mind for a weekend road trip."

I drew a shuddering breath and tried to summon my training. "Okay. Lux Bellator agents," I reminded myself aloud. "This is exactly why they drilled us on first contact."

Door ajar, I climbed out into the scented gloom of damp earth and moss. Every hair on my arms prickled. The air tasted faintly of old magic, sour and sweet at once. The phooka watched, hooves silent on the leaf-carpeted ground, ears swiveling like restless sentinels.

Mustering confidence, I spoke up. "Hello. We—uh—didn't mean to intrude, sir?" My throat tightened over that last word. Please be male, I begged the forest.

Suddenly a voice, smooth as riverstone and rich with an Irish lilt, echoed inside my mind: Greetings, young witch. 'Tis been many moons since one of your kind dared these hidden groves.

I staggered back, mind reeling. Behind me, Kat's startled gasp confirmed she'd heard it too.

"We…we're sorry," I said, forcing calm into my tone. "We were told this was a shortcut to New York City. We're new Lux Bellator recruits, on our way to our first assignment."

In an instant, the horse's dark form wavered and resolved into a tall, striking man—his skin pale as moonlight, eyes still ablaze like coals, wild hair tumbling over his shoulders. His coat, woven from shadow and starlight, billowed around him.

"Lux Bellator, is it?" he purred, pacing around us with feline grace. "Guardians of the hidden world, yet you blunder through my realm as though strolling a village lane." He laughed—a tinkling, ominous sound, like chimes stirred by a sudden wind. "Ah, perhaps your order's standards have slipped since last I watched over mortals."

A spark of indignation flared in my chest. "We may be new, but we aren't helpless. Now—will you guide us through, or stand in our way?"

For a heartbeat he froze, dark brows arching. Then he threw

back his head and laughed again, wild and liberating, as though the forest itself shivered with delight.

"Ah, I like you, little witch," he said, voice softening. "You've got fire in your belly and steel in your spine. Very well—pass you may. But first, a test."

He snapped slender fingers, and before us the mist parted to reveal three trails, each winding into gloom. The one on the left curved gently, almost inviting. The center path plunged straight ahead, dappled with moonlight. The third slithered into darker shadows that whispered secrets only the desperate would hear.

"Choose wisely," he murmured, eyes dancing with mischief. "One path delivers you to your city. One circles you here 'til eternity claims your souls. And one…" He paused, lips curving into a half-smile edged with warning, "one leads to corners of despair no mortal should ever glimpse."

I exchanged a glance with Kat, who had quietly come to stand beside me. Her eyes were wide, but I could see the determination in the set of her jaw.

"Any ideas?" she whispered.

I closed my eyes, reaching out with my magical senses. The air around us thrummed with energy, each path pulsing with its own unique signature. I focused, trying to discern the subtle differences between them.

The first path felt… slippery somehow, like trying to grasp smoke. The second pulsed with a steady, rhythmic energy that felt almost hypnotic. But the third… the third path had a vibrant, electric quality that resonated with my own magic.

I opened my eyes, meeting the phooka's amused gaze. "The third path," I said with more confidence than I felt. "That's the one that leads to New York."

The phooka's grin widened, showing teeth that seemed just a bit too sharp to be human. "Clever witch," he purred. "You trust your instincts well. Very well, you may pass."

He snapped his fingers again, and the other two paths vanished, leaving only the one I'd chosen stretching out before us.

"But remember," he added, his voice taking on an ominous tone, "the path you walk is treacherous. New York is not the city it once was. Dark forces are stirring, and the balance teeters on a knife's edge. Tread carefully, young Lux Bellator."

With that cryptic warning, he shimmered and transformed back into his horse form, galloping off into the misty forest and disappearing from sight.

Kat let out a shaky breath beside me. "Well," she said, trying to inject some levity into her voice, "I guess that's one way to start our New York adventure. Think we can get AAA out here to jumpstart the car?"

I couldn't help but laugh, the tension of the moment breaking. "Somehow, I don't think your insurance covers 'magical forest breakdowns,'" I replied. "But I might have a spell that can get us going again."

We walked back to the car while Orion began meowing indignantly from his carrier. I couldn't shake the phooka's warning from my mind. Dark forces stirring in New York... it seemed our assignment might be more complicated than we'd anticipated.

I placed my hands on the hood of the car, closed my eyes, and began to murmur an incantation. I felt the magic flow through me, into the vehicle, coaxing the engine back to life. With a splutter and a roar, the car started up.

"Nice work, witch," Kat grinned, sliding back into the

driver's seat. "Now let's get out of this creepy forest before anything else decides to test us."

As we drove down the path the phooka had revealed, the mist seemed to part before us, guiding our way. The trees gradually thinned out, and soon we found ourselves merging onto a highway that definitely hadn't been there before. In the distance, the New York City skyline loomed, a forest of steel and glass replacing the magical woodland we'd just left behind.

"Well," I said, letting out a long breath, "I guess we're really doing this."

Kat nodded, her eyes fixed on the road ahead. "Yep. New York City, he we come!"

My heart raced as we crossed into Manhattan, the energy of the city palpable even through the car windows.

"Holy crap," Kat breathed, her eyes wide as she tried to take in the dizzying heights of the skyscrapers around us. "This is insane. How are we supposed to find anything in this concrete jungle?"

I chuckled nervously, feeling equally overwhelmed. "I guess that's part of the challenge. At least we have the address of our new apartment."

As we navigated through the busy streets, I couldn't help but marvel at the sheer blend of people and creatures around us. It was a far cry from our small Indiana town. The air thrummed with a different kind of energy – not just the usual bustle of a big city, but something more. Something magical.

"Can you feel that?" I asked Kat, my skin tingling with the sensation.

She nodded, her nostrils flaring slightly. "It's like… a mix of everything. Human, supernatural, good, bad. It's all here, isn't it?"

"No wonder they call New York a melting pot," I mused, my senses on high alert. Every street corner seemed to pulse with hidden energy, every alleyway potentially concealing supernatural secrets.

Traffic is bad inside the city. It's five lanes of bumper-to-bumper cars and trucks complete with a symphony of horns.

Kat, who navigates traffic about as well as a cat navigates a bathtub, was in full-blown road rage mode, yelling like a banshee with a megaphone.

"Move it, dipshit!" she hollers at a bike courier who dared to venture a bit too near her bumper. I cringed as Kat's outburst bounced around the car.

"Whoa, calm down there, tiger—or should I say, lioness. We're not trying to headline the evening news for a street fight on our first day in the city."

Kat let out a low growl, her eyes gleaming with a wild hint of gold. "I swear, if one more jerk cuts me off—"

"And then what? You'll morph into a lioness right here in the middle of Manhattan traffic?" I quipped, arching an eyebrow at her. "I'm sure the Lux Bellator would just love that."

She exhaled sharply but reluctantly backed off the horn. "Fine. But I still get to maul Nathan if he pisses me off."

"Get in line," I muttered, glancing at the GPS on my phone. "Alright, we should be closing in on our new digs. Take the next right."

When we pulled up to our new apartment building, a nondescript brownstone in a quieter part of the city, I was hit with both relief and trepidation. This was it – our new home, our new life.

"Well, here goes nothing," Kat said, putting the car in park.

"Ready to start our big city adventure, witch?"

I took a deep breath, glancing at Orion in his carrier. He meowed encouragingly, as if to say, "You've got this."

"Let's do this," I replied, pushing open the car door. The cacophony of city sounds hit me immediately – car horns, distant sirens, the chatter of pedestrians. But underneath it all, I could sense the thrum of supernatural energy, a subtle undercurrent that seemed to pulse through the very streets themselves.

5

Witch, There's a Demon in My Living Room

As we lugged our battered duffel bags up the narrow, creaking staircase, each step groaned beneath our weight. The peeling wallpaper curled at the edges, and a single bare bulb overhead cast a sickly yellow glow that made every shadow seem alive. I couldn't shake the prickling sense that unseen eyes tracked our progress. Every few steps I glanced over my shoulder, heart thumping, but the hallway lay deserted—silent except for the echo of our boots and the distant drip of a leaky pipe.

We reached the third floor, where twin apartment doors sat side by side. I'd insisted on separate living quarters because, as much as I adored Kat, her apartment back home looked like a cyclone had blown through—clothes strewn everywhere, dishes piled high, ancient pizza boxes on the floor. It drove me insane.

The building itself was structurally sound—stucco walls, sturdy brick façade—but you could feel a weight in the air, an almost tangible hush that smothered the lobby's potted ferns and faded welcome mat. It was the kind of place where the wallpaper seemed to hold its breath, waiting.

"Paranoid much?" Kat called from behind me, her voice echoing in the corridor. She leaned casually against the banister, ruffling her blonde hair with one hand.

"Just… adjusting," I muttered, my fingers brushing against the cold brass of my doorknob. The key slid in with a clink, and I twisted it, half-expecting some hidden lock to groan open.

My apartment swung inward to reveal a compact living space bathed in morning light. Two tall windows framed a slice of the city skyline, and the faint scent of new paint mingled with the warmth of worn wooden floors. It was small but welcoming: a threadbare rug covered the center, a narrow bookshelf lined one wall, and a mismatched set of chairs huddled around a tiny square table. I dropped my bag and released Orion from his carrier. He sprang free, fur rippling, but trembling with curiosity, as he padded along the floorboards as though greeting old friends.

Kat bounded in after me, dropped onto the sagging, mustard-yellow couch that the landlord had thrown in with the furnished apartment, and let out a contented sigh. "Hey, this isn't half bad," she said, peeling off a pair of dust-caked sneakers. Her own place was a mirror image—same paint chips, same flickering overhead bulb—like twins separated at birth.

I set my bag by the coffee table and smoothed my hair out of my face. "So, when do we meet the Dream Team?" I asked, glancing down at Orion, who was now investigating a loose floorboard.

"Monday morning," Kat replied, fishing a crinkled pamphlet from her pocket. "Their training facility. Six A.M." She leaned back, letting the couch cushion swallow her shoulders. "Better get your beauty sleep."

I laughed, but there was steel behind it. "I need to look hot when I see Nathan again—not to impress him, exactly, but to remind him of everything he can't have." My lips quirked in a half-smile. "Petty Thy Name Is Sadie."

After that, Kat retreated to her apartment to unpack. When she returned an hour later, she carried a cardboard box of kitchen supplies: chipped mugs, an enamel saucepan, mismatched Tupperware. I unwrapped a set of cotton napkins, the fabric rough beneath my fingertips. As I folded them, the reality of Monday crawled up my spine like an ice-cold finger. In just two days, we'd be standing face-to-face with Nathan Blackwood and his legendary team. Anxiety bubbled in my chest, mingling with old resentment until I felt like I might erupt.

"You know," Kat said over the soft tear of packing tape, "maybe Nathan's changed since that training retreat. Five years is a long time."

I snorted, pressing a fork into a box with more force than necessary. "People like him don't change, Kat. They only get more arrogant with each new adoring fan."

"Maybe," she murmured, sliding onto one of the kitchen stools. Her phone glowed in her hand, screen illuminating her face in cool light. She scrolled. "But I did some digging. Nathan's team—they're kind of a big deal in the supernatural world."

"Great," I snapped, folding a T-shirt until the crease burned my fingertips. "As if his ego needed any more of a boost."

Kat's eyes flicked up, sparkling. "No, seriously. Last year they dismantled a rogue vampire coven trying to spawn an army of newborns in Brooklyn. The creatures were—" she shuddered slightly "—barely sentient, all bones and pale skin, but there were dozens of them."

I paused mid-fold. "Okay, that's… impressive."

"Then," Kat continued, "the year before, they stopped a pack of feral werewolves tearing through Central Park during a full moon. The ground was littered with shredded park benches and mauled trash cans."

I inhaled sharply, despite myself. "Alright," I admitted, voice softer. "That's pretty badass."

Kat grinned. "Looks like not much has changed with Mr. Blackwood. He's still the paranormal golden boy."

I shrugged, trying to appear indifferent. "What about the uptick in activity around the city? You think it's demons?"

Her expression sobered. She set her phone on the counter with a soft thunk. "Nobody knows for sure. But it's not just one faction acting up. Vampires are more daring, wandering the subways at night. Werewolves can't control their shifts outside the full moon. Fae—bad ones—are everywhere, leaving broken glass and nightmares in their wake. And demon sightings? Off the charts."

A cold knot formed in my gut. "This isn't normal fluctuations," I whispered. "It's like something's… stirring them all up."

"Exactly," Kat said, voice low. "And the Lux Bellator are seriously worried."

I ran a hand through my hair, eyes flicking to Orion, who had settled on the counter and was purring against my wrist. "And they're calling us in now? In the middle of this chaos?"

She shrugged, tension tightening her shoulders. "Maybe they need all hands on deck. Or maybe they think—"

"Think what?" I pressed, heart hammering.

She met my gaze, unwavering. "They think fresh eyes like ours might spot something the others have missed."

I let out a shaky laugh. "No pressure, then."

Silence settled between us, thick as the dusk creeping in through the windows. Orion nudged my hand again, a small, comforting weight. I scratched behind his ears, drawing strength from his soft purr.

"Well," I said at last, lifting my chin, "I guess we'll find out soon enough what we're really up against."

Kat pushed herself up, forcing a grin that trembled just a little. "Hey, at least you'll get a chance to remind Nathan just how badass you've become."

A flutter of nerves danced in my stomach, but I returned her smile. "Yeah," I whispered, "that might almost make dealing with his ego worth it."

I haul my suitcase into the bedroom. I begin unpacking and meticulously organizing my grimoires and spell components on the wobbly bookshelf. Suddenly, a shiver runs down my spine and I stop in my tracks. My hand hovers over a vial of powdered moonstone.

"Kat," I whispered, not daring to turn around. "Do you feel that?

Kat, who had been sprawled on the couch playing on her phone, sat up abruptly. Her eyes narrowed, and I could almost see her lion senses kicking into overdrive.

"Yeah," she murmured, her voice low and tense. "Something's not right."

The air in my apartment pulsed with raw, crackling energy, each breath tasting of ozone and brimstone. Orion's fur stood on end like quills, his back arching into a perfect bow as he unleashed a guttural hiss that rattled my bones.

A white-hot dread ignited in my chest. My hand jittered with magic. At my side, Kat's spine elongated in a blur of sinew and fur—muscles rippling into a massive lion's form, every movement taut with lethal intent. I snatched my athame from my bag; the blade thrummed with violet fire, scorching the air in my palm.

Kat settled low, paws splaying on the worn carpet, her rumble vibrating through the floorboards. Then he materialized— tall as a skyscraper's shadow (okay, I'm exaggerating), skin the color of midnight oil. Eerie red orbs flared above a cruel grin. Sulfur and scorched air drifted around him.

"Well, well," he rasped, voice like gravel sliding over steel. "Fresh prey in the Big Apple. How…delicious."

My fingers clenched the athame's hilt until the veins on my forearm stood out like rope. "Wrong apartment," I snarled, forcing steadiness into my voice as fear surged through me.

He laughed—an ice-cold rasp that crawled up my spine. "Oh, I don't think so, witchling. We've been waiting."

Waiting? My pulse thundered.

"Waiting?" Kat's snarl shook the plaster from the walls. She circled wide, fangs bared in a crescent of gleaming bone.

"Word travels fast through Hell," he said, voice smooth as oil. "Power like yours doesn't cross the River Styx unnoticed." His gaze slid back to me, unblinking. "Sadie Baker—quite the prize."

My stomach knotted. His calling my name was a curse in itself.

He advanced, dragging a trail of sulfurous wind. With a flick of his wrist, shadows seeped from the corners, clawed tendrils gouging deep rune-like slashes into the walls.

Kat's growl rolled like thunder.

"Last chance," I warned, veins aglow, every inch of me humming with raw magic. "Leave or die."

His grin split his face, rows of razor teeth gleaming. "Show me, witch."

I unleashed my power through the athame in a single, blinding bolt. It slammed into his chest with a thunderclap, hurling him back—but he only laughed, smoke curling from his scorched tunic.

"Insolent," he mocked. "Is that all you've got, Lux Bellator?"

Lux Bellator? How did he know—

Kat vanished in a cyclone of gold and shadow, pouncing with inhuman speed. Furniture splintered under their collision, books and spell jars shattering like crystal fireworks.

Seizing the moment, I channeled every stolen spark into my blade. A crackling wave of magic shot right into his heart. He roared, flesh hissing where the magic bit, but staggered only a step.

He flung Kat aside as if she were a rag doll, sending her crashing into a bookshelf. Herbs and scrolls rained down.

"Kat!" I yelled, my heart lurching.

His claws slashed the air where my head had been a heartbeat ago. I rolled free, grit and despair mixing in my throat as he advanced, red eyes glittering.

"You're out of your depth, witch," he hissed, stalking me like prey. "New York will digest you."

I slammed power into the athame until it blazed like a miniature star. "I'm stronger than you know." I thrust out my palm—an explosion of raw force ripped from my soul— and punched it into his torso. He stumbled, smoke spiraling from his skin.

His eyes flared white-hot fury.

He lunged.

This time I was ready. I invoked the forbidden spell I'd practiced in secret. The apartment shuddered as spectral shards of energy ripped from the air, slashing toward him in a blizzard of lights.

From the corner of my eye, I saw Kat recover. With a roar that shook the rafters, she slammed into the demon from behind, jaws clamping onto his shoulder with a sickening crunch.

We needed to finish this now. I raised my free hand, every nerve screaming with power, and unleashed a colossal beam of blinding light. The room erupted in a supernova of magic. The demon's howl pierced the blast as he flew through the shattered window, glass spraying like deadly rain.

Kat launched herself after him, leaping through the shards and landing—an embodiment of fury—on the sidewalk below. I barreled down the stairs two at a time, adrenaline fueling every step.

Out front, the demon clawed at the pavement, trying to rise. Kat pinned him in a vice of claws and teeth. I burst through the door and dove into the fray. With one swift motion, I drove the athame through his heart. His scream cracked the air, then faded into a raspy sigh as darkness swallowed him.

Silence flooded the street. Kat reared back, roaring victoriously. I stood beside her, chest heaving, ash-scented wind whipping my hair.

That was one hell of a welcome to New York.

6

New Team, Who Dis?

The New York City Lux Bellator training center was a marvel of modern architecture and supernatural ingenuity. As we stepped through the sleek glass doors, I couldn't help but feel a healthy dose of awe and intimidation. The lobby alone was larger than our entire facility back in Indiana, with high ceilings and walls adorned with ancient symbols and modern tech in equal measure.

"Whoa," Kat whispered beside me, her eyes wide as she took in our surroundings. "This place is insane."

I nodded, trying to keep my composure despite the butter-flies in my stomach. "Yeah, it's - something else."

As we neared the reception desk, an intimidating figure emerged from one of the side corridors, casting a long shadow that seemed to stretch across the room. My heart did a little tap dance as recognition hit me like a ton of bricks - Nathan Blackwood. He was even more intimidating than I remembered, around 6'3, he towered like a Greek god, with piercing blue eyes that could undress you in a single glance, dark brown hair that probably had its own fan club, and skin that glowed like he'd just returned from a vacation in the sun. That smug expression was still plastered on his annoyingly handsome face as he strutted over, eyes giving us the kind of scrutiny usually reserved for suspicious tax returns. Why was I even surprised?

Nathan approached us with the deliberate, measured strides of a man who knew he looked damn good doing it, his gaze dissecting us like we were the main course at a fancy dinner. You could almost feel the testosterone wafting off him like cheap cologne. Despite lacking Michael's wings, Nathan's presence screamed of his own formidable power. Nephilim like Nathan were unnaturally fast, ridiculously strong, and could wield an angelic blade with the kind of precision that made surgeons jealous.

Crossing paths with them was a great way to ensure your life insurance policy wasn't wasted.

"You must be the new recruits," he declared, his voice deep and commanding, like a commercial for luxury cars. "I'm Nathan Blackwood, leader of this team."

"Katerina Volkov," Kat introduced herself, extending a hand with the confidence of someone who'd just nailed a job interview. "But everyone calls me Kat."

Nathan gave her hand a brisk shake, then turned his laser-like focus on me. A wave of irritation washed over me at his obliviousness, but I shoved it down like last night's regretful taco binge.

"Sadie Baker," I said, keeping my voice steady enough to rival any zen master. "Witch."

His eyebrow arched with the kind of intrigue usually reserved for reality TV drama. "Ah yes, Michael's protégé. I've heard… interesting things about you."

I fought the urge to unleash a snappy comeback, instead letting a sharp, sardonic smile dance on my lips, my eyebrow lifting in a clear signal of my unimpressed attitude. His ego would survive the hit. "We'll do our best not to disappoint," I replied, my words dripping with enough sarcasm to fill a swimming pool.

Nathan's eyes narrowed slightly, a flicker of irritation flashing across his face before he covered it with a mask of professional indifference. "Well, let's see if you live up to the hype. Follow me."

He spun on his heel and stomped down the corridor, not even glancing back to see if we were dogging him. Kat shot me a "we're not following the Pied Piper, right?" look, as we hustled after.

As we jogged, Nathan threw his voice over his shoulder like a bored game show host. "You'll meet the rest of the crew soon: Hadeon, Silas, and Chloe. We don't do participation trophies around here—so pull your weight."

"Trust me, I hate coddling," I murmured. Kat jabbed me in the ribs—note to self: sarcasm is a risky sport.

We spilled into a space that looked like Tony Stark's basement on steroids: at least five times the size of our sad little gym at home, crammed with gadgetry I couldn't name. One corner held a baby thunderstorm in a forcefield; another had holographic targets doing more evasive maneuvers than my last Tinder date.

Three figures eyed us. Hadeon, the deadpan fae; Silas, a vampire with red contact lenses straight out of a bad horror flick; and Chloe, the wolf-shifter, giving us the stink-eye.

"Team," Nathan announced, voice booming, "meet our new recruits: Katerina Volkov, lion-shifter, and Sadie Baker, witch."

Hadeon nodded politely—"I could kill you with a look" vibes. Silas offered a toothy grin that screamed "hope you like neck bites." Chloe barely glanced up, then muttered, "Fresh meat. How—quaint."

My magic trembled under her sneer, but I swallowed it.

Barely.

Hadeon stepped forward, his fae skin shimmering slightly. "Welcome to New York," he said, his voice deep and melodious. "I hope you're prepared for the challenges ahead."

"Oh, we got a sneak peek last night," I said, smirking. "Tiny housewarming demon crashed our pad. Real classy touch."

Nathan blinked. "A demon?"

Kat hopped in, grinning like she'd found free pizza. "Yeah, this one thought our living room needed redecorating. Sadie sent it flying, and I used it as a chew toy. No biggie."

Their jaws collectively dropped. Silas whistled so low it could've summoned a banshee. Chloe's face twisted in doubt.

"Please," she scoffed. "Rookies versus a demon. Cute fairytale."

Heat spiked behind my eyes. Time to show this barking dog some bite. "Wanna see proof?" I said, all silky challenge.

Chloe's eyebrow arched. "You're bluffing—memory orb's a one-in-a-million feat."

I gave her my best "bite me" grin and whipped up a glowing sphere the size of a bowling ball in my palm.

The orb flared to life, replaying our demon rodeo: the shrieks, my blast, Kat's claws shredding spectral goo. Even Nathan looked like someone swapped his latte for nitro.

When it faded, silence roared louder than a hurricane. Chloe's sneer was toast—replaced by grudging respect. Silas let out another low whistle.

"Well, well," he said, grin widening. "New blood's got teeth."

Hadeon's face remained passive. "Impressive. Maybe we judged you too soon."

I crossed my arms. "One odd thing: the demon called me by name. Any thoughts?"

Silas's red eyes glinted. "A demon that names names? Not standard hellspawn behavior. Someone's got you personally in their crosshairs."

Chloe's brow furrowed deeply, her expression flickering with disbelief as she processed the shocking revelation. "That's... impossible. You've only just arrived. How could any demon possibly know you, or even know to seek you out here?"

"It claimed it was waiting for me," I reiterated, the chilling memory wrapping icy tendrils around my spine. I shot a glance at Kat, who nodded with a grave seriousness that amplified my dread. "It... knew things." My voice wavered under the weight of the room's piercing gaze, each pair of eyes like a scalpel dissecting my every word. "It knew I was Lux Bellator. Called me a prize." My voice cracked, and Michael's warning echoed ominously in my mind: Power that stands out draws the sharpest daggers.

For the first time, Nathan's eyes betrayed something beyond his usual arrogance. His gaze was calculating, rapidly assessing the gravity of the risk and threat. "This must be reported to the Council immediately," he declared, his words clipped and urgent. "There should be no breaches in operational security. Not at this level. For now, we'll proceed with the tour, but a report is imperative once we conclude."

7

Bite Me, Blackwood

After meeting the rest of his team, Nathan led us to a few other locations in the building, pointing out their importances as we went. As we continued our tour of the facility, I couldn't help but notice Nathan's eyes repeatedly darting in my direction. His earlier dismissive attitude had been replaced by a wary curiosity, and I had to admit, I was enjoying his discomfort.

"This is our tactical room," Nathan explained as we entered a sleek, high-tech space filled with holographic displays and advanced computer systems. "We plan all our major operations here."

Kat whistled, impressed. "Fancy. Makes our old planning sessions around a folding table look pretty sad."

I nodded in agreement, trying not to look too awestruck. "It's certainly… elaborate."

Nathan's lips twitched in what might have been the ghost of a smile. "We spare no expense when it comes to protecting the city. The supernatural threats here are unlike anything you've faced before."

"I'm sure we'll manage," I replied.

Moving on, Nathan led us to a heavily reinforced door. He placed his hand on a scanner, and the door slid open with a soft hiss, revealing a vast chamber filled with an eclectic array of magical artifacts and weaponry.

"This is our armory," Nathan explained, his voice taking on a note of pride. "We have tools here to combat nearly any supernatural threat you can imagine."

Kat and I exchanged impressed glances as we took in the room. Shelves lined the walls, filled with everything from ancient-looking tomes to sleek, high-tech devices. In the center of the room, various weapons were displayed on stands - swords that glowed with ethereal light, crossbows with arrows tipped in what looked like liquid silver, and even what appeared to be a set of brass knuckles etched with intricate runes.

"Wow," Kat breathed, her eyes wide as she took it all in. "This is incredible."

I nodded in agreement, my fingers itching to examine some of the more intriguing magical items. A staff in the corner seemed to pulse with an otherworldly energy, and I could have sworn I saw runes flickering across its surface.

I wonder when they'll let me try it out. Judging by Nathan's stern gaze, not any time soon. As we moved through the armory, I couldn't help but notice Nathan's eyes following me, curiosity paramount in his gaze. I pretended not to notice, instead focusing on the array of magical items around us.

"This is quite the collection," I remarked, running my fingers lightly over the spine of an ancient-looking grimoire. "I don't suppose we get free rein in here?"

Nathan's lips twitched in what might have been amusement.

"Hardly. Each item here is carefully catalogued and monitored. You'll be assigned equipment as needed for missions."

I may have actually pouted at that.

We made our way towards the exit of the armory, Kat in the lead when I had one of my more graceful moments, tripping over thin air. Nathan's hand shot out, catching me before I could fall. His grip was firm, his skin warm against mine. For a moment, our eyes locked, and I felt a jolt of... electricity? Magic? Probably just plain old attraction. The man is gorgeous. Too bad he knew it.

"Careful," he murmured, his voice low in my ear. "Some of these artifacts are sensitive to touch."

I quickly regained my footing, trying not to shiver at his closeness. "Right," I said, trying to keep my voice steady. "Thanks."

As we exited the armory, I could feel the weight of Nathan's gaze on me. I resisted the urge to look back, instead focusing on Kat's animated chatter about the weapons she'd seen.

"And did you see that crossbow? I bet I could take down a wendigo from a hundred yards with that baby," she gushed.

I nodded, only half-listening to Kat's excited chatter. My mind was still reeling from that brief moment of contact with Nathan. What was that spark I felt? And why did it unsettle me so much?

As we made our way back to the main training area, Nathan cleared his throat. "Right, now that you've seen the facilities, it's-"

He's interrupted by the shrill ringing of his phone. Nathan's expression turned serious as he answered the call. "Blackwood," he said tersely, listening intently to the voice on the other end. His brow furrowed, and he began pacing as the conversation continued. After what felt like an eternity, Nathan ended the call and turned to face us, his blue eyes intense.

Kat and I exchanged glances. This could be our first real test with the team. We were both ready to prove ourselves, excited by the prospect.

Nathan's face twisted into the most condescending expression imaginable. "Ladies, I have an extremely crucial task for you," he said a little too jovial for the situation, his evil smirk firmly in place. As we leaned in, a sense of dread settled over us, knowing full well we wouldn't appreciate the assignment. "You'll be managing crowd control while we move in to apprehend the suspects," he declared, leaving us simmering with frustration and disbelief.

That rat bastard.

"Crowd control?" I repeated, my voice dripping with sarcasm. "Wow, how generous of you to entrust us with such a crucial task."

Nathan's expression remained impassive, but I could see a hint of smugness in his eyes. "Oh, it's truly my pleasure."

I wonder what the consequences would be for punching the Lux's golden boy. I do believe we are about to find out. "You can't be serious right now."

Nathan's smirk only grew more infuriating, taking a step closer to me, invading my personal space. "Deadly serious. This is a delicate situation, and we need experienced agents to handle the actual apprehension. Your job is to keep civilians back and maintain the illusion of normalcy. Think you can handle that?"

I could feel my magic crackling beneath my skin, begging to be released. I held it in though. We'll play it his way. For now.

I took a deep breath, trying to calm the magic beneath my skin. "With all due respect," I said, my voice contradicting my words, "I think our skills would be better utilized in the field, but you're the boss. We will go where you want us." Then under my breath, "we wouldn't want to outshine you." Though he must have heard me if his glare was any indication. While his eyes flashed with anger at my comment, Nathan quickly composes himself. "Good. Glad we understand each other. Now, let's move out."

As we piled into the team's big black SUV, I could feel the tension crackling in the air. Kat nudged me with her elbow, giving me a look that clearly said, "Cool it."

The drive to midtown was tense and silent. I watched the city blur past us, trying to calm my frustration. When we arrived at the scene, chaos had already erupted. People were running and screaming, fleeing from something we couldn't yet see.

"Alright, team," Nathan barked, his voice authoritative. "You know the drill. Hadeon, take the high ground. Chloe, flank from the sides. Silas, you're with me. And you two-"

"Crowd control!" I say, in my best cheerleader tone, which earned me another glare from Nathan.

"Crowd control, got it," Kat repeated quickly, grabbing my arm and pulling me away before I could say anything else to antagonize Nathan further. I could feel his gaze burning a hole in my back as we walked away.

As the rest of the team moved swiftly into action, Kat and I positioned ourselves at the edge of the commotion. People were still fleeing in panic, and in the distance, I could hear the sounds of destruction - crashing metal, shattering glass, and an inhuman roar that sent shivers down my spine.

"Okay, Sadie," Kat said, her eyes scanning the crowd. "Time to put on a show. Think you can whip up an illusion to keep these folks back?"

I nodded, inhaling deeply to center myself amidst the tension swirling around us. With a graceful wave of my hand, I conjured an illusion spell, meticulously crafting the appearance of a formidable police barricade. The illusion was complete with glaringly bright flashing lights and stern-looking officers who seemed to emanate authority, their expressions unyielding.

8

Rescue and Roasting: A Double Feature

We waited. Seconds bled into minutes, minutes into an eternity of awkward breath and wasted lives. Still no team. Not a peep on the radio—just the echo of our own nerves rattling around. After thirty excruciating minutes, Kat and I exchanged a look that said: screw it, let's get a move on. My illusion spell was watertight; it'd keep the rubberneckers busy while we snuck in.

Inside, the silence was oppressive—like the universe was holding its breath to screw with us. Each footfall sounded like a marching band in an empty church. Rounding the corner, we found our elite strike squad huddled in the middle of the room, imprisoned by swirling arcs of iridescent magic. They looked more trapped than my ex at a singles bar.

I mean, these were supposed to be the best demon-hunters in the biz. How do four seasoned agents end up in a sparkly force field surrounded by garden-variety demon scum? My last insult—getting benched—still burned, but seeing them here almost made me forget my bruised pride.

Nathan Blackwood, our team lead and resident ego, glared at me through the shimmer. He looked like a cornered bad boy at a bachelor party—hot, furious, and desperate to break free. The glare was meant to slice me in half, but it lost its edge when he was trapped in a glittering cage of doom. I couldn't help smirking.

I fell my fingertips graze the familiar heft of my athame, a trusty companion in battle. Instead of unsheathing it; however, I whipped out my phone. "Gotta get this," I muttered, toggling the camera. Snap. Snap. The shutter clicks felt like little barbed compliments to Nate's trapped derrière.

"Sadie, what the hell?" Kat hissed, eyes flicking between my grin and our ensnared colleagues. Her tone was pure "I love you, but don't die because your ego needs attention."

"Just documenting our first day on the job," I replied with a mischievous wink, unable to suppress the bubbling excitement in my voice as I turned to grab a selfie complete with Nathan's glare in the background. "You know, for our scrapbook." My words dripped with irony, and I could feel the weight of my amusement dancing in the air around me.

The rest of the team wore expressions that ranged from sheepishness to outright annoyance, their faces a spectrum of red hues. Nathan's face, however, was a tempest of fury, his eyes blazing like storm clouds ready to unleash a downpour. His jaw was clenched so tightly that I feared he might shatter a tooth under the pressure. "If you're done playing paparazzi," he growled, his voice a low rumble that seemed to echo off the walls, "maybe you could actually help us out of this situation?"

With a playful smirk still lingering on my lips, I couldn't help but goad him more. "Oh, I don't know. I thought we were just supposed to handle crowd control. Wouldn't want to overstep our bounds as 'untrained rookies', right?" My tone was light, teasing, but it carried the weight of a challenge.

Kat elbowed me sharply, her jab a reminder of the seriousness of the situation. "Sadie, come on. We can gloat later." Her voice was firm yet held a hint of urgency.

"Alright, alright," I sighed dramatically, slipping my phone into my pocket. "I suppose we should probably help them out." My sigh was a theatrical concession, a performance of reluctant agreement.

Kat nodded, her posture shifting as she steeled herself for action. Her muscles tensed beneath her skin like a coiled spring ready to be released, every fiber primed for the impending confrontation. "What's the plan?" she asked, her voice laced with unwavering determination, her eyes glinting with a fierce resolve as she prepared to take charge of the unfolding chaos.

I scanned the dimly lit room, taking in the grotesque figures of the demons and the shimmering magical barrier that flickered ominously. "Follow my lead," I instructed, my voice steady as I turned to face the demon lurking to the right.

"Hey, big guy," I began in my sweetest, most clueless tone akin to a lost tourist seeking directions. "We seem to be in a bit of a bind here. My boss over there and his merry band of idiots have managed to land themselves on the wrong side of that magical barrier and, unfortunately, want me to get them out. Mind letting them out?"

The demon—fur matted like it'd been living in mothballs, drool dripping off jagged teeth—fixed me with cold red eyes. It snarled, deep enough to rattle your fillings, then flicked its spiky tail and muttered a resounding, "No." The smell of sulfur gave me a contact high.

Absolutely charming.

"No?" I questioned, addressing its retreating back before turning towards Nathan and the others with a regretful look etched into my features. "He said no. Best of luck."

Silas, trapped amid the vortex of energy, burst out laughing. I couldn't tell if he was freaked out or found me hilarious. Either way, points for morale.

Nate's face went full 'volcano.' "This isn't a game, Sadie! Get us out, damn it!"

I sighed dramatically, turning back to face the demons. "Well, you heard the man. I guess we'll have to do this the hard way."

With a fierce growl, I thrust my hand forward, channeling my magic into a concentrated blast of energy. The sheer force of it sent the demon hurtling across the room, crashing into the far wall with a sickening crunch.

The other demons, all identical in appearance, finally snapped out of their surprise and began to converge on us. "Whoa, trippy." I quipped watching the matching bunch come at us from every angle.

Kat, sensing the danger, shifted into her lion form with a deafening roar that shook the very foundations of the building. She pounced on the nearest demon, her razor-sharp claws raking across its chest.

I gripped my athame tightly, my fingers practically glowing from the surges of magic coursing through them. As two more demons charged towards me, I swung my blade with precision, sending arcs of pure energy slicing through their defenses. They howled in agony as the magic seared their flesh.

The battle is intense and chaotic, but we are determined to prevail. One by one, we begin to make quick work of our opponents, wondering how our colleagues were ever captured by these creatures in the first place.

As we fight, I can feel the intense gaze of Nathan and his team upon us, their eyes following our every move with unwavering focus. The thrill of showing off for them tugged at my muscles, but I knew the mission was more important.

Kat is a blur of fur and claws, moving with a lethal grace as she tore through our enemies. We fought in perfect synchronization, anticipating each other's moves and providing cover from all angles. My heart swelled with pride for my best friend as she effortlessly took down opponent after opponent.

In one fluid motion, I flicked my wrist and sent a demon hurtling towards the magical barrier containing Nathan's team. The creature let out an ear-piercing shriek as it collided with the barrier, its body sizzling and turning to ash upon impact. The barrier shimmered and trembled under the strain but still held strong against our assault.

With each swipe of her claws, Kat's determined cries echoed through the battleground. Her movements were swift and precise as she fought off another demon.

Using one final blast of magic to defeat my own opponent before turning towards the shimmering wall of energy that separated us from our target. I could feel the dark magic pulsing within it, a tangled web of malevolence that threatened to consume us all.

"Everyone, stand back," I commanded, my voice trembling with equal parts fear and determination. Raising both hands towards the barrier, I closed my eyes and drew deep from my well of power. The air around me began to crackle with electricity, causing my hair to stand on end as if caught in an invisible breeze.

I began to chant, ancient words of power flowing effortlessly from my lips. Words I've never learned yet somehow come instinctively to me.

The barrier pulsed and writhed, fighting against my magic with every ounce of its strength. Beads of sweat formed on my forehead as I pushed harder, feeling the strain in every fiber of my being. Just when I feared I couldn't hold on any longer, I felt the barrier give way.

As the barrier fell, Nathan and his team leaped into action with renewed vigor. Despite the exhaustion that threatened to overtake me, I couldn't help but admire their skills.

Nathan moved with inhuman speed and grace, his angelic heritage evident in the way he seemed to almost fly between opponents. Hadeon took the high point, unleashing powerful blasts of fae magic from above. Silas was a blur of fangs and claws as he tore through demons with ferocious efficiency. And Chloe shifted rapidly into a fierce wolf form, keeping our enemies off-balance with her unpredictable attacks.

Together, we were an unstoppable force fighting for our lives against the forces of darkness.

But even as I admired their skill, I couldn't help but feel a twinge of satisfaction. We had saved them, after all. And I wasn't about to let Nathan forget it.

As the last demon fell, the room fell into an eerie silence, broken only by our heavy breathing. Nathan turned to face us, his expression unreadable.

"Well," I said, unable to keep the smugness out of my voice, "I guess crowd control came in handy after all, huh?"

Nathan's jaw clenched, but before he could respond, Silas let out a low whistle. "Damn, rookie. You've got some serious power there." Nathan, finally finding his voice, begrudgingly added. "I… appreciate your assistance," he said, the words seeming to physically pain him. "Your skills are… adequate."

I couldn't help but smile sweetly at him. "Oh, no need to thank us. We were just doing our job. You know, crowd control and all that."

Kat, now back in her human form, snorted with barely contained laughter. The rest of the team shifted uncomfortably, clearly unsure how to react to the situation.

Nathan, ready for another fight, whipped around in my direction, but before he could respond, Hadeon stepped forward, his hand outstretched in a playacting gesture. "What Nathaniel is trying to say," he interjected smoothly, "is that we're grateful for your help. Your skills are impressive, and we underestimated you. It won't happen again."

Nathan shot Hadeon a look that could have melted steel but nodded stiffly in agreement. "Yes… what he said."

I couldn't help but smirk, enjoying Nathan's discomfort perhaps a bit too much. "Well, I'm glad we could be of service. Always happy to lend a hand when the 'experienced agents' find themselves in a bind."

Nathan's eyes flashed dangerously, but before he could retort, Silas stepped between us, his fangs glinting in a wolfish grin. "Alright, alright, let's not start round two."

"Well," I said, unable to keep the smirk off my face, "that was fun. Shall we call it a day?"

Nathan momentarily froze, his eyes narrowing. "We'll discuss this more at headquarters first thing in the morning."

I gave him a little wink that almost sent him into orbit. Trying to keep the smugness out of my voice and failing miserably. "You got it boss, we're just here to learn from the best, right?"

Nathan's eye twitched at that, but he managed to keep his cool. "Right. Well, let's finish up here and head back to headquarters and call it a day. We will need to debrief Stephen in the morning."

Stephen is the big boss of New York by the way.

As the team began to move about the room, checking for any remaining threats and gathering evidence, I couldn't help but notice Nathan's gaze continually drifting back to me. His expression was the embodiment of frustration. The ride back was tense, to say the least. I could feel Nathan's eyes on me in the rearview mirror, his gaze a healthy dose of anger with a side of curiosity. The rest of the team seemed unsure what to make of the tension between me and their leader.

Silas finally broke the silence, "How about we grab a drink to celebrate our new teammates' impressive debut?"

I could see Nathan bristle at the suggestion, but Chloe chimed in before he could object. "That sounds like a great idea. I, for one, could use a stiff drink after being trapped in that barrier."

Kat nodded enthusiastically. "I'm in. Nothing like a near-death experience to work up a thirst."

I glanced at Nathan, raising an eyebrow in challenge. "What do you say, boss? Care to join us mere mortals for a drink?"

Nathan seemed like he wasn't going to respond, but after a moment, he let out a resigned sigh. "Fine."

9

Unfinished Business

Once we eased the SUV into a narrow bay deep in the underground parking garage of the Lux Bellator building, the engine's hum died amid the echoing clang of distant metal doors. Harsh amber lights flickered overhead, casting elongated shadows on the stained concrete floor. We tumbled out of the vehicle, jackets rustling and boots squeaking, the team fracturing off in different directions like wary birds. I was about to follow Kat into the dim corridor when a firm hand clamped onto my forearm.

I turned to find Nathan standing there, his frame tense, cobalt eyes blazing in the low light. The hairs on my neck prickled. "Sadie, my office—now," he ordered in a low growl. "The rest of you, go home."

I lifted one eyebrow, trying to steady the quick beat of my heart. "Your office? I thought we were grabbing drinks." My voice was light, teasing, even as my pulse thudded against my ribs.

Nathan's grip tightened, knuckles pale against my jacket sleeve. His gaze was steel. "Drinks can wait. We need to talk—privately."

"Okay, okay," I retorted with a shrug, forcing a casual smile. "But you don't have to be so pushy. If you want to spend more quality time together, just ask."

For a moment, his expression flickered between rage and something darker, but then he released me and strode down the hall, footsteps hollow on the concrete. I fell in behind him, the heavy door to his office hissing closed on its hydraulic hinges, sealing us off from the rest of the world.

Inside, the office felt like another planet. Floor-to-ceiling windows spanned one wall, revealing the glittering New York skyline beneath a violet dusk. The sunset cast long orange beams across a sleek mahogany desk, its surface meticulously organized—file folders stacked in perfect symmetry, pens aligned like soldiers in a row. Leather-bound books lined glass-fronted shelves, and a single pot of white orchids softened the room's otherwise severe lines.

Nathan crossed the polished hardwood floor in three purposeful strides, then pivoted to face me. His posture was rigid, shoulders squared, every inch of him exuding control.

"Sit," he commanded, nodding toward the high-backed leather chair before his desk.

I hesitated—then slid onto the seat, crossing one leg over the other. I leaned forward slightly, meeting his intense gaze. "So," I said, tapping the armrest, "are we here to discuss my exceptional crowd-control skills?"

His jaw twitched. Lightning flashed behind his blue eyes. "Cut the crap, Sadie. What the hell was that back there?" he growled, voice low enough to vibrate through the room.

I folded my arms and tipped my head, feigning innocence. "I'm not sure what you mean."

"Don't play dumb," he snapped, stepping closer until the scent of his cologne—oakmoss and cedar—filled my senses. "The attitude, the showing off. You've been antagonizing me since the moment you arrived. Why?"

I leaned back, the leather creaking under me, and stared him down evenly. "Oh, I don't know. Maybe it's because you dismissed us as 'untrained rookies,' lumping us with crowd-control when you clearly thought we were useless in the field."

His eyes narrowed to icy slits. "You disobeyed a direct order."

I scoffed, folding my arms tighter. "An order that almost got you, and your entire team, trapped—and possibly killed—inside a demon barrier. Face it, Nathan: if Kat and I hadn't intervened, you'd still be stuck in there, powerless."

He ran a hand through his dark hair, tugging at the roots in frustration. The city lights danced on the sharp planes of his face. "That's not the point," he said, voice low and fierce. "The point is you need to learn obedience, Sadie. You need to learn to follow orders and trust the team."

I uncrossed my legs and leaned forward again, voice cool as steel.

"Rich coming from you. From what I saw today, you're doing the very thing you accuse me of."

"I have a team to protect. I am not here to cater to you and your friend's feelings. My job is to make sure my team is safe and successful."

"Don't blame the job for this. You've always been an arrogant ass!"

That stumps him. "What are you talking about."

"Nothing. Forget I said anything."

"Not likely. What does that comment mean?" He asks, with something akin to suspicion. Is he starting to remember me, or does he get suspicious of anyone who doesn't fawn all over him?

I sighed, realizing I'd let my frustration get the better of me. "Look, it doesn't matter. Ancient history."

Nathan's eyes narrowed, studying me intently. "No, I want to know what you meant by that. Have we met before?"

Ugh, I don't want to do this right now. "Look, if there's nothing else, I need to get going. I'm still tired from the move and I used a lot of energy today."

Nathan's eyes narrowed further, his posture tensing as he stepped closer to me. "No, we're not done here. Answer the question, Sadie. Have we met before?"

I sighed heavily, realizing there was no easy way out of this conversation, but I was going to try anyway. "Yes, we have. Not that I'd expect you to remember. That's also all I will be saying on the matter. If you have any other questions about it, well, tough."

Nathan's eyes flashed with frustration and curiosity. He took a step closer, his imposing presence filling the space between us. "That's not good enough, Sadie. If we've met before, I want to know when and where. It could be relevant to our working relationship."

I stood up, refusing to be intimidated by his proximity. "Our 'working relationship' is just fine as it is, Nathan. Professional and nothing more. The past is irrelevant."

He ran a hand through his hair, clearly agitated. "Damn it, Sadie. Why are you being so difficult about this?"

I couldn't help but let out a bitter laugh. "Oh, please. Mr. High-and-Mighty himself, questioning why someone else is being difficult. Hilarious." I take a deep breath to compose myself. "Look, the past is in the past. It's not a big deal anyway.

Nothing that would affect our working together. So, let's just drop it."

Nathan stared hard at me, I could practically hear his teeth grinding. For a minute, I thought he might actually let it go. But of course, I wasn't that lucky.

"It's on the tip of my tongue," he muttered, almost to himself, eyes darting over my face as if he could conjure a memory by sheer willpower. "The way you looked at me today. The way you talk. I know you from somewhere, Sadie." His voice was low, intense, searching for a crack in my armor.

I didn't flinch. "Maybe in another life," I said, breezy and unimpressed—a feat, considering my heart was threatening to beat out of my ribcage. "Maybe in your dreams. I bet I'll be the star of those. Does it really matter?"

He was still for a moment, watching me with predator's patience. "If you're hiding something," he said, voice low, "I'll find out."

I shrugged, all nonchalance. "Can't wait to see you try."

He looked like he might say more, but then his phone buzzed on the desk with a shrill, intrusive alert. He snatched it up, eyes scanning the screen, the anger bleeding off his face as his jaw slackened into something wary.

"I have to take this," he said, already turning away, the tension still tethered between us like a highwire. "We're not finished, Sadie."

I was halfway out of his office before I let myself breathe again. The walls in the Lux Bellator HQ seemed to press in from every side, shadows pooling in the corners like spilled secrets. Kat found me in the hallway, arms folded, one eyebrow cocked. "You look like you just survived a firing squad."

"Not far off," I muttered. "He's got a sixth sense for being insufferable."

She snorted. "And yet you stood your ground. That's my girl." We headed for the exit, our footsteps muffled by the plush, unnecessary carpet. "So, what did your prince of darkness want?"

I glanced back at Nathan's office, the closed door humming with the aftershock of our conversation. "To 'talk,' apparently. To reestablish his dominance. Same old, same old."

Kat shook her head and grinned, eyes ultra-bright. "You do realize you're baiting the beast, right? And that's not an insult. I saw his face; that man hasn't met a challenge he didn't want to wrestle to the ground."

The elevator bay was empty except for a cleaning sprite boredly buffing the marble floor. I gave it a nod and headed for the doors. "He thinks our history is relevant to our work relationship. I told him the opposite."

Kat grinned. "What's the move here, witchy?"

"Easy. Ignore it. Outperform him."

"Outperform the golden boy?" Kat stretched, feline satisfaction in every muscle. "You know, I do believe I like this version of you."

I looked at my reflection in the mirrored elevator doors, the faintest shimmer of magic still wreathed around my head like an afterimage. "Yeah, well. He doesn't know what's about to hit him." I pressed the elevator button with more force than necessary, and the doors slid closed with a soft, mechanical sigh.

The ride down was silent except for the hum and click of cables, and the faint whispered echoes of our own ragged breathing. I tried to shake Nathan's words free from my mind, but their barbed hooks caught and snagged in the softest places.

Kat didn't comment further, just leaned against the wall with her arms crossed, watching the numbers above the door tick steadily downward.

10

Cosmic Showers and Complicated Feelings

"Well, that was intense," a voice said, making me jump as we exited the elevator. My eyes snapped to the side where I find Silas leaning casually against the wall right outside of the elevator, a knowing smirk on his face.

"Jesus, Silas," I gasped, my hand flying to my chest. "You saw our little talk?"

He shrugged, his fangs glinting as he grinned. "Impossible not to hear the end of your little tête-à-tête with our fearless leader. Gotta say, I'm impressed. Not many people stand up to Nathan like that."

I groaned, running a hand through my hair. "Were you eavesdropping?"

"Vampire hearing," he said, tapping his ear. "It's both a blessing and a curse. But don't worry, your secrets are safe with me."

I eyed him warily, "And I can trust you?"

Silas's grin widened. "My dear Sadie, I have a feeling you and I are going to be great friends. Anyone who can ruffle

Nathan's feathers like that is alright in my book."

He fell into step beside Kat and I as we made our way through the vast and opulent lobby fit for royalty. Sunlight poured in through floor-to-ceiling windows, casting golden beams on the marble floors and ornate furnishings. It's going to take some getting used to.

Silas gestured grandly, "After you, my feisty new colleague."

I rolled my eyes but couldn't help the small smile that tugged at my lips. "Thanks, Silas."

"So," Kat begins, a sly edge to her voice. "Let's talk about the tension between you and Nathan. What all did you say to each other in his office?"

I sighed, running a hand through my hair. "It's a long story. One that definitely requires alcohol to tell properly."

Silas clapped his hands together, his fangs glinting in the lobby lights. "Well then, ladies, shall we adjourn to the nearest watering hole? I believe we were promised celebratory drinks."

Kat's eyes lit up. "Drinks sound perfect right about now," Kat said, linking her arm through mine. "I want to hear all about what happened with Nathan."

I groaned, "Trust me, you really don't."

Silas chuckled, leading us out of the building. "Oh, I think we all want to hear this story. It's not every day someone gets under Nathan's skin like that."

As we stepped out into the bustling New York night, the city's energy seemed to pulse around us. The lights, the sounds, the sheer vitality of it all - it was a far cry from our quiet Indiana town.

"So, where to?" I asked, glancing between Kat and Silas.

Silas grinned, his fangs glinting in the streetlights. "I know just the place. It's a little supernatural hotspot, off the beaten path."

He led us through the bustling streets, weaving between crowds with practiced ease. After a few blocks, we turned down a narrow alley that I would have missed if I wasn't following closely. At the end of the alley was a nondescript door with a small, glowing rune etched above it.

Silas placed his hand on the door, and the rune flashed briefly before the door swung open. "Welcome," he said with a flourish, "to The Witching Hour."

As we stepped inside, I was immediately struck by the atmosphere. The bar was dimly lit, with floating orbs of soft light hovering above each table. The air was thick with the scent of herbs and incense, and I could feel the hum of magic pulsing through the room.

"Wow," Kat breathed, her eyes wide as she took in the scene.

"This place is incredible," I agreed, feeling the thrum of magic in the air. It was comforting, like slipping into a warm bath after a long day.

Silas led us to a secluded booth in the corner, the plush velvet seats a deep, rich purple. As we slid in, a menu materialized on the table in front of us, the text shimmering and changing as we looked at it.

"The house special is to die for," Silas said with a wink. "Literally, in some cases. But don't worry, they have plenty of options for the living."

I scanned the menu, my eyebrows rising at some of the more exotic offerings. "Blood of the Innocent? Essence of Eternity? What kind of place is this, Silas?"

"Relax, you'll love it." Silas said, leaning back with a mischievous grin.

The waitress, a human oddly enough, sauntered over to take

our orders. Her expression was far from friendly and could even be described as hostile. It seemed like she didn't want to be bothered by us.

Too bad.

After we ordered she slank back to whatever corner she wandered out of as Silas picked the conversation right back up where we left off.

"So, who's ready to spill the tea on what went down with our illustrious leader?"

I sighed, ready to respond just as our drinks were delivered with a pointed slam. Bitch has some nerve; I'll give her that.

Taking a long sip of my drink - a shimmering concoction called "Cosmic Shower" that tasted like liquid starlight. "Alright, alright. I suppose I owe you both a longer explanation."

Kat leaned in eagerly, her eyes sparkling with curiosity. "Spill it, sister. What happened in that office?"

I recounted the confrontation with Nathan, watching as Kat's and Silas's expressions shifted from surprise to amusement to something like admiration.

"Wait," Kat interrupted, her brow furrowed. "You mean to tell me he doesn't remember you at all?"

I sigh, completely over this whole conversation already.

"Why would he? I didn't stand out. I wasn't fighting for his attention like all the other girls there."

Silas leans forward, interest written all over his face. "I'm lost, what are we talking about? You've met Nathan before?'

Kat shot Silas one of her patented "You're in for it now" grins. "Oh, it's good, Silas. Sadie had a little moment with Nathan at the Lux Bellator retreat back when we were kids. She's been carrying the wounds ever since."

Silas's eyes flared, as if this was juicier than synthetic blood.

"Please, elaborate. Don't be shy."

I drained half my drink, feeling the magic tingle through my chest, and set the glass down a little harder than intended. "Fine. If it'll shut you both up." I pressed my fingers to my temples, summoning the memory.

"Picture me at sixteen, still a dork, not allowed to use my real powers. Nathan's nineteen, already the golden boy, strutting around like he runs the place—which he basically did. I'm minding my own business, practicing the lamest spells because Michael said, under no circumstances, could I show off. Nathan saunters over and…" Even now, embarrassment and anger shoot through me at the memory. "He calls me out. Tells me not to hurt myself with 'parlor tricks.' Then walks off laughing." I finished my drink, savoring the electric aftertaste. "I mean, the first boy you ever notice, and he goes full jerk on you."

Silas studied me, his gaze a little softer than before. "And now you're almost his equal and you get to rub it in his smug face every single day. Poetic."

"Too bad he doesn't remember it. Or maybe, it's better this way." I say conflicted. "Either way, I can tell he has a problem with me now."

Silas's grin widened, a knowing look in his eyes. "Oh, I think I might have an idea about that."

I raised an eyebrow, both curious and wary. "Care to share with the class?"

Silas leaned in, his voice dropping to a conspiratorial whisper. "Well, let's just say our fearless leader isn't used to being challenged. Especially not by someone he underestimated. You, my dear Sadie, have managed to do both in spectacular fashion."

Kat nodded enthusiastically. "He's right. You should have seen Nathan's face when you took down that barrier. He looked like he'd been hit by a truck."

I felt a sense of pride at their words. "That doesn't mean anything. He was probably just shocked that the 'rookie' saved his ass."

Silas chuckled. "Sure Sadie, it has nothing to do with him finding you intriguing not to mention sexy."

I nearly choked on my drink at Silas's words. "Sexy? Are you kidding me? Nathan doesn't find me sexy. He finds me annoying at best."

Kat and Silas exchanged knowing looks that made me want to sink into my seat.

"Oh honey," Kat said, patting my hand. "You really don't see it, do you?"

I rolled my eyes. "See what? That Nathan Blackwood, Mr. Perfect Nephilim himself, secretly has the hots for me? Yeah right."

Silas leaned back, a smirk playing on his lips. "You'd be surprised. Nathan may act all high and mighty, but he's still a man. And you, my dear, are quite the beautiful woman."

I felt my cheeks flush, though I tried to play it off. I was about to protest further when my phone buzzed. I pulled it out to see a text from Chloe in our group thread:

"Where is everyone at? I thought we were getting a drink?"

Oops. We all look at each other guiltily. I couldn't help but feel bad for leaving them behind. In all the drama with Nathan, we'd completely forgotten about the rest of the team.

"Should we invite the others too?" I asked, glancing between Kat and Silas.

Silas shrugged, a mischievous glint in his eye. "Why not?

The more, the merrier. Besides, I'm sure they'd love to hear all about your little pow wow with Nathan."

I groaned, burying my face in my hands. "Can we please stop talking about Nathan?"

"Not a chance," Kat grinned, nudging me playfully. "This is prime gossip material."

Thirty minutes later the door swung open, Chloe, Hadeon, and Nathan walked in. I felt my stomach do a little flip. Nathan's eyes immediately locked onto mine, his expression unreadable.

"Well, well," Silas drawled, raising his glass in greeting. "Look who decided to join the party."

Chloe slid into the booth next to Kat, while Hadeon pulled up a chair. Nathan hesitated for a moment before taking the only remaining seat - right next to me. I could feel the heat radiating off his body, our arms nearly touching in the cramped space.

"Fancy seeing you here," I said, unsure of what to say. "Drink?"

Nathan gave a small shake of his head. "I'm good, thanks."

"Nice place," Chloe remarked, looking around appreciatively. "How'd you find it?"

Silas grinned, his fangs glinting in the dim light. "A vampire never reveals his secrets. Now, what can I get you all to drink? First round's on me."

As Silas took drink orders, I couldn't help but notice Nathan's eyes flickering to me every few seconds. I was acutely aware of his presence beside me. The booth suddenly felt much smaller, and I found myself trying not to fidget.

"So," Chloe said, leaning forward with a mischievous glint in her eye, "what have we missed? Any juicy gossip?"

I shot a warning glance at Silas and Kat, silently pleading with them not to mention my earlier conversation with Nathan. Silas, of course, ignored me completely.

"Oh, just discussing our new teammates' impressive debut," he said with a grin. "Sadie here was just telling us all about her little chat with Nathan after the mission. Turns out they have a past."

That gets everyone's attention. I resist the urge to kick Silas under the table.

Chloe perks up, eyes practically glowing with gossip-fueled hunger. "A past? Details, please."

Nathan's jaw goes rigid, but he keeps his gaze trained on his untouched glass. "It's not important," he says, voice clipped.

But Chloe isn't deterred. "Oh, I think it's extremely important," she purrs. "Especially if it explains why the two of you can't be in the same room for five seconds without trying to set each other on fire. Figuratively or literally."

I shoot Silas a dirty look, but he just flashes his fangs in an unapologetic grin. "What can I say? I have an ear for good stories."

Hadeon, who's been quietly observing the dynamic with unreadable fae cool, finally speaks up. "If there is a prior relationship, it can only benefit unit cohesion if it is addressed openly." He says it like he's reading from a training manual, but I sense a shade of amusement behind the words.

I glanced sidelong at Nathan. His face was blank, but his knuckles were white where he gripped the edge of the table. "It's nothing. Just ran into him at a training retreat years ago. He doesn't remember it. It's ancient history. Not a big deal." I glance over at Nathan to see his brow furrowed in thought. He definitely doesn't remember.

Chloe raised an eyebrow, clearly not buying it. "Uh-huh. And that's why you both look like you're about to jump out of your skin right now?"

I felt my cheeks flush and took a large gulp of my drink to hide my discomfort. The liquid sparkled as it went down, leaving a warm, tingling sensation in its wake. I started to feel lightheaded, what was in this thing?

The conversation continued to swirl around Nathan and me, with the team speculating and teasing. I could feel the tension radiating off Nathan beside me, I bet he wished he didn't come after all.

"Okay, that's enough," Nathan finally said, his voice tired. "What happened between Sadie and me is nobody's business but our own."

The way he said it made it seem like we'd been involved in some scandalous escapade. I gulped down more of my drink, wishing I could vanish faster than a slice of pizza at a frat party. The room wobbled slightly, courtesy of the intoxicating concoction I was sipping. I blinked, trying to regain focus as the chatter around me blurred into a symphony of nonsense. Nathan's presence was as overpowering as cheap cologne, his arm occasionally grazing mine and sending little jolts of static electricity through my system.

"You okay there, Sadie?" Kat's voice cut through the pulsing neon and laughter, her brow knitting as she studied my dazed expression. Behind her, the bar's magical lanterns cast drifting patterns of violet and gold against the polished wood. I stared down at the crystalline glass in my hand, the Cosmic Shower's iridescent liquid swirling with miniature bursts of stardust. With a shaky sigh, I slid it away. "Yeah, I think you're right.

This stuff is stronger than I thought."

Nathan pivoted toward me, the low glow highlighting his sharp jawline and the concern flickering in his cobalt eyes. "Do you need some air?" His voice was soft, almost private, and I felt a shiver trace my spine at how close he leaned. "I'm fine," I managed, though the room tilted beneath me. "Just need a minute."

"I think some fresh air would do you good." He rose smoothly, extending a steady hand. Outside, an abrupt gust of icy wind rushed in through the open door as I accepted it, the electric shock of contact sending a tiny spark through my palm. Around us, our teammates paused mid-conversation, their curious glances following our retreat.

The alley's narrow strip of sky glimmered above us, the night air tasting of damp brick and distant rain. Nathan led me toward a shadowed alcove beside a barred window, its yellow light a soft halo on the wet cobblestones. He slipped an arm around my waist, guiding me onto a cold, wrought-iron bench. "Sit," he whispered, his hand warm at the small of my back. "Breathe deep."

I inhaled, the air crisp in my lungs, and let it out slowly, eyes closed. When I opened them, Nathan's face hovered close, his gaze tender, laced with something unspoken. "Feeling better?" His tone held an unexpected gentleness.

"Much," I said, pressing a palm to my temple. "These magical cocktails… they sneak up on you."

He let out a soft laugh, the sound richer than the echoing runes inside. "They're not like ordinary drinks. One wrong mix, and your head's in a spin."

I offered a weak smile. "Lesson learned. Thanks for dragging me out here."

Nathan was silent for a heartbeat, then leaned in so I could feel the warmth of his breath. I braced for a kiss; my heart pounded against my ribs as his blue eyes searched mine. But he pulled back, conflict flashing across his features. "Sadie, I…" He swallowed.

"What is it?" My voice fell to a whisper, disappointment knotting in my chest.

He ran a hand through his dark hair, unusually flustered. "I want you to know I respect your abilities. What you did today was impressive."

Surprised, I blinked. "Oh. Um, thanks."

He nodded gravely, then his tone shifted. "But that doesn't mean you can disregard direct orders."

My cheeks burned. The fragile warmth between us drained away. "Seriously?" I scoffed, pulling back. "We're back to this?"

Nathan straightened, shoulders rigid, yet his voice held none of its earlier edge. "You're right. I'm sorry."

His apology landed between us, awkward and brittle as the frost on the bricks. We sat, the cold night stretching silent around our unspoken thoughts.

"Are the rumors about an uptick in activity around the area true?" I ask when the silence becomes suffocating.

He gives me a surprised look, clearly not expecting that question. He waits a beat, leaving me wondering if he is ever going to respond when finally, he gives a small nod.

"Yeah, the past six months have been wild. We aren't sure what exactly going on, but we suspect it has something to do with demonic energy.

I considered Nathan's words carefully. "Demonic energy? That's concerning. Have you been able to pinpoint any specific source or pattern to the increased activity?"

Nathan shook his head, his expression grim. "Not yet. It's been frustratingly elusive. Every time we think we're getting close to figuring it out, the trail goes cold."

I nodded thoughtfully. "Well, maybe a fresh perspective could help. Kat and I might see something you've missed."

Nathan studied me for a moment before nodding slowly. "You're right. I shouldn't have been so quick to dismiss your abilities earlier. Your skills could be valuable in this investigation."

I felt a small thrill at his admission. "Does this mean you'll actually let us participate in real missions now instead of just crowd control?"

The corner of Nathan's mouth twitched in what might have been the ghost of a smile. "We'll see. You've certainly proven yourselves capable today."

We lapsed into silence again, but this time it felt less awkward, more contemplative. I found myself studying Nathan's profile in the dim light, noticing the way his brow furrowed slightly as he seemed lost in thought.

Finally, Nathan broke the silence. "We should probably head back inside before the others start getting ideas."

I couldn't help but smirk. "Too late for that. I'm pretty sure Silas already has us married off in his imagination."

Nathan groaned, running a hand through his hair. "Fantastic. Well, shall we face the music?"

As we stood to go back inside, I felt a wave of dizziness hit me again. Nathan's hand shot out to steady me, his touch sending a jolt through my system.

"You okay?" he asked, concern evident in his voice.

I nodded, trying to ignore the way my skin tingled where

he touched me. "Yeah, just still a bit woozy from that drink. I'll be fine."

Nathan's hand lingered on my arm for a moment longer than necessary before he pulled away. "Right. Well, let's get you some water and then call it a night. We've got a big day tomorrow with the debriefing."

As we walked back into the bar, I couldn't help but feel that something had shifted between us. The hostility from earlier had faded, replaced by… something else. Something I wasn't quite ready to name.

One thing was certain though - working with Nathan Blackwood was going to be far more complicated than I'd initially thought.

11

Office Hours and Power Plays

I make it to headquarters for my debriefing with Nathan and Stephen. Stephen's secretary leads me to an office door at the end of the hallway. She knocks once before entering with me in tow. Sitting behind the desk is the head of the Lux Bellator's New York Chapter, Stephen Donaldson.

Stephen is legendary in the paranormal world for his heroic combat, however nowadays he is the man in charge, no longer in the field. On the other side of the desk sits my new team lead, Nathan. He spares me a quick glare. I guess we are back to that. I'm beginning to think he doesn't like me. Pity. Next to him is an empty chair meant for me, I'm assuming.

"Ah, Ms. Baker, welcome," Stephen says, rising from his chair with a warm smile. "Please, have a seat."

I slide into the empty chair next to Nathan, flashing him a cheeky grin. "Miss me?"

He responds with a barely audible grunt.

I turn to Mr. Donaldson giving him my most winning smile.

"Pleasure to meet you. I've heard so many... well, some things about you."

His weathered face crinkled with amusement as he shook my hand. "Miss Baker. Your reputation precedes you as well."

"All bad things, I hope?" I quipped.

"Depends on who you ask," Nathan muttered under his breath.

I shot him a sidelong glance. "Careful, Nathan. Your sunny disposition is showing again."

Stephen chuckles. "We do like to keep things exciting around here. But onto business. Nathan here will be personally overseeing your training and integration into the team."

I turn to Nathan, batting my eyelashes. "Oh goody, more quality time together. I can already feel our friendship blossoming."

Nathan gives a curt nod as his eye twitches. "I look forward to it," he says, his tone suggesting he'd rather swallow nails.

"We'll begin your training first thing tomorrow morning." He continues. "6 AM sharp."

"6 AM?" I gasped in mock horror. "Do supernatural threats not believe in sleeping in?"

"Evil doesn't wait for your beauty sleep, Miss Baker," Nathan replied dryly.

"Clearly," I retorted, eyeing Nathan's disheveled appearance. "Though I'd argue my wit is sharper when I'm well-rested."

Stephen cleared his throat, drawing our attention back to him. "I'm sure you two will work out a… mutually agreeable schedule. Now, Sadie, there's one more matter we need to discuss."

I straightened in my chair, sensing the shift in tone. "I'm all ears."

"Here at Lux Bellator, there is another aspect of being an operative with us. When not out in the field, agents have a lot of paperwork and investigative duties, you get the idea. You will be working in the office next to Nathan where I will have you working as his assistant until you get more acclimated with our organization."

That sounds like a lot of time with Mr. Tall, Dark, and Brooding. I want to protest, but since I just got there, I figured I shouldn't burn my bridges too soon.

Nathan has no such issue. His complaints are almost instant.

"With all due respect, sir," Nathan interjected, his voice tight with barely contained frustration, "I don't need an assistant. Especially not one who—"

"Who what, Nathan?" I challenged, unable to resist. "Who might actually bring some fun to your dreary little world?"

Nathan's teeth smash together, his face promising a scathing reply. But, before he can retort, Stephen holds up a hand. "This isn't up for debate. Sadie needs to learn our protocols, and you, Nathan, could use the help. Your last three reports were late."

I couldn't help but smirk at Nathan's discomfort. "Aww, having trouble keeping up with your paperwork, sunshine?"

Nathan's glare could have melted me on the spot. "I assure you, sir, I'm perfectly capable of—"

"It's decided," Stephen said firmly, his tone brooking no argument.

"Fantastic," I chirped, clapping my hands together. "Nathan and I, office buddies. This is going to be so much fun."

Stephen chuckled at our exchange, his eyes twinkling with amusement. "I can already tell you two are going to keep things interesting around here." He leaned back in his chair, regarding me with a thoughtful expression. "Now, Sadie, I understand you and your partner Katerina had quite the eventful first day yesterday."

I nodded, feeling Nathan tense beside me. "You could say that, sir. We encountered some unexpected… challenges."

"Challenges?" Nathan scoffed. "Is that what we're calling blatant insubordination now?"

I turned to him, batting my eyelashes innocently. "I prefer to think of it as creative problem-solving."

Stephen held up a hand, silencing us both. "I've read the reports, and while I understand there were some… unorthodox decisions made, I can't argue with the results." He fixed his gaze on Nathan. "Sometimes, Nathan, we need to be open to new approaches. Rigidity can be our downfall in this line of work."

Nathan scowled like a petulant child, but he nodded stiffly. "Understood, sir."

I couldn't help but feel a small thrill of victory at Stephen's words. "I promise to bring plenty of new approaches to the table," I said with a grin.

Stephen chuckled. "I'm counting on it, Miss Baker. Now, is there anything else either of you would like to discuss before we wrap this up?"

I glanced at Nathan, who was still looking like he'd swallowed something sour. "I think we're good," I said, flashing a saccharine smile at Nathan. "Right, partner?"

Nathan shot me a withering look before turning to Stephen. "Yes, sir. We're fine."

"That will be all then," Stephen said, his tone final. "Sadie, get settled in. Nathan, show her to her office."

Before we left, Stephen called out, "Oh, and Sadie? Try not to drive Nathan completely mad on your first day in the office together. We do need him functional."

I placed a hand over my heart in mock offense. "Me? Never. I'll be the very picture of professionalism."

As we left Stephen's office, I couldn't resist needling Nathan a bit more. "So, 'office buddy', ready for our grand adventure in paperwork?"

Nathan stopped abruptly, turning to face me with an intensity that almost made me take a step back. Almost. "Listen carefully, Sadie," he said, his voice low and controlled. "I don't know what game you think you're playing, but it ends now."

Ha! Please, son.

"Understood. So....boss, what's our first order of business tomorrow? Coffee run? Alphabetizing your journal entries?"

Nathan pinched the bridge of his nose, looking pained. "Our first order of business will be establishing some ground rules."

"Ooh, kinky," I teased.

"Rule number one," Nathan growled, "No more jokes."

I gasp in mock horror.

"No jokes?" I clutched my chest dramatically. "You wound me, Nathan. How will I ever survive in such a humorless environment?"

Nathan's eye twitched again. I was starting to think it was a nervous tic. "You'll manage," he said dryly. "Now, if you're quite finished with the theatrics, I'll show you to your office."

We walked down the hallway, our footsteps echoing off the marble floors. I couldn't help but notice the tense set of Nathan's shoulders, the way his jaw clenched every time I opened my mouth. It was almost too easy to get under his skin.

"So, Nathan," I began conversationally, "what's your deal anyway? Were you born this uptight, or did you have to work at it?"

He stopped abruptly, turning to face me with a look of exasperation.

"Listen Baker," Nathan said, his voice low and controlled, "I'm thrilled to see you're in a better mood and I understand that you find this situation amusing. But I assure you, our work here is no laughing matter. Lives are at stake. The fate of the world often hangs in the balance. So forgive me if I don't find your constant quips and jabs particularly entertaining."

Okay, he's really starting to piss me off. "Now you listen here Nathan Blackwood. I'm joking around, trying to make the best of a situation, I really don't want to be in. I've been fighting these demons long before you and your merry band of clowns came into my life."

I can tell he is thrown off guard by my change in persona. I tried the lighthearted way to no avail, so allow me to introduce him to my bitch side.

He opened his mouth to say more, but before he could utter a word, I pressed on.

"I'm not here to be your friend, Nathan," I snapped, my previous joviality evaporating. "But I am here to do a job. A job that, I'm no more a fan of than you. So how about we skip the posturing and get down to business?"

Nathan blinked, clearly taken aback by my sudden shift in demeanor. He had stopped outside of an office I assumed was for me. For a moment, he just stared at me, his blue eyes searching my face as if seeing me for the first time.

"Fair enough," he said, his voice losing some of its edge, but certainly not all. "You're right."

"Damn straight I am," I replied, crossing my arms, stepping back into the office. "So, now, if you will excuse me, I want to check out my new office." I then slammed the door in his face feeling satisfaction through every fiber of my being.

That dude is an asshole.

* * *

Later that evening, I am in my new apartment, trying my best to get used to the city life. It's really not my thing. I'm laying on the couch watching my fourth true crime episode of the evening with Orion. We were just getting into the investigation when there was a knock at my door. Grumbling under my breath, I get up to answer.

Silas and Chloe are waiting on the other side.

"Hey girl," Chloe says when I open it. "Get dressed, we're going out. Where's Kat?"

I glanced down at my sweats wondering why I answered the door. "Um, I'm kind of tired. With the move and all, you know?"

She nods in false sincerity and says, "too bad, this is a bonding experience with your new teammates at a supernatural bar down the street."

"I've already bonded with Nathan enough for one day," I say, grumbling.

"I don't think he'll be there. It's usually me, and Chloe, and sometimes, Hadeon." Silas informs me.

I glance between the two of them noticing the determination on their faces and relent.

"Fine, give me a bit to go get dressed." I motion to the couch, "Make yourselves at home."

12

The Pixie Dust Incident (Classified, Obviously)

Thirty minutes later, I emerged from my room, fully dressed and prepared for the evening ahead. My hair cascaded down my shoulders in soft, flowing waves, catching the light with each movement. My makeup was an artful balance, with dramatic smokey eyes that created an air of mystery, contrasted by the subtle, neutral tones on my lips and cheeks, lending a touch of understated elegance. I completed my ensemble with a short, form-fitting black dress that hugged my curves, paired with slender stiletto heels that added a touch of sophistication. Kat was bubbling with excitement; she never missed an opportunity to revel in the night.

We arrived at a supernatural bar whimsically named The Cloak of Invisibility. Cute, indeed. As we stepped inside, I was immediately enveloped by the vibrant and eclectic mix of patrons that filled the room. Vampires lounged at the bar, elegantly sipping on blood cocktails, their alabaster skin casting an otherworldly glow beneath the dim, ambient lighting. In the far corner, a group of werewolves engaged in a lively game of pool, their boisterous laughter mingling with the occasional playful growl, creating a symphony of camaraderie. Toward the back, a pair of fae sat at a table, their ethereal beauty and shimmering wings captivating everyone around them with an almost magnetic allure. "Welcome to our little slice of supernatural heaven," Silas declared with a grin, his sharp fangs catching the light and adding an extra glint to the already enchanting atmosphere.

Chloe nodded, a small smile gracing her lips as she absorbed the lively atmosphere around her. The room buzzed with the low hum of conversation and the clinking of glasses, a haven for those seeking refuge from the day's challenges. "This is our sanctuary after a long day of saving the world," she said, her voice carrying a lighthearted tone. "Or, you know, getting ensnared by some low-level demons."

I couldn't help but snort, a grin tugging at my mouth. "Hey, at least you guys have a sense of humor about it. Unlike a certain brooding team leader we all know."

Silas chuckled warmly, guiding us toward a cozy booth nestled in the corner, away from the main throng. "Trust me, we're not usually that incompetent. Yesterday was… an anomaly," he assured, his eyes twinkling with amusement. "As for our fearless leader, don't let his gruff exterior fool you—beneath that tough shell, he's just a big teddy bear."

"A teddy bear with anger management issues and a stick up his ass, maybe," I muttered.

Chloe laughed, her shoulders shaking from amusement. "You're not wrong. He's been extra grumpy lately. But he's good at what he does, and a great leader."

As we settled into the booth, a waitress with mint green hair and shimmering skin approached. "Welcome to The Cloak!

What can I get for you lovely creatures tonight?"

I glanced at the menu, impressed by the variety of supernatural-themed cocktails. "I'll have the 'Witch's Familiar', please," I said with a grin.

"Bloody Mary for me," Silas quipped, winking at the waitress. "And make it extra bloody."

Chloe rolled her eyes at Silas' antics. "I'll have the 'Shifter's Surprise'."

As the waitress left with our orders, I turned back to my new teammates. "So, tell me more about this place. How'd you guys find it?"

Silas leaned back, a nostalgic smile on his face. "Ah, now that's a story. It was about two years ago, right after a particularly nasty run-in with a coven of dark witches..."

As Silas launched into his tale, I found myself relaxing for the first time since arriving in New York. There was something comforting about being surrounded by other supernatural beings, not having to hide who I was or what I could do.

"So, there we were," Silas continued, gesturing animatedly, "covered in some potion - the nasty kind, not the unicorn kind- and desperately in need of a drink. We stumbled down this alley, half-dead on our feet, when suddenly we see this shimmering doorway appear out of nowhere."

Chloe jumped in, her tone conveying her excitement as she recalled the memory. "At first, we thought it was a trap, you know? But then we heard the music, smelled the booze, and figured, hey, if we're going to die, might as well do it with a drink in hand."

I listened intently as Silas and Chloe recounted their amusing tale of discovering the bar. Their animated storytelling and obvious camaraderie made me smile. As they finished, our drinks arrived - my Witch's Familiar cocktail glowing an eerie green.

Hadeon arrives a little while after us, his presence marked by an easy camaraderie with Kat. It appears they have connected quite well, their heads bent together in a deep, private conversation that piques my curiosity. Their words, though inaudible, seem to flow smoothly between them, hinting at shared interests or secrets.

Meanwhile, Chloe shifts her position, her shifter eyes catching the light and shimmering as if woven from moonbeams. She leans forward, her eyes gleaming with interest. "So, Sadie," she inquires, her voice a soft melody, "what's your story? How did you find yourself among the ranks of the Lux Bellator?"

I lifted my glass to my lips, pondering just how much of my tale to reveal. "Well," I began, "it's a bit of a long story, but the short version is that I've been training with them since I was a kid. My mentor, Michael, spotted my potential early on—or so he claims—and took me under his wing." Silas arched an eyebrow, a flicker of admiration crossing his features. "Michael? As in Michael the Nephilim?" he asked, his voice tinged with awe. "He's a legend in our circles." The mention of Michael's name seemed to reverberate, like the echo of a mythical saga told around countless campfires.

I nodded, feeling a swell of pride for my mentor. "Yeah, that's the one. He's hardcore, but an excellent teacher. Taught me everything I know about magic and the supernatural world."

"So, you've been in this life since childhood?" Chloe asked, her eyes wide with curiosity. "That must have been intense."

I shrugged, taking another sip of my drink. "It was... different, for sure. While other kids were learning algebra and worrying about prom dates, I was mastering protection spells and learning how to banish demons. Kat came into the picture when she was sixteen and she and I have been inseparable since then, training together and dreaming of the day we'd become full-fledged agents."

As the night wore on, the conversation flowed as freely as the drinks. I found myself genuinely enjoying the company of my new teammates, their stories of past missions and supernatural encounters both thrilling and hilarious. I'm also relieved to see that Nathan is not present at this little impromptu get together. I'm just not in the mood for his shit tonight.

"So," Silas said, leaning in conspiratorially, "want to talk about you and Nathan? The tension between you two is thicker than a vampire's bloodlust at midnight."

I rolled my eyes, taking another sip of my drink. "He and I just don't click. We have a mutual dislike for one another. I feel, that given the right amount of time together, it can blossom into a full-blown hatred. It's all very inspiring."

Chloe raised an eyebrow, her form shimmering with curiosity. "Oh, come on, there's got to be more to it than that. Spill the tea, witch."

I sighed, realizing they wanted more. "It's not that exciting, really. It's like I told you guys last night. We met at a training retreat years ago, he was an ass, I flipped him off, now we have reunited to irritate one another again. For the record, he started it."

Silas leaned back, a knowing smirk on his face. "Oh, I doubt that's the end of the story. The way you two snipe at each other? There's definitely more to it."

I rolled my eyes at Silas's insinuation. "Trust me, there's nothing more to it. Nathan and I just clash, plain and simple. He's uptight, arrogant, and takes himself way too seriously. I, on the other hand, am a delight."

Chloe snorted into her drink. "A delight who nearly gave Nathan an aneurysm today, from what I heard."

I grinned, raising my glass in a mock toast. "What can I say? It's a gift."

Chloe leaned in, her form shimmering with excitement. "Oh come on, Sadie. You can't tell me you don't find him even a little bit attractive. I mean, have you seen those arms?"

I snorted into my drink. "I've seen better," I lied. Okay, so maybe Nathan was objectively attractive, in that brooding, chiseled-jaw kind of way. But his personality more than canceled out any physical appeal.

"Besides," I added, "I don't mix business with pleasure. Especially not when that 'pleasure' comes with a side of constant irritation."

Speak of the devil. Damn, I thought too soon. Looking over Chloe's head I see him, Nathan, talking with a group of people all dressed as though they were headed to a regatta rather than your local everyday bar. He was standing next to a pretty woman with red hair and a look of distain on her face. Who'd have guessed?

I couldn't help but roll my eyes at the sight of Nathan with his preppy posse. Of course he'd hang out with people who looked like they stepped out of a J. Crew catalog. And is that jealousy simmering in my stomach? Of course, not.

"Looks like Mr. Sunshine decided to grace us with his presence after all," I muttered, taking a sip of my drink.

Chloe followed my gaze and grinned. "Oh, that's just Nathan's old crowd from his boarding school days. They like to get together and reminisce about their glory days on the rowing team or whatever."

"Fascinating," I drawled. "I'm sure discussing trust funds and yacht clubs makes for riveting conversation."

Silas chuckled. "Don't let the preppy exterior fool you. Nathan's actually a pretty badass fighter when it comes down to it."

I raised an eyebrow skeptically. "Oh really? I'll have to take your word on that."

Hadeon chuckles at that. "The redhead next to him is Tiffany. She's a viper. They've been on and off since kids. Both trust fund kids with parents in the right circles. I'm guessing they're on again this week."

"Best of luck to them both," I say in a grumbling tone.

When I look back his way, I notice Nathan approaching our table, his preppy posse thankfully staying behind. He was dressed more casually than I'd seen him before, in dark jeans and a fitted black t-shirt that showed off his muscular build. I hated to admit it, but he looked good.

Nathan's expression held a healthy dose of wariness as he spotted me. "Well, well. I didn't expect to see you here," he said, his tone neutral but with an undercurrent of tension.

I plastered on my sweetest smile. "Nathan! What a surprise. We were just discussing how much fun we're going to have working together."

His eyes narrowed slightly, clearly not buying my saccharine act. "Is that so? And here I thought you'd be too busy plotting ways to drive me insane."

"Oh come now, Nathan," I replied, batting my eyelashes innocently. "Driving you insane is a small bonus. My real goal is world domination, obviously."

Silas snorted into his drink, while Chloe tried to hide her grin behind her hand. Even Hadeon's lips twitched in a small smile.

Nathan's eyes flickered with amusement before he quickly masked it. "World domination? Ambitious. I'd start smaller if I were you. Maybe try conquering your inbox first."

I gasped in mock offense. "Are you implying I can't handle a little paperwork, Mr. Blackwood? I'm new at this, but I'll catch on. Besides, that's why I have you. To mentor me."

Nathan's eyebrow quirked up at that. "Mentor you? I thought I was just here to be the target of your endless sarcasm."

"Oh Nathan, you're so much more than that," I said, my voice dripping with faux sincerity. "You're also here to fetch my coffee and sharpen my pencils."

The rest of the table burst into laughter at our exchange. Even Nathan's lips twitched in what might have been the ghost of a smile.

"We'll see about that," he replied dryly. Then, to my surprise, he turned to the others. "Mind if I join you?"

Silas and Chloe exchanged a quick glance before Silas shrugged. "Sure, boss. Pull up a chair."

As Nathan settled into the empty seat next to me, I couldn't help but tense slightly. His presence seemed to fill the entire booth, and I was acutely aware of his arm brushing against mine as he reached for a menu. The scent of his cologne - something woodsy and masculine - wafted over me, and I had to resist the urge to lean in closer.

"So," he said, his voice low and smooth, "what have I missed?"

Silas grinned, his fangs glinting in the low light. "Oh, just Sadie here regaling us with tales of her magical prowess and her plans for world domination."

I rolled my eyes, but before I could retort, Chloe jumped

in. "Oh, you know, just the usual. Swapping war stories, comparing battle scars. Sadie was just about to tell us about her most embarrassing moment as a witch."

I shot Chloe a glare. "I was not."

Nathan leaned back, a mischievous glint in his eye that I hadn't seen before. "Oh, now this I have to hear. Come on, Sadie. Regale us with tales of your magical mishaps."

I narrowed my eyes at him, not about to let him get the upper hand. "Nice try, Blackwood. But I don't kiss and tell… or in this case, fail and tell."

I continued to glare at Chloe, who was grinning mischievously. "There's nothing to tell. I'm a paragon of grace and competence at all times."

Silas snorted. "Come on, Sadie. Everyone's got at least one embarrassing story. Even our fearless leader here has a few."

Nathan's eyes narrowed at Silas. "We agreed never to speak of that incident with the pixie dust again."

My curiosity was piqued. "Pixie dust incident? Do tell."

"Not a chance," Nathan said firmly, but I caught a hint of a blush on his cheeks. "We're here to hear about your embarrassing moments, not mine."

I sighed dramatically. "Fine, if you insist."

"About a year ago, I was sparring with Michael and thought it would be brilliant to test out a levitation spell. Well, turns out I had no clue what I was doing and ended up dangling upside down for nearly an hour," I confess, my voice tinged with embarrassment. "And to top it off, I was wearing a sundress that day, so the whole gym got an unintentional peep show of my undies. Let's just say, I became the unplanned entertainment for the day!"

As I finished recounting my embarrassing levitation mishap,

the table erupted in laughter, the sound echoing warmly against the walls. Even Nathan, who was usually composed, let out a chuckle. His eyes crinkled at the corners in a way that softened his usual demeanor, making him appear almost… charming, as if the laughter had unveiled a different side of him.

"Well," he said, his grin lingering, "I suppose we all have our moments. Though I have to say, the mental image of you floating upside down in a skirt is pretty priceless."

"How did you finally get down?" Chloe asked, wiping tears of mirth from her eyes.

I grinned sheepishly. "Well, after about an hour of failed attempts to reverse the spell, Michael finally stepped in to counteract whatever I'd done. I swear I couldn't look him in the eye for weeks after that." I surveyed the table as everyone burst into laughter at my magical misadventure. "Yeah, yeah, get it out of your system. At least I didn't have a 'pixie dust disaster' like some people."

Nathan's grin wavered. "We're not discussing it."

Silas leaned in, his fangs gleaming with playful menace. "Oh, but we absolutely are. You see, Sadie, a few years back, we had a case involving a rogue pixie peddling contraband dust."

Nathan's eyes widened, panic creeping in. "Silas, don't you dare…"

But Silas was already diving into the story with gusto. "We were chasing this pixie through Central Park at midnight. Nathan, ever the eager beaver, insisted on leading. What he didn't expect was the pixie's penchant for booby traps."

Nathan groaned, hiding his face in his hands. I leaned forward, utterly intrigued.

"Continue," I urged Silas, my grin wicked. I tapped Nathan's arm teasingly. His arm tensed briefly before relaxing again.

"Well," Silas went on, "Nathan sets off this trap, and suddenly he's plastered head to toe in glittery pixie dust. And not just any pixie dust - this was the premium stuff. Highly potent. He was more pixie-dusted than a Vegas showgirl." Silas continued, his eyes dancing with mischief, "So there's Nathan, sparkling like a disco ball and high as a kite. And let me tell you, seeing Nathan in that state is both a party and a half."

Nathan groaned deeper into his hands. "I despise you all," he grumbled.

I couldn't suppress my delight. "Oh, this is priceless. Silas, spare no detail."

"Well," Silas beamed, "First, he started giggling. And I mean full-on, uncontrollable giggling. Then he decided he could fly."

"Oh no," I gasped, torn between horror and amusement.

"He climbed up on a park bench, spread his arms wide, and yelled some nonsense spell at the top of his lungs. Then he jumped."

I gasped, my hand flying to my mouth. "He didn't!"

Nathan groaned again, his face now a deep shade of red. "Can we please change the subject?"

But Silas was on a roll. "Oh, it gets better. When he realized he couldn't actually fly, he decided the next best thing was to become one with nature. We found him hugging a tree, telling it all his deepest, darkest secrets while only dressed in his underwear."

The mental image of Nathan in only his underwear gave me a pause. I bet he looked good naked…wait, what was I thinking? Not important. I took a deep breath, enjoying the delightful despair on Nathan's face.

"I really hate you all," Nathan said, but his ears were red and his annoyance had lost its bite. He looked at me, blue eyes full of reluctant amusement. "I'm glad you're enjoying this, Baker."

"Immensely," I said, unable to hide the grin. "You in your underpants hugging a tree is officially my new happy place."

A flicker of something passed between us—a flash of mutual understanding, camaraderie, possibly even attraction, though I'd rather eat glass than admit it out loud.

I tried to compose myself, wiping tears of laughter from my eyes.

"Oh Nathan, who knew you had such a wild streak? Hugging trees and those spectacularly botched flying attempts—I'm seeing a whole new side of you." Nathan shot me a withering glare, though I could see his lips twitching, barely suppressing a grin. "Yes, well, we all have our moments of… indiscretion." "Some more dazzlingly exposed than others," I quipped, setting off another round of laughter from the table. "But hey, here's the silver lining: both our tales ended with an audience getting an unplanned peek at us in our underwear, so at least we have that in common."

As the laughter subsided, I found myself observing Nathan with a newfound intensity. There was an unexpected allure in witnessing this rare vulnerability in his otherwise unyielding demeanor. For a fleeting moment, our hostile relationship seemed to fade into the background. Nathan met my eyes, and for once, there was no trace of irritation or contempt. Instead, he offered a subtle, sincere smile that made my heart flutter with a combination of surprise and confusion. I quickly averted my gaze, disturbed by the unsettling warmth that spread through me.

Almost.

"Well," Nathan said, his voice a bit rough as he cleared his throat, "I suppose I should get back to my friends. Try not to enjoy yourself too much at my expense."

An unfamiliar tension lingered in the air as I watched him retreat to his circle of friends. He paused halfway, turning back to cast one last lingering glance at our table, or perhaps directly at me, before rejoining his group.

13

Sparkles, Spite, and Supernatural Politics

As the conversation carried on with stories shared around me, I found myself stealing glances at Nathan, struggling to pull my gaze away. Part of me felt undeniably drawn to him, yet another part cringed at how helplessly captivated I was. It was as if I was caught in a tug of war with my own emotions.

At some point, an imposing shadow falls over our table, casting a dark veil that is quickly followed by a shocked silence, an almost palpable pause in the lively hum of the bar. I glance up to find a dark-haired elf standing before us, exuding a regal aura interwoven with an undeniable air of pomposity. His presence is as commanding as it is unexpected.

Elves are infamous for their deeply ingrained superiority complex, a trait that is invariably accompanied by an utter disdain for any being lacking their distinctively pointed ears. To describe this unexpected visit as unprecedented would be a gross understatement, for elves are known to interact exclusively with their own kind, shunning any form of engagement with outsiders.

"I beg your pardon," the elf begins, his tone a curious blend of condescension and politeness, a verbal dance of superiority masked in courtesy. "My prince has requested you to join him for a drink at his table, my lady," he concludes, his gaze unwaveringly fixed upon me, as if daring me to refuse the unexpected invitation.

I certainly have a knack for drawing attention to myself. It seems as though every eye in the room is fixated on me, scrutinizing my every move. The air is thick with anticipation, and I can almost feel the weight of their gazes pressing against my skin. I flash a warm smile in his direction, my heart pounding in rhythm with the subtle tension in the air. Despite the flutter of nerves, I don't dare decline his invitation. "You lead the way," I say, my voice steady and inviting, as I gesture for him to take the first step.

We weave our way over to the elegantly roped-off table I noticed when we first entered. Seated prominently in the middle is the elven prince who, it seems, I left quite an impression on. As we approach, he rises with a graceful fluidity, his silvery blonde hair catching the light, and gestures toward the seat beside him with an inviting smile. He's handsome. More than handsome, he's beautiful in that Legolas kind of way. I accept his offer, settling into the chair and returning his smile with a touch of my own.

"Greetings," his voice resonates, deep and mysterious like the whisper of an ancient forest. "I am Prince Rothilion of Elnora."

"Hi, nice to meet you, Roth," I reply, a playful lilt in my voice as I anticipate the challenge of his full name. "I hope that's okay because there's no way I'm gonna be able to pronounce that. I'm Sadie Baker of Indiana."

My title may not hold the same allure, but it's what I have.

The elven prince's eyes twinkle with amusement, catching the light in a way that makes them shimmer like polished gemstones. "Indiana? I'm not familiar with that realm. Is it a place of great power and magic?" he inquires, his curiosity genuine and open.

I couldn't help but laugh. "Oh yeah, tons of magic. We're known for our enchanted cornfields and mystical basketball courts."

Prince Rothilion's brow furrowed slightly, clearly unsure if I was being serious. I decided to take pity on him.

"I'm just teasing. Indiana is actually quite ordinary by supernatural standards. I'm new to New York, just joined the Lux Bellator."

His eyes widened with recognition. "Ah, the Lux Bellator. A noble organization.

As our conversation continued, the atmosphere around us subtly transformed. The lively chatter and clinking glasses of the bar gradually faded into a distant hum, a mere backdrop to the increasingly bewildering exchange between us. We plunged into an array of topics, from the intricacies of politics to the mysteries of paranormal activity, each subject captivating us with its depth and complexity. Our mutual curiosity drove the conversation, a dance of ideas and insights that was both thrilling and enlightening.

Yet, amidst this engaging dialogue, I couldn't shake off the constant weight of curious stares from around the bar. It appeared that a human engaging in an animated discussion with an elven prince was quite the spectacle, drawing eyes like moths to a flame.

As I surveyed the dimly lit room, the warm glow from the

overhead lights casting soft shadows, I noticed the absence of my teammates and silently hoped that Nathan hadn't discovered my whereabouts.

The intensity of the gazes only seemed to grow with each passing moment, their scrutiny turning the air heavy and causing a flutter of discomfort within me. But I steeled myself against the unease, determined to savor this once-in-a-lifetime opportunity to connect with an elven prince on such a personal level.

"So, tell me, Sadie of Indiana," Rothilion said with a charming smile, "what brings a witch like yourself to join the Lux Bellator? Surely there are more… entertaining pursuits for one of your talents."

I shrugged, taking a sip of my drink. "Oh, you know, the usual. Save the world, kick some supernatural butt, maybe learn a few new spells along the way. Plus, the medical plan is to die for."

Rothilion chuckled, clearly amused by my flippant response. "You're quite unlike any human I've ever met before."

I laugh along with him. "Oh, you have no idea."

As laughter bubbled up around Rothilion and me, an unexpected chill crept down my spine, leaving me unsettled. The familiar sensation of being watched prickled at the back of my neck. I tried to casually scan the bar, my eyes inevitably finding Nathan's across the room. His gaze pierced through the crowd, his jaw set tight, focusing intently on me and the Elven prince. I struggled to decipher the look in his eyes—was it anger simmering beneath the surface? A flicker of concern? Or perhaps jealousy snaking its way through his thoughts? Each possibility twisted knots in my stomach, leaving me torn between wanting to confront him and fearing what I might discover.

I turned back to Rothilion, trying to shake off the feeling.

"So, tell me more about your realm, Roth. I bet it's way more exciting than Indiana." Roth began to describe the Elven kingdom, but my mind was a whirlwind, unable to focus on his words. Nathan's image kept invading my thoughts. No, Sadie. Concentrate on the captivating elf in front of you. Yet, Nathan's intense gaze felt like it was searing into my back, making it impossible to concentrate.

"Is everything alright, Sadie?" Rothilion asked, his voice tinged with concern as he noticed my distraction. "You seem… preoccupied."

I forced a smile, trying to shove thoughts of Nathan into the background. "Oh, I'm fine. Just taking in all the wonders of your realm. It sounds absolutely magical." My words felt hollow, a façade to hide the turmoil within.

Rothilion beamed, clearly moved by my feigned interest. "It truly is. Perhaps one day I could show you around personally." The idea was enchanting, yet I couldn't shake the feeling that my heart was being pulled in two different directions.

Before I could formulate a response, a familiar voice sliced through our conversation with the precision of a blade. "I hate to interrupt, Your Highness, but I'm afraid I need to borrow Sadie for a moment," Nathan declared, his voice taut with barely suppressed tension. "Lux Bellator business."

I swiveled to face Nathan, unable to mask the irritation etching across my features. "I'm sure whatever it is can wait until tomorrow, Nathan. I'm in the midst of a conversation," I retorted, my words laced with exasperation.

Nathan's voice held a fervent intensity, his blue eyes sparking with an emotion that bore a striking resemblance to jealousy. "I'm afraid it can't, Sadie. It's urgent," he insisted, his tone brooking no refusal.

Prince Roth cast a glance between us, his brow knit in perplexity. "Is everything alright? If there's an emergency—" he began, his concern evident.

"No emergency," I reassured him quickly, casting a sharp glare at Nathan. "Just my overzealous boss being... well, overzealous," I added with a hint of sarcasm.

Nathan's eyes narrowed at my dismissive remark, his demeanor unyielding. "Sadie, a word. Now." His voice resonated with a finality that left no room for debate.

With a dramatic sigh, I turned back to Rothilion, offering an apologetic smile. "I'm so sorry about this, Roth. Duty calls, apparently. It was lovely meeting you," I said, my tone tinged with regret.

The Elven prince nodded graciously, though confusion still clouded his expression. "Of course. Perhaps we can continue our conversation another time?" he suggested, his voice filled with hope.

"I'd like that," I replied, deliberately ignoring Nathan's impatient huff beside me, determined to savor the lingering connection with Rothilion for as long as possible.

As I stood to follow Nathan, I couldn't help but feel aggravated at whatever game he was currently playing. What could be so urgent that he'd interrupt my conversation with royalty?

Nathan led me to a secluded corner of the dimly lit bar, his posture rigid and tense as he turned to face me with eyes that burned with intensity. "What do you think you're doing?" he hissed, his voice low but sharp, cutting through the ambient chatter. His irritation was crystal clear, barely concealed beneath the surface.

I responded in kind, my voice a whispered retort, "What am I doing? What's so urgent you needed to drag me away right now? Couldn't it have waited until my conversation with the prince was finished?"

Nathan's eyes narrowed, a dangerous glint flashing in his piercing blue eyes. Without a word, he gripped my arm with a firm but not hurtful hold, guiding me to a more secluded hallway away from prying eyes and ears.

"What were you thinking?" Nathan hissed again, his voice a torrent of what sounded an awful lot like jealous anger that echoed softly in the narrow space. "Do you have any idea how dangerous it is to get involved with the elves?"

I stood my ground, crossing my arms defiantly as I met his fierce glare with one equally fierce. "Involved? We were just having a friendly conversation, nothing more. And as I recall, I'm a grown woman who can choose to talk to whoever I please," I replied, my tone steady and unwavering, matching the fiery tension between us.

Nathan raked his fingers through his hair, frustration radiating from every tense muscle in his body. "This isn't a game, Sadie. The elves are ancient, formidable forces with their own agendas, and their involvement leads to... complications. They don't just strike up conversations with humans for kicks."

I couldn't help but scoff. "Complications? Like what? Am I going to wake up with pointy ears or something?"

Nathan's expression grew stormy. "This isn't a joke, Sadie. The elves are notorious for manipulating humans to fulfill their own desires. They're dangerous and not to be trusted."

"Oh, and suddenly you're the all-knowing sage on elven matters?" I retorted sharply. "Maybe Prince Charming over there just wanted a conversation that didn't involve trust funds and yacht clubs."

Nathan's eyes narrowed, bristling at the jab.

"This isn't about me or my… connections," Nathan said, his voice dropping to a taut, warning tone. "It's about your safety and the integrity of the Lux Bellator. We can't afford to have our newest recruit getting tangled up in elven politics in her first week."

I felt my anger rising. "Tangled up? It was a single drink, Nathan. I wasn't signing my soul away or promising my firstborn to the elven realm."

"You don't grasp the intricacies at play here," Nathan insisted, pinching the bridge of his nose in exasperation. "Every interaction with the elves is a loaded game of chess with hidden meanings and potential repercussions. They never act without a calculated purpose."

"Oh, and I suppose you're also the resident expert on elven etiquette now?" I scoffed.

Nathan sighed long and hard, clearly trying to rein in his frustration. "Look, Sadie, I know you're new here and you're still learning the ropes." He stated in the most pretentious and condescending tones I have ever heard. "But there are certain… protocols we follow when it comes to interacting with other supernatural beings, especially ones as powerful and unpredictable as the elves."

"Oh really?" I challenged, gritting my teeth. I was this close to throat punching him. "And where exactly are these 'protocols' written, Nathan?"

He gave me an arrogant look and scoffed as though shocked I questioned his words.

"What I really think is going on here," I continue because

I'm on a roll now. "Is that you are jealous."

Nathan's mouth dropped, and for a moment he looked utterly thrown. "Excuse me?" His voice pitched upward, almost comical in its disbelief.

I arched an eyebrow, taking a perverse pleasure in watching him squirm. "You heard me, Blackwood. I think the only thing you hate more than elves is the idea that someone might find them more interesting than you."

He sputtered, searching for a retort and coming up empty. Finally, he gave up, settling for glaring at me with all the intensity of a man denied the last life preserver on a sinking ship. "That's absurd," he finally muttered. "I don't care who you do—talk to." The correction was sharp, and I filed it away for future use.

I leaned in, grinning. "Sure, Nathan. Whatever helps you sleep at night."

For a moment we just stood there, the air practically crackling with unspoken challenges and unresolved whatever-it-was between us. Then Nathan seemed to realize how close we were standing. He took half a step back, just enough to put some safe space between us, but not so far that he couldn't reach out if I tried to make a break for it, which, let's be honest, was probably the only part of this "protocol" he genuinely cared about.

"You are impossible," he said, shaking his head.

I shrugged, pride blooming in my chest. "I've been called worse."

Before we could explore our little heart to heart further, our team found us in our little corner.

"That was AMAZING!" Chloe gushed. "I've never seen the elves interacting with anyone but themselves. Incredible!"

Getting an idea in my head, I run with it. "Hey Chloe, is it against the rules of Lux Bellator to hang out with the elves?"

Nathan looks like he's ready to interject when Silas busts out laughing. "What? No way. You can talk to whomever you like. Where'd you get that idea from?"

I couldn't help but smirk at Nathan's discomfort as Silas unwittingly called out his bluff.

"Interesting," I drawled, fixing Nathan with a pointed look. "Because someone seemed to think there were all these protocols about interacting with elves. Guess that was just a misunderstanding, huh?"

Nathan's jaw clenched, his eyes flashing with barely contained frustration. "I was merely trying to caution you about the potential risks—"

"Risks?" Kat chimed in, her brow furrowed in confusion. "What risks? The elves may be aloof, but they're not dangerous. If anything, this could be great for diplomatic relations!"

I raised an eyebrow at Nathan, enjoying his comeuppance. "Yeah, Nathan. What risks exactly?"

Nathan didn't flinch, he met my eyes with the force of a thousand glares. "I was merely trying to explain the delicate nature of supernatural politics to our newest recruit."

"Delicate nature, my ass," I scoffed. "You practically dragged me away like I was consorting with the enemy."

Silas chuckled, clapping Nathan on the shoulder. "Come on, man. Sadie can handle herself. You saw her file - she's not exactly a damsel in distress."

We glared at each other for a moment before Hadeon interjected, "Alright you two, that's enough.

Hadeon's intervention seemed to diffuse some of the tension, but I could still feel Nathan's eyes boring into me.

"Nathan," a sultry voice calls from behind us.

I turn to see the redhead giving us a look of disdain before turning her gaze back to Nathan, "Are you coming back or what?" She practically pouts.

He looks back at us, clearly torn about what to do but the effect of her voice is instant: whatever heated current had kept us tethered snaps, and Nathan schools his expression to impassivity. "Excuse me," he mutters, backing away from our little circle. But before he turns, his eyes lock with mine, and for the first time, I see something like regret flicker across his face. Then he's gone, swaggering back to the trust-fund table like he didn't just have his reality publicly upended by a nobody from Indiana.

Kat elbows me in the ribs, hard enough to make me grunt. "Damn, Sadie. You just got the Golden Boy good." She says with pride.

"He was being a prick," I mutter, though I'm already replaying the look on his face. It'll haunt me, in that way only mutual shame can.

Chloe raises her drink in salute, eyes bright with the kind of laughter that comes from genuine camaraderie. "Don't think I've ever seen Nathan rattled before. I live for this drama." She glances across the bar to where Nathan's confab with the redhead is all sparkly smiles and brittle tension. "Though, oof. Tiffany is going to have opinions." Kat still riding high on the drama excitedly gushes, "An elven prince and Nathan Blackwood in a jealous standoff? You realize you're living out every supernatural romance plotline ever, right?"

I scowled at her, but the effort was half-hearted. "Don't start."

"Too late, darling. I've already cast you in the role." Silas said eyeing Roth. Then he turns his attention back to me. "You, my dear Sadie, have made work a whole lot more interesting."

I tried to ignore the steady pulse of adrenaline that lingered in my veins. All the showmanship at the bar was one thing, but the way Nathan had stared at me—like I was some dangerous entity threatening to detonate the clean, ordered world he'd built for himself—felt like an even bigger problem than any demon outbreak.

I ordered another drink and tried to exhale the nerves away, but the tension was now a living thing, following me home and curling up on my pillow like a cat made of thumbtacks.

14

Swords, Sweat, and Sexual Tension

The next morning, I dragged myself out of bed at the crack of dawn, feeling the chill of the early hours seep into my bones. I arrived at the imposing Lux Bellator headquarters with a precious 10 minutes to spare, the building casting long shadows in the pale morning light. Today, I was scheduled to train with Nathan, which promised to be anything but smooth given our strained encounter the previous night.

Nathan had mastered the art of being hot and cold. In novels, people seem to adore the drama of love-hate relationships, but out here in the real world, it was nothing short of exhausting and, to be honest, downright irritating. The training room was an expansive area, with ceilings that soared high above and walls adorned with an impressive array of exercise equipment and weapons, gleaming under the fluorescent lights. As I stepped inside, I spotted Nathan already there, his back turned to me as he meticulously arranged a row of target dummies, each one standing ready for whatever rigorous session he had planned.

"Morning, sunshine," I shouted with a teasing lilt, relishing the way his shoulders stiffened at my voice, like a taut bow-string ready to snap. "Ready to show me the ropes?" Nathan spun around, his face a fortress of cold professionalism. "Good morning, Sadie. I trust you're prepared for a rigorous session." His words were clipped and precise, a stark contrast to the storm of anticipation swirling between us. How very formal of him.

I leaned back, cracking my knuckles with a grin. "Always ready. Though, I must admit, I'm a bit let down. I was expecting some trust falls or maybe a game of 'Pin the Tail on the Demon' to start things off." Nathan's eye twitched ever so slightly, but he kept his composure. "We'll begin with fundamental defensive maneuvers. It's imperative you know how to protect yourself in close combat."

"Protect myself?" I chuckled, raising an eyebrow. "Haven't I already shown I can handle myself?"

He scoffed, eyes narrowing. "Let's put that claim to the test then." He stepped onto the training mat, beckoning me forward. "Show me what you've got, Baker."

I sauntered onto the mat with a smirk. "With pleasure. Just remember, I warned you."

We circled each other slowly, our eyes locked in a tense, silent challenge. Nathan struck first, lunging with a quick jab. I sidestepped smoothly, using a touch of telekinesis to nudge him as he went past. He stumbled but quickly regained his footing.

"Nice trick," he growled, steadying his stance again. "But magic won't always save you in a real fight."

"No," I conceded, "but it certainly makes things more interesting."

I launched my attack, feinting left. Nathan blocked it effortlessly, but I used the momentum to spin away, narrowly dodging his swift counter-strike. His Nephilim blood granted him the extra speed and strength that made it seem effortless. This was going to be more challenging than I had anticipated.

"Not bad," he conceded reluctantly.

Nathan's words were abruptly cut off as I swiftly swept his legs from beneath him, sending him crashing to the mat. I lunged, pinning him down with my forearm pressing firmly across his chest. Using my magic to reinforce my hold.

"You were saying?" I taunted, savoring the blend of surprise and frustration flickering in his eyes.

For a tense moment, we remained locked in this position, our faces mere inches apart, both of us panting heavily. I couldn't help but notice the intense blue of his eyes up close, or the subtle twitch of his cheek as he strained against my grip.

Then, with a decisive grunt of effort, Nathan bucked his hips and deftly flipped us over, reversing our positions. Now he was the one pinning me down, his weight pressing into me with a commanding presence.

"Never let your guard down," he murmured, a hint of smug satisfaction in his voice. This was precisely what Michael had been trying to convey when he warned me against my overconfident approach to combat.

I scowled, determined not to let him see how breathless he'd left me. "Is this how you plan to teach me, Blackwood? By sitting on me?" Despite the bite in my voice, my pulse was thundering with something disturbingly close to fascination. He didn't move. "If you're waiting for me to apologize, don't hold your breath." "You're heavier than you look," I grumbled, squirming beneath him, magic prickling at my fingertips. He leaned in, lowering his voice, and for a split second I thought he was about to kiss me, the tension jagged and electric. "You're not half as clever as you think, Sadie." His eyes lingered on mine, and abruptly he rolled off, offering a hand to pull me up. I lay there, ignoring his hand, a breathless tangle of limbs and adrenaline, trying to steady myself. "Lesson learned," I croaked, pushing up on my elbows. "Seriously, what do they feed you Nephilim? Because I'm going to need a protein shake and a new spine."

Nathan's mouth twitched, almost a smile, before he caught himself and reverted to Sergeant Mode. His eyes slid away as if the last ten seconds hadn't happened. "Again," he said, hauling a practice blade from the wall and tossing it to me. "This time, with weapons."

I caught the blade on reflex, the hilt familiar and right in my hand. For a moment, I wondered if he'd seen the way my fingers trembled.

"Don't underestimate a demon with a blade," he said, squaring off. "A lot of them were swordsmen before they fell." He didn't have to specify who he was talking about; the stories of fallen angels and their penchant for mayhem were the backbone of Lux Bellator bedtime stories.

This time Nathan didn't wait. He closed the gap in a blink, steel flashing as he aimed a precise slash at my shoulder. I parried, stepping into the blow, letting our blades catch and ring, the jolt vibrating up my arm and into my teeth. He pressed, relentless, forcing me back step by step until the mat edge bit at my shoes.

When he finally let up, it was only because I feinted a stumble. He advanced, overcommitting, and I spun low, sweeping his knees as I'd done before but this time jabbing upward with the blade. He twisted aside so fast it left an afterimage, caught my wrist mid-swing, and in a blur had me spun and pinned—my arm braced behind my back, blade at my throat, both our chests heaving.

We stood like that for a breathless second, then he released me—not with the roughness I expected, but with a slow, deliberate uncurling of his fingers, letting the heat of his palm linger just a moment too long.

"Not bad," he said, breathing hard. "But you'll need to do better."

He reached for a towel and wiped the sweat from his brow before tossing it aside, the movement casual but oddly intimate for reasons I choose not to examine. "Again," he repeated, but softer, and this time I could sense the edge of a smile. We sparred until my muscles shook and sweat soaked through my clothes. Nathan kept up a running commentary: "Watch your left flank." "You drop your shoulder on every backswing." "Don't let me get inside your range." Half of it was annoying—no, all of it was—but I found myself learning, not despite his criticism but because of it. He never once gave me an inch; every time I landed a hit, he made sure I bled for it, even if it was only metaphorically. After an hour, he finally called a halt. "You're done," he said, voice hoarse. I collapsed to the mat, gasping for air. "What, no motivational speech? No hearty pat on the back?"

Nathan gave me a flat look. "You survived. It'll have to do." "High praise." I let my head thump back onto the mat. "So, am I trainable?" He didn't answer right away. Instead he paced in a tight, restless circle, like he still had more energy to burn. Eventually he crouched next to me, elbows on his knees. "You're reckless. You rely too much on your magic to compensate for technique. You push yourself until you break, and you never accept help." He paused, his gaze unwavering. "But you're not afraid to get hit, and you don't give up." "Aww, that's the nicest backhanded compliment I've gotten in a while," I say with a goofy smile on my face. "Does this mean I am promoted out of crowd control?"

He tossed the towel over his shoulder, glanced at me sidelong, mouth twitching. "You don't know how to quit. That can get you killed, or it can make you a hero. Depends on the day." He looked away, a muscle in his jaw working. "Maybe both." I sat up slowly, feeling every bruise as I did. "I'll take those odds." For the first time, Nathan actually smiled. Not a smirk, not a sneer—a real smile, fleeting, but enough to make me wonder if maybe I'd misjudged him after all. The room fell into a companionable silence. I realized I liked the sound of our breathing, rough and exhausted but alive, filling the echoing space. After a moment, I snagged a water bottle from a nearby table and took a long swig, then passed it to Nathan. He took it, drank, wiped his mouth with the back of his hand. "Next time we're on a mission, you can be on point with me. You're off crowd control." I was so excited, without even thinking, I launched myself at him, giving him a huge hug and feeling the heat of his body, the rock-solid tension of his arms as he caught me midair, stunned. For half a second we just hung there, me wrapped around his chest, the scent of his sweat and aftershave mingling intoxicatingly, before he seemed to realize what was happening and gingerly set me down, palms lingering at my waist just long enough to spark a new shiver through my bones.

I stepped back, coughing into my elbow to cover my embarrassment, and to my horror, could feel a blush crawling up my neck to my cheeks. "Sorry," I stammered, forcing a laugh. "I guess I'm just not used to being… promoted."

He shook his head, but the freeze in his eyes had thawed. For a second there was even a kind of warmth, a brother-in-arms solidarity, like he was seeing me—not as the world's worst practical joke, but as an actual person.

He checked his watch, then looked back at me. "Debrief in thirty. Clean up and be there." I limped to the locker room and stood under a pounding shower until the water ran cold, thinking about the way Nathan's face changed when he lowered his guard. I couldn't tell if he liked me, hated me, or both. But I knew now that I wanted to find out, and that was almost worse than the actual bruises.

15

Witchfire & Whiskey

That became our routine over the next several weeks. Combat drills at sunrise, followed by a debrief with the team, with Nathan watching me through a lens of cautious hope instead of outright skepticism. Evenings were a grab bag: sometimes a mission, sometimes paperwork, sometimes drinks with the squad at one of Manhattan's three exclusively supernatural bars. The days blurred into a sequence of bruises and breakthroughs, sarcasm and silences slowly turning into small, grudging trusts. Kat was thriving, crushing the physical challenges and soaking up every ounce of city life. She'd gotten close with Hadeon—like, coffee-in-the-park, inside-joke close—and they'd become an inseparable duo. Despite her attention on Hadeon, even she noticed that something changed in the dynamic between Nathan and me. "Don't let it go to your head," I grumbled one night, scraping a dried bloodstain off my favorite pair of jeans. "Just because I'm not actively plotting to murder our team lead doesn't mean I've gone soft." Kat grinned and flicked a peanut at me. "Tell that to Silas, he says you're in love with him." I threw a pillow at her, but even I could tell my heart wasn't in it. Because the truth was, Nathan and I worked. Not in the way rom-coms sell you, not in the grand, fated, soul-deep way, but in the way that fire recognizes fire: we could be a disaster, but at least we'd burn together. I found myself thinking about Nathan at odd hours, replaying the nuances of our sparring sessions, the brief flashes of vulnerability or humor that caught me off guard.

Kat started a betting pool with Silas and Chloe about how long it would take for us to hook up. (Silas gave it three weeks. Chloe said two if there was another demon attack. Kat was the holdout, rooting for slow burn.) Hadeon, who was as subtle as a sunrise, told me in confidence that while fae typically found human relationships "tedious," he found my ongoing feud with Nathan "riveting, at least." High praise from a guy who once described falling in love as "like eating cheese—enjoyable in small doses, but frequently regrettable."

Life at Lux Bellator never settled into anything that could remotely be called routine. The city thrummed with supernatural incidents—sometimes small, like a hexed subway train that turned all the commuters' MetroCards into cursed objects (there was a week where midtown office workers kept hissing and flaring gills), sometimes huge, like the time a rogue vampire clan tried to set up an impromptu blood-speakeasy in the Flatiron Building and got so deep in over their heads that even Silas blushed when he saw the aftermath. We responded to all of it, usually with Nathan barking orders and the rest of us pretending we weren't impressed. But the real change came on a muggy Friday in June, when a mission turned into an ambush. It started simple: an uptick in poltergeist activity at a condemned hotel in Hell's Kitchen. Intel said it was a single

Class Three, maybe a Class Four if we were unlucky, but the moment we hit the lobby, the temperature dropped hard and every light in the place shattered, raining glass like confetti. We moved as a unit—Kat and Hadeon on point, Chloe and Silas flanking, Nathan and me bringing up the rear. That was the plan, anyway. The first sign things were off was the heavy, chemical stink in the air—like ozone and burning oil. The second sign was when Chloe, who could take a bullet and not flinch, stopped cold, hackles up, and said, "Something's eating the ley lines." Normally, that would mean nothing to a human. To a Lux Bellator team on a mission, it meant very bad things. As we inched down the crumbling corridor, spells at the ready and weapons drawn, the walls themselves seemed to vibrate, alive with a low, guttural drone. Hadeon cursed in a language that sounded like knives scraping on glass. Then Kat, ahead of us by half a step, whirled and yelled, "Lay the hell down!" I was already yanking at Nathan's collar, both of us hitting the floor as a wave of black fire roared over our heads, charring the faded wallpaper to cinders. I felt the heat on my scalp, smelled the scorched hair, and didn't even care because Nathan was whispering, too low for human hearing, his lips pressed to the side of my head as he shielded my body with his own. The words—Latin, I thought, but twisted into something that scraped the ear—stripped the oxygen from the air and chased the shadows back just far enough for me to see. The whole ceiling of the corridor was writhing, a living mass of something unclean, like smoke but thicker, curdling the gaslights in gelatinous whorls. He quickly yanked me to my feet with a grip like iron. We sprinted, ducking another blast, and slid into a service alcove where the rest of the team had regrouped, faces pale, eyes wide. Silas wiped a blackened bit of debris from his cheek, panting. "That's not a Class Three," he spat. "That's a damn demon Duke of Hell at least." Before anyone could even begin to devise a plan, an ominous, bone-chilling voice thundered from the direction we had just fled. "We are here for the girl. Sadie Baker." A surge of icy dread surged through my veins as every pair of eyes whipped towards me, their gazes reflecting the same fear I feel in me. Panic clawed at my insides, and I couldn't fathom why these relentless demons were so hell-bent on pursuing me. Nathan, in a single motion shoved me behind him, the bench and wall crackling with the pressure of his magic as he took a defensive stance. Huh, I had no idea Nephilim could wield magic. "Nobody's taking her anywhere," he growled. Kat bristled, claws half-formed, and the rest of the squad snapped to my side like a snapping jaw. But it was me they wanted. It was always me. The sense of being hunted, of being the crimson thread yanked through the eye of every needle, spiked so hard it choked my breath. The lobby turned to hell in a heartbeat. Columns of black flame ripped through the air, chasing us through the buckling marble. The demon—Duke or whatever—manifested as a roiling knot of shadow-glass and bone, its eye pits gouged from the void. It smashed toward us, every impact setting my skull vibrating like a bell. We fought. That's what we did. Nathan's sword rang with angelic fire, Kat's lion form flanked and bit, Chloe and Silas tag-teamed it with magic and teeth. I did my part, hurling hex after hex, drawing fire, trying to keep the thing's full attention away from my friends. The demon only wanted me. It spoke in a voice that was agony poured into words, and somewhere in the crack between a shriek and a curse, it said, "He will be here soon, Sadie. Your power will soon be his." Then, in a moment that felt like falling off the sharp lip of a nightmare, the whole world upended and we were falling—literally, the marble beneath our feet splitting open into a vertical shaft that dropped us three floors directly into the basement.

We landed in a tangle, bodies slamming against stone, half the air knocked from my chest before Kat half-dragged, half-rolled me behind what was left of a concrete pillar. Above us, the Duke's cackling echo slithered down the rubble. I saw Silas and Chloe scrambling for footing, blood streaming down Silas's arm, Chloe with a sizzling burn across her shoulder. Hadeon was attempting to sit up. Pain blurred the edges of my vision but Nathan's hand gripped my wrist, grounding me in the here and now. "You with me?" His voice was a rasp, but all the old coldness was gone, replaced by a grim, fierce urgency.

"Yeah," I gasped, finding my feet. "What's the plan?"

He glanced upward, where the black mass was oozing through the ceiling like living tar. "We need to spread out—divide and conquer. If we attack from all sides, we can banish him back to hell where he belongs!" His voice was sharp, slicing through the tension as he formulated the strategy. "We'll split into pairs. Hadeon, Kat, you're together. Silas, Chole, stick close." He whipped around to meet my eyes; his gaze momentarily clouded with fierce worry. "Sadie, you and I—we're a team."

I offer him a subtle nod, my gaze unwavering as I advance a step closer. After weeks of intense sparring sessions each morning, an unspoken camaraderie has developed between us, a bond forged in sweat and determination. This moment marked the pinnacle of our training, the ultimate test of our abilities. We were about to diverge from our team, setting out alone to assume our positions on the outside circle. He grabbed my hand and pulled me behind a shattered chunk of cinderblock. "Do not do anything reckless," he hissed. "I know it's your signature move but try to stay alive for once." I ignored the command. All I could focus on was the voice from before, the way it had said my name—like it owned me, like it had already marked me as its next meal. Nathan must have seen the panic simmering under my skin, because he bent down to my level, leaned in so close I could smell the ash in his hair, and whispered, "You are not alone in this. "We do it like in practice," he continues, eyes glinting in the dark. "Draw him out, break his focus, then you bind and I banish." I nodded, heart hammering so hard it made my teeth ache. There was no sarcasm in me now, no shield to hide behind.

"I'm scared," I admitted, feeling the tension coil inside me like a spring ready to snap. If I didn't let it out, I feared I might explode. His hand found mine, warm and reassuring, fingers interlocking in a firm squeeze as he drew me into a tight embrace. I could hear the steady rhythm of his heartbeat against my ear, a comforting metronome in the chaos of my thoughts. His voice, a gentle murmur, whispered into my hair, "You're a badass, Sadie. You know this. I'll be right there with you the whole way." The words wrapped around me like a protective cloak, infusing me with a sense of strength and solidarity. We pulled apart, and just like that, the moment was over—replaced by the grinding reality of our predicament. Nathan's arms slid from my shoulders, but his hand lingered on my elbow, guiding me into the next cover. All around us, the basement pulsed with a moving midnight: walls seeping shadow, the air thick with a basso thrum that worked its way into your guts, looking for a place to hollow out and nest.

"Ready?" he mouthed, barely a whisper. I angled my head to where the demon was coalescing above, black limbs drooling from the torn ceiling like molten plastic, forming grotesque implements as it searched for us. "Yeah," I mouthed back. "Go." We sprinted along the wall, criss-crossing debris and half-submerged pipes. I caught sight of Kat flanking the other side, her lion form battered but alive, teeth bared in a snarl. Hadeon was with her, blood running down his arm but eyes bright with adrenaline. I didn't see Silas and Chloe, but hoped they were still moving, still fighting. The demon's eye sockets glittered, fixed on me even as I ran. Shadows wormed over the concrete, trying to trip and grab, but Nathan swatted them aside with enchantments that flickered like starlight, each one burning a hole in the darkness. We reached the far wall, back to back, breath coming in ragged bursts. Nathan whispered the first part of the plan: "Draw his attention. He's fixated on you, use it." I nodded, ducked out, and called up the brightest flare of witchfire I could muster. The room went nuclear-white for a half-second, and the demon howled, flickering back from the light as if slapped. Its voice shrilled again, scraping at the inside of my skull: "BAKER. COME." "No. You come here, I'm not walking all the way back over there," I yelled, bolting toward a ruptured stairwell as the demon lunged after me, shearing metal and stone in its wake. I ran on legs made of panic and caffeine, slamming through the maze of the basement, using every trick from every morning practice: dodge, stutter-step, fake left, sprint. The shadows writhed, and the demon peeled itself from the ceiling, reforming midair with a splatter of darkness and noise like a broken radio—voices in every tongue, all of them cursing, all of them hungry. It swooped, claws out, howling. For a second I froze, watching it close in so fast the air warped, every nerve ending petrified by the certainty that this was really happening, not a training exercise, not a drill. Then Nathan's hand hit my back, hard, shoving me out of the way at the last instant. The demon smashed into the ground with enough force to crater the concrete, black ichor splattering the walls. Up close, it reeked of wet earth and sulfur, its form flickering between razor-edged bone and a shape so human it made my scalp crawl.

This was it. I did what we'd practiced a hundred times in the gym: I kept moving, arms weaving the spell, voice low and steady even when my knees wanted to buckle. The demon chased, but Nathan was on it, sword blazing cold white as he drove it back, step by step, howling ancient curses that sounded like they'd been torn from some forbidden gospel. It lunged for me and he intercepted on one side, blade meeting claw, as Hadeon and Kat attacked from the other.

It staggered, a flailing tangle of jaws and smoke, then pivoted, ignoring the fae and the lion and fixing all its focus on me. That made sense. Everything in my life wanted one thing lately: to possess, corrupt, or consume my soul.

I took a stance in the center of the debris field, hands up and athame flickering with blue-white fire, the words of Michael's binding spell coiling on my tongue. I tried not to imagine the demon's shadow arms slipping down my windpipe. I tried not to imagine the raw hunger in its voice.

"Now!" Nathan roared, and everything seemed to slow: Chloe's wolf form caught the demon's leg, Silas vaulted over a heap of broken pipe and seized the other arm, Kat dug in and bit down on its spectral midsection, holding the thing in place for just a moment. All I had to do was finish the ritual.

I heard Michael's voice in my head, not stern but calm, like a hand cupping the back of my neck: "Intent is everything. Focus on the target, not yourself. Forget the noise. Be the force in the circle." I found the center of my mind, opened my senses, and spit the words like bullets:

"Verbum vinculum, lux et motum—"

The demon shrieked, a sound that split every nerve. My vision blurred at the edges but I kept going, the Latin burning inside me like a fever. The shadow buckled inward, ribs snapping, claws slashing at every anchor point. Hadeon hurled fae-bolts that stuck like phosphorescent nails; Nathan's blade flared and cut again, the silver scream of it nearly as bright as my own panic. We were winning, but only by inches and only for now.

"Lux et motum, anima inimicum."

The binding circle was a pitiful excuse, scratched in concrete dust and blood, but it held. The demon slammed against its edge, flailing, spitting curses in a dozen lost languages. Black fire licked the ceiling, curling back on itself as if even the inferno was afraid to touch what we'd caged.

This was the moment it usually went wrong. That was the lesson: at the final step, when you think you've won, that's when they get you. But not this time. The demon convulsed, imploding into a knot of glass and shadow so dense it seemed to swallow the light itself. Then, in one excruciating flash, it was gone. Absorbed, banished back to the hellhole that had spawned it. The silence afterward was almost violent. I swayed, knees buckling, and Nathan caught me under the arms, half-carrying, half-dragging me behind the shelter of a boiler. I could hear the others regrouping, their voices trembling in the cavernous quiet. Chloe was licking her wounds, Silas and Hadeon grunting through the pain as they checked for more threats.

We waited, breath held, but nothing else came. I slumped against the boiler, heart crashing against my ribs as I tried to process what had just happened. I stared at my hands, the faint blue shimmer of spent magic pulsing over my skin before it faded, leaving every nerve in my arms screaming for mercy. We'd done it. But the fear didn't leave—not really. Even with the demon gone, its words lashed through me like barbed wire pulled through raw flesh.

Nathan hovered above me, face so close I could see the smeared streaks of ash and blood across his cheek, the barely contained tremor in his clenched jaw. He let go of my arms and knelt, one hand bracing me upright, the other pressing gently at my neck as if checking for a pulse. "You still with me?" he asked, voice fraying at the edges.

I tried for a joke, but my mouth only worked enough for a croaked "Define 'with.'"

He laughed, hoarse and brittle, and for a second I hated how much I liked the sound. Then his eyes changed, shifting from sarcasm to something raw and unfiltered.

"They're not going to stop," he said, barely more than a whisper. "Whatever's after you, it wants you bad."

"Tell me something I don't know," I muttered, but the words felt heavy with all the things I didn't want to admit.

Nathan's grip tightened a moment, and then he let go, raking his hand through his hair as he scanned the ruined basement. The others were limping back, Kat supporting Hadeon, Chloe and Silas dragging up the rear. We made our way out. There was a moment, standing in the residue of hellfire and dust and adrenaline, when I almost teared up. Not because of pain—I'd hurt worse, and more privately, a thousand times—but because in that bombed-out hole, surrounded by the only people who could possibly understand, I felt less like a misfit and more like someone who belonged to a pack.

Kat was the first to talk, "Next time we do this," she said, voice gone all husky from smoke, "I'm booking a spa day first. If I die, I'm at least gonna have nice nails." Chloe snorted, chin streaked with blood, and even Nathan let out a slow exhale that might have been a laugh if you squinted.

"Is everyone okay?" Nathan barked, dropping back into command voice only long enough to stop and count heads. Chloe answered with a shake of her coat, Silas with a grunt. Hadeon was pale as copy paper, but flashed a thumbs-up.

My knees were still jelly, so I just nodded.

"Let's move," Nathan said, "before the building collapses." He took point, head high and sword at the ready. Kat and I brought up the rear, our steps slow and clumsy over the cracked concrete.

"Hey," she said, sidling close enough to bump my shoulder, "You alright, witchy?"

I didn't trust my voice so I just jerked a half-smile.

"That was some Big Damn Hero energy," she said, and under her bravado I heard the tremor. For a second, we clung to each other, arm in arm, and the cold sweat running down my neck finally felt like relief instead of dread.

We staggered out of the hotel into the muggy evening, the city around us going about its noises and lights like nothing had happened. Nathan made a quick call and within five minutes a black SUV, standard-issue for Lux Bellator, screeched up to the curb. No sirens, no fuss—just business as usual. We collapsed inside, bodies tangled and filthy, reeking of sweat, blood, and metaphysical ozone.

Nobody said much on the ride back. The adrenaline had worn off, leaving only exhaustion and that guiltless, end-of-the-world euphoria you get after barely surviving something designed to kill you. Kat leaned her head on my shoulder and dozed, hair matted with blood from someone else's cut. Hadeon sat ramrod straight, eyes closed, lips moving in a private fae mantra. Silas and Chloe, bruised but already bickering, had their heads together plotting what sounded suspiciously like a post-mission bar crawl.

Nathan sat across from me, knees almost touching mine, arms folded so hard they trembled. He was staring out the window, jaw clenched, but every so often his gaze flicked to my face, as if checking to see if I might dissolve at any moment.

At headquarters, we were herded to the infirmary for the usual checks. The nurse on duty—Pix, a stoic vampire with a crocheted bunny headband—patched up our wounds with the efficiency of someone who'd seen a thousand worse. Once we were released—patched, bandaged, still vibrating with the aftershocks—we headed for the nearest bar. By some unspoken consensus, even Nathan came along. The place was half-empty, a two-fisted joint where the seats were vinyl and the drinks were poured heavy, and for the first time in a while, the entire team sat together in a single battered booth, battered but alive.

Kat and Hadeon claimed the side with a view, their knees pressed under the table. Chloe sprawled out beside Silas, who looked like he'd kill for an IV tap of O-negative. Nathan sat at the head of the table, arms folded, his face in its usual mask, but the air around him was softer, like he'd let go of something huge in the hotel back there and wasn't ready to let anyone see what replaced it.

Someone ordered a round of shots. We passed them up and down, the alcohol catching in the raw places left by adrenaline and fear. Nobody spoke first.

Finally, Silas said, "Anyone else want to admit they pissed themselves even a little when that thing came through the ceiling?" He raised his glass, and Chloe matched it, deadpan.

"I thought that was you," she said, prompt as a trigger, and the table cracked up—a jagged, exhausted laughter that hurt to let out but wouldn't be stopped. Even Hadeon, usually as lively as a statue, cracked a tight smile.

Kat elbowed me gently. "Not bad for a Midwest girl," she whispered, her voice part pride, part awe. "You took on a fucking Duke of Hell and didn't even die."

I wobbled a shrug and grinned, still tingling from the demon's words and the afterburn of raw magic. I tried to make light of it, but people kept glancing my way, their eyes never quite leaving my face. Even after the banter died down, the team's attention stuck to me like dried blood.

Nathan, for his part, didn't say a word the whole night. When the waitress came by and offered a discount for anyone with battle scars, he just nodded, eyes locked somewhere deep in a glass of neat whiskey. I wanted to ask if he was okay— really ask, not in the bullshit "you good, bro?" way—but the words wouldn't come. Instead I watched him, searching for cracks in the armor.

The evening wore on. The air in the bar turned gold around

the edges, thick with the chemical comfort of bourbon and sweat. Chloe and Silas staked out the jukebox and promptly monopolized it, trading off between sulky 90s hits and the kind of indie-rock you only hear on college radio stations. Hadeon nursed a single lager and watched, amused, as Kat goaded him into trying every bar snack on the menu. I let myself relax, limbs unwinding into the sticky vinyl as I nursed a beer and ignored the way my brain looped Nathan's last words to me like a curse I'd accidentally hexed myself with.

At some point, Kat and Hadeon decided to get some "air" and moved, whispering secrets in a corner booth near the bathrooms. Chloe and Silas disappeared in the direction of the arcade den, leaving the table abruptly too large for just the two of us left behind. Nathan waited a minute, then finally looked up, meeting my eyes for the first time since the basement.

"You did good today," he said. Not the formal, lofted praise he used on subordinates, but something softer, as if the words came from a place he'd never meant to show to anyone. He fidgeted with the glass, thumb tracing the rim in slow, even laps. "You did more than good, actually. You kept the team alive." I felt my face heat, embarrassment and pride mixing like chemicals in a beaker. "Thanks," I managed. "I… couldn't have done it without you."

He shook his head, a breathless little sound escaping. "You probably could have. You're a force of nature, Baker. It's why they want you—to break you or to claim you. That's got to feel… heavy."

It did, but the way he said it made the truth less terrifying, like we were sharing the burden instead of letting it rot me from the inside out. The jukebox cut out for a second, leaving the words suspended in an odd hush. Nathan watched me, expectant and unguarded, and I shrugged.

"I guess I never really thought about it. The breaking or claiming part, I mean. I just… do what I can. And hope it's enough."

Nathan's mouth quirked, half-sad. "It is. More than enough." He said it with a conviction that rattled me. A silence stretched, that strange, tightrope silence where everything mattered but neither of us could say what we meant. I fidgeted with the torn label on my beer, chewed my lip, and risked, "Is this where you give me a 'we're in this together' speech? Because if so, you're really underselling the pep talk."

Nathan's laugh was a hot breath of surprise. "You don't need a speech." He paused, licking his bottom lip. "You need someone to have your back. That goes for me, and for everyone in this room. Even when you piss us off."

I grinned, a thin, tired thing, but real. "Good to know you're finally admitting I piss you off." "Only most of the time," he said, but his eyes were warm now, the ice long since melted. Silence again, this time not the tightrope kind, but companionable, like the pause before a shared joke. He grinned slyly, a flash of the boy I'd glimpsed years ago at the Lux Bellator retreat—a little less haunted, a little more alive.

For a while we said nothing, letting the noise of other people's lives fill the space between us. I could feel my defenses thinning, all the old barbs and armor dulling just enough for the next thing to slip in unnoticed. That was the trouble with surviving: it left you open, if only for a second, to something you'd never meant to feel. Nathan tapped the edge of my glass with his own. "Here's to not dying."

I raised mine to meet him, the clink small and strangely intimate. "Not dying is my favorite hobby. Right after making you miserable."

He smirked, then tipped back his glass, and for the first time instead of wanting to slap it out of his hand, I wanted to ask if maybe he'd stay for a second round.

At home later that night I stripped off my jacket and collapsed onto the couch, every joint in my body singing a separate hymn of protest. I let Orion, tail high and righteous, sniff me with elaborate disgust before hopping up to knead my bruised thighs. The city's bright light spilled through my blinds, painting stripes of gold across the ceiling and making the air look thick enough to chew. I didn't want to move. I didn't want to think about Demons, or rituals, or about how my heart still thrashed in my chest every time I replayed the words: "He will be here soon, Sadie. Your power will soon be his."

16

Jealousy Looks Good on You, Actually

The next morning, I dragged myself into work feeling like I'd been hit by a truck. Saving the day was exhausting work. As I shuffled towards the break room in desperate need of caffeine, I nearly collided with Nathan.

"Whoa there, Baker," he said, steadying me with a hand on my arm. "You look like death warmed over."

I glared at him through bleary eyes. "Thanks. You really know how to make a girl feel special."

The corners of his mouth twitched.

"You're welcome." He let go, but not before squeezing my arm just enough to make sure I was steady on my feet. "There's coffee in the kitchenette. Chloe brought in donuts, too. I'd hurry if you want one; Kat's already circling like a shark."

The image powered me through the next twenty feet, and I managed to claim a cup of coffee and a lopsided maple-cream donut before Kat swooped in for the kill. She looked bright-eyed, per usual, even though I doubted she'd gotten any more sleep than I had. Her hair was wild, and she had a new bandage over her eyebrow—a badge of honor from last night's brawl.

"Morning, witch," she said, plopping down next to me at the communal table. "You sleep at all?"

"Define 'sleep,'" I answered, trying not to spill hot coffee on myself as I tore into the donut.

"Yikes." Kat made a sympathetic face, then leaned in, voice dropping to a confiding whisper. "So. You and Nathan. What's the deal?" She held up a finger: "And don't give me the 'he's my boss and I hate him' routine, because you two were making eyes across the vodka sodas last night."

"That's not what was happening—"

"Babe." Kat's eyes gleamed. "It's exactly what was happening.

Don't get excited, Kat. The only thing Nathan and I are making is each other's lives hell," I retorted, though the words felt hollow even to me. Kat picked that up instantly. She nudged my coffee cup closer and gave me a look that was more therapist than friend.

"Look, I know you. I know when you're lying. And I know something changed down there. You can tell me or you can tell me, but either way, I'm not going to stop pestering until you spill."

I took a scalding gulp and scowled at my own reflection in the surface. "He's just…less of a jerk than he used to be," I muttered. "And for some reason that makes it worse."

Kat grinned like a cat who'd just cornered the world's last canary. "Feelings. Ugh, right?"

I shot her my signature death glare, but her mirth was impenetrable. "Go away," I said, but she just propped her chin on her hand and waited. "So, what did you do after our night out, last night?" She asked, switching gears.

"Oh, the usual. Went home, laid on the sofa with a certain green-eyed gentleman. Then went to bed." I said in a depressed huff.

Before she could respond, a sharp gasp cut through the room. I whipped around, my heart pounding, to see Nathan standing there, his eyes icy and detached, piercing me with their frigid gaze.

"Really?" His voice sliced through the air, sharp and cold, his expression darkening with a fury that rivaled a brewing storm. "I thought you had more sense than to consort with the elves after our discussion."

My mind reeled, momentarily lost in the whirlwind of his sudden, explosive shift in mood. Then clarity struck like lightning - he believed the green-eyed gentleman I mentioned was the elven prince from the bar. I was about to enlighten him, to reveal that the green-eyed gentleman was actually my cat, but it dawned on me that Nathan had no right to such knowledge. Moreover, it was none of his concern who I chose to date, be it cat or elf.

Not that I was dating a cat. Or an elf.

The point was, he had no authority to cast judgment on my personal affairs, especially when he was entangled with a girlfriend himself. Let him think I was involved with the elf. In fact, I relished the thought of him stewing in that misconception.

With a defiant shrug, I decided to fuel the fire of his assumptions. "A girl's gotta have some fun after a hard day's work. Now, if you'll excuse me, I have paperwork to attend to."

I brushed past him, savoring the surge of satisfaction that coursed through me at his stunned silence. Who did he think he was to meddle in my life?

I could feel Nathan's eyes boring into my back as I walked

back to my office. He followed me in, shutting the door behind him. His blue eyes flashing with something that looked suspiciously like jealousy. "I thought I made it clear that getting involved with the elves was a bad idea."

I raised an eyebrow, crossing my arms defensively. "And I thought I made it clear that you're not the boss of my personal life, Nathan. What I do in my free time is none of your business."

"It is when it affects the team," he growled, taking a step closer. "Do you have any idea how dangerous—"

"Dangerous?" I say, voice low, "I'm a big girl, Nathan. I can handle myself."

"Can you?" he snapped, his blue eyes hard. "Because from where I'm standing, it looks like you're making reckless decisions left and right."

This guy.

"I seem to remember you praising my moves last night" I stepped closer, glaring up at him. "I don't know what your problem with me is, but that is, in fact, a YOU problem, not a me problem. Worry about yourself and leading the team. I don't say a word about your girlfriend; you don't get a say in my personal life."

Nathan went taut, his jaw flexing. His eyes flicked away for a second, then back to mine, as if he'd recalibrated mid-argument. "Tiffany is—" he started, then stopped, the words catching on raw edges. "This isn't about her," he managed, quieter. "It's about you getting targeted, again and again, by things that shouldn't even know your name." He ran a hand over his face and for once looked less like a statue carved to intimidate and more like a twenty-four-year-old who'd been handed the keys to the world's most dysfunctional doomsday machine. "You can date whoever you want," he said, but there was a catch in it, a fine hairline crack of something less self-righteous and more... vulnerable. "Well, that's a relief," I shot back, but even I could hear the strain in my own voice. It was like waiting for the other shoe to drop, and knowing it would always land on your throat. I was sick of that other shoe.

I turned my back on him, tried to busy myself with a pile of case files, but my hands were shaking and I couldn't even focus on a single word. After a moment Nathan's shadow clouded the desk; he was still standing there, arms crossed over his broad chest, determination radiating off him in waves. "So," he said, "are you going to see him again?" I peered at him through my lashes, calling up every drop of sarcasm I possessed. "What, the elf? Probably. But, I don't know when." I shrugged, unable to stop myself from goading him. He has Tiffany, why does he even care?

A muscle throbbed in Nathan's cheek. He opened his mouth, then shut it again, the silence between us pressed so tight you could slice it with a letter opener. When he finally spoke, his voice was so controlled it almost sounded artificial. "You're so naive, Sadie." Nathan says, derision setting into his tone. "You'll only end up hurt."

"That's for me to worry about, not you." I clap back.

"Fine," he finally bit out. "Do whatever you want, Baker. Just don't come crying to me when it blows up in your face."

"Trust me, you'll be the last person I come to," I snapped back.

He let out a frustrated laugh, one with no joy in it, all bile and static. I watched him from the corner of my eye as he spun on his heel and strode out, tension snapping in the empty space where he'd been. The door didn't slam, but I could imagine the echo anyway. I sank into my desk chair and stared at the case files. My pulse pounded like I'd just run a marathon, and I was lightheaded with the migraine of Nathan's intensity. I didn't understand how he could slide so easily, so aggressively, between concern and contempt. Or why it mattered so much to me, except it did. Maybe Kat was right. Maybe there were feelings. I wasn't sure I'd know if there were—my emotional compass had been chewing on metal shavings for years. I let out a breath, then pulled the notebook closer and got to work. There were demons on the loose, and they wanted me. If I didn't figure out more, and soon, I'd be dead or worse.

17

Vodka, Vengeance, and Very Bad Ideas

That night, Kat and I met up at The Cloak of Invisibility. She was already there, whirling vodka in her glass, the ice cubes clacking out a rhythm as she scanned the room for drama. "You look like you got dragged backwards through a sewer," she said by way of greeting.

"I'm on theme, then," I replied, slumping into the vinyl seat. "Got a bar tab big enough to buy me a round?"

She flagged the bartender with two fingers. "Whiskey, neat, for my emotionally stunted friend." Kat's smile was all teeth and mischief, but there was a softer edge underneath. "Rough day at the office?"

I shook my head, rubbing at a spot behind my ear that still hummed with the aftershocks of the morning's argument. "Nathan's been a disaster. And now, on top of everything, the demons are getting bolder. I don't know how long I can keep up this whole 'devil-may-care' witch attitude before I actually become a cautionary tale."

Kat snorted. "You are already a cautionary tale." Then her expression sobered. "But you're also the best witch I know.

Whatever demon is after you, you're not alone."

The bartender set down the whiskey, and I drank, letting the burn settle my nerves. "I'm terrified, Kat. That demon said someone was coming. Someone who wanted my power. I just—" I couldn't finish. I didn't have the words.

She didn't push. Just squeezed my hand in a way that was utterly un-magical and therefore more comforting than any spell.

Across the bar, the usual suspects were in attendance: the pack of werewolves hunched around, Chloe, Silas, and Hadeon are in our usual booth, Silas beckoning us over. "There she is," Silas said, voice bright as always, though one of his hands nursed a fresh bandage. "Tough week, huh?"

I slid in next to him, Kat following close. "Tough doesn't even cover it. " I downed the rest of the whiskey, felt it settle somewhere near my solar plexus.

Chloe grinned, her canines catching the light. "You did good, though. Held that binding circle like a pro."

"She did better than good," Hadeon added, gaze oddly soft on me. "Rumor is the Duke was not expecting resistance. Or a witch who could spell in three dead languages at once."

I shrugged, drawing circles in the condensation left on my now-empty glass. "Guess that's what years of study and trauma drills will get you."

Silas flagged the bartender again, ordered another round for the table. "Let's toast to trauma, then," he offered. "Best teacher I ever had." We all raised our glasses, clinked them over the sticky wood. It felt good, that sound—a punctuation mark on a sentence I hadn't realized I was writing.

Hadeon, ever the fae, cocked his head. "This demon after you. Why now? Why not before?" His brow furrowed as he toyed with a silver ring on his hand, like he was weighing the question on some internal scale.

I thought about it. About Indiana, about the quiet months leading to this year. About Michael, and how he'd appeared in my life like he'd always known exactly when to step out of the shadows. "I don't know," I admitted, rubbing at the spot behind my ear until the skin tingled. "Maybe I'm just unlucky. Or maybe someone's changing the rules."

"Or maybe," Hadeon said, eyes going flinty, "someone's calling in an old marker."

The table went still. Even Silas seemed to pause mid-joke, the smile flickering at the edge of his mouth. I didn't know what to say. The air in the bar went thin for a moment, like it was waiting for me to fill it with something final. I looked down at my hands, the faintest blue shimmer still haunting my wrists where the spell had burned through me.

"Maybe," I repeated, wishing—stupidly, for once—that I could just be normal, whatever that ever meant.

Kat broke the silence first. "Doesn't matter why," she said, glass thumping down with finality. "If they want you, they have to go through all of us. Right, team?"

A chorus of "hell yes" and "over my dead body" followed, and for a second, I realized that all my little terrors, all the paranoia and dread, had grown itchy and awkward around these people. These friends, not-quite family, but something wedged in between that wouldn't be shaken.

The night rolled on, and with every hour I felt the weight on my shoulders get a shade lighter. Every war story, every inside joke and bitch session, knitted us closer together.

Around 9 that evening, Nathan and his polo posse showed up. Tiffany latched to his side. The gut punch I felt seeing them together was equal parts shameful and infuriating. I turned back to the table, refusing to watch her whisper into his ear, laughing in ways I'd never seen him laugh, all soft and easy. Good for them. I hoped she had a stunning personality to balance out that soul-leech of a smile. Silas, ever the meddler, noticed my mood and nudged me with a pointed elbow. "Don't let the Barbie show get to you. You know he only brings her here to piss you off." He whispered loud enough for only us to hear. "I think it's good he's found someone as vapid as he." I whisper back.

"I know, right?" Kat cut in, her voice sharp with glee. "She could never handle a quarter of what we do, let alone survive a single mission. It's hilarious. He looks bored out of his mind." I chanced another glance at Nathan and caught his gaze, sky-blue and cold, trained on me for a split second. I turned away effectively dismissing him. For a guy who supposedly didn't care, he sure spent a lot of time keeping tabs on me. I made a show of ignoring the both of them, throwing my arm around Kat and laughing like we'd just heard the filthiest joke in existence. If jealousy was a game, I had practice at pretending not to care. We made our way out to the dancefloor once the buzz started to kick in. I had no idea Kat could dance like that—ferocious, all elbows and hips, her hair a wild mane as she spun under the colored lights. I tried to keep up, tried to match her energy and forget about Nathan and every demon, literal or personal, that wanted a piece of me. It almost worked. By the fourth song, sweat glued my shirt to my spine and laughter spilled from me, real and unchecked. The ache in my throat was relief, not panic.

When we finally staggered off the floor, we're sandwiched between Chloe and Silas, both looking slightly less put together than usual, eyes glassy with drink and adrenaline. "If I die tomorrow," Chloe gasped, fanning herself dramatically, "I want you to know this is how I want to be remembered: as a disco ball of pure, raw shifter energy."

"Noted," I said, looping an arm around her waist for balance. Kat pressed a glass into my hand, something cold and neon with a fruity tang that insisted on being fun. I tipped it back, let the burn chase away the last dregs of anxiety from my system.

It was only when a familiar shadow loomed across the bar that I remembered we had an audience. Nathan stood at the fringe, arms folded, eyes narrowed, disappointment on his face. We were all drunk. Really drunk and it was a work night.

Kat caught sight of him and stage-whispered, "Uh oh, Dad's here." It broke whatever spell the music had over us and sent the table into a fit of giggles. I made a point not to look his way, but I could feel the disapproval radiating across the room, icy and absolute.

Eventually, nature and the effects of three vodka tonics called; I navigated the overcrowded hallway to the restroom and fumbled my way inside, catching myself in the mirror. My mascara was halfway to my cheekbones and my hair looked like someone had tried to hex it into sentience. The face in the glass was unfamiliar—flushed, wild-eyed, and, weirdly, happy.

I did my business, splashed cold water over my wrists and cheeks, bracing myself before stepping back out into the neon-lit chaos. The hallway was deserted except for Nathan, leaning against the opposite wall, arms folded so tight his knuckles went white.

"Enjoying yourself?" he asked, voice low enough not to carry, but edged with something that could cut glass.

I sidestepped, but he blocked the hall with one arm. "Do you have a problem?" I snapped, more sharply than intended.

"You tell me," he shot back, eyes flicking over my face, not missing a single smudge or stumble in my stance. "You're not supposed to be on duty hungover."

"We're not on duty, Nathan, unless you're planning to bust a demon for grinding too enthusiastically on the dance floor." I tried to push past again, but he didn't move.

He leaned in so his mouth was almost touching my ear, and for a second the press of people and music vanished; there was only his breath on my skin, the wall cool at my back.

"Don't be reckless," he said, but it didn't sound like an admonition. It sounded like a plea. I laughed, but it was shaky. "I'm not the one standing in the girls' hall at midnight, Nathan. Why don't you go find your girlfriend."

He drew back, just far enough for me to see the lines creased in his brow, the raw corners to his eyes. "Sadie—" He stopped, jaw flexed.

Then he did something unexpected. He smiled. That sardonic twist coloring his features. "You're jealous."

I snorted so hard I nearly choked. "Please. I don't care who you date. I'm just pointing out the double standard. If anything, you're jealous of my princely admirer." I finish in a haughty tone.

Nathan studied my face, searching for some sign of weakness, or maybe just some sign at all. I refused to give up anything. He had his little perfect girlfriend, and I had… what, exactly? A recurring role as demon bait and a standing invitation to every supernatural bar in Manhattan? Go me.

"So you think I'm jealous of some pretty-boy elf?" he scoffed, but the edge in his voice was unmistakable. "Have at it, Baker. They'll eat you alive."

"Isn't that half the fun?" I fired back, swaying a little as the hallway tilted under my feet. Either the vodka or the presence of Nathan Blackwood was doing funny things to my inner ear.

He caught my shoulder, steadying me with the gentlest touch I'd ever gotten from him. His hand lingered, just for a second. "You're not as invincible as you think."

"And you're not as tough as you think," I retorted, my words laced with an anger I couldn't quite control. "I thought things were improving between us. I really did. I believed we were becoming friends. But here we are again. You've reverted to the person I met at that retreat all those years ago—arrogant and rude." Even as the words left my mouth, a wave of regret washed over me. After all, he didn't even remember that interaction.

The hallway's ambient roar faded to a brittle silence. Nathan just looked at me, his expression a storm cloud of emotions. For a moment, I saw flicker in his eyes—a hurt that cut through all the bravado and left only something raw behind. He was about to say something, maybe even apologize, but the door to the bar flung open and a pair of werewolves staggered out, howling into their phones and reeking of spilled tequila. The spell was broken. He straightened, all business, and jerked his chin toward the main room.

"You're right," he said, voice suddenly flat. "I'm being an ass. Enjoy your night, Baker. Try not to start any wars." And with that, he walked away, his back a solid wall of retreat.

I waited until the door shut behind him, then slid down the wall, the concrete cold against my shoulder blades. The vodka was catching up with me, seeping into all the cracks Nathan had managed to pry open. God, I was exhausted. I snuck out the side, not feeling particularly social. When I finally made it back to my apartment, the city was in a rare lull, clouds glowing dirty orange over the harbor like the aftermath of some distant, polite disaster. I locked the door and let out a long, shaky sigh. Orion blinked at me from inside a laundry basket, one paw trailing a string of mismatched socks like a flag of surrender. I tossed my keys, peeled off my boots, and sat on the edge of my bed, replaying the night in my head until the humiliation smoothed into numbness. I was so tired I felt hollow. There were days when I wanted something more— wanted to be the protagonist of my own story, not just a pawn in someone's cosmic pissing match. But mostly I just wanted tomorrow to be easier than today and for nobody to need me quite so much. I fell asleep still in my clothes, shoes half-on, Orion burrowing into the curve behind my knees.

18

Heat of the Moment

I was jolted awake by the piercing shriek of my alarm clock, a sound so sharp it cut through the silence of dawn like a knife. Today, I have a training session with Nathan, a prospect that loomed over me like a nightmare you can't shake. I'm sure it won't be awkward at all, I thought, with a twinge of sarcasm flickering in my mind.

I rolled out of bed, too tired to care that I was still wearing last night's jeans, and dragged myself to the bathroom. Staring in the mirror, I saw the dark smudges under my eyes and wondered if maybe, just maybe, I should switch to decaf and keep the whiskey to a dull minimum. But who was I kidding? The city, the job, the endless grind of being a twenty-something with supernatural baggage—none of it worked on decaf. I washed away the mascara streaks, splashed cold water on my face, and got myself presentable enough for headquarters. Orion wound between my legs, purring like a tiny engine, and I bent to scratch his head before heading out the door. The dawn was grey and sticky, already hinting at a suffocating summer day. By the time I reached Lux Bellator's front steps, my shirt was glued to my spine and my hair was a frizzed halo around my face. The lobby was mercifully dark and cold, the only person visible was the Nephilim at the security desk who didn't even spare me a glance, too engrossed in whatever hellish paperwork passed for entertainment in that job. I made it to the gym with two minutes to spare and found Nathan already there, stretching in a way that was both infuriatingly competent and, annoyingly, kind of impressive. He was back in his usual training gear—a black compression shirt and loose sweatpants that somehow hid nothing and everything at once. He didn't acknowledge me right away, just finished his routine with a crisp efficiency that said he could have done this in his sleep. I dumped my bag and stood there, waiting for the snarky comment or arched eyebrow I'd come to expect. Instead, Nathan finished his stretch, straightened, and faced me with a blank, neutral expression. "You ready?" he asked.

I tried to match his chill, keeping my voice even. "Always. What's the plan, Blackwood?"

He hesitated—a split-second pause, but enough for me to catch it. "Sword work," he said, then gestured to the practice rack. "Pick your poison." I went for the weighty hilt of the Lux Bellator standard-issue longsword, my favorite among the mocked-up arsenal, and caught a sideways smirk from him. "Classic," he murmured. Then, aloud: "I want to see if your footwork's improved since last time."

We squared off on the mat, the early-morning hush settling over us like a held breath. He circled, feinting a jab, and I parried, muscle memory guiding me through the patterns we'd drilled for weeks. The rhythm was familiar, almost comfortable. Our blades met with a satisfying clang, the vibration running up my arms and rooting me, for a moment, in the present instead of the mess of my head.

Nathan pressed the attack, moving quicker now, sweat already glistening on his forehead. My movements were slow, my attacks sloppy. I could tell he was ready to yell at me when he just stopped, hands at his hips, and let out an exasperated huff. "Sadie! Focus!" He barked.

"Oh, bite me, Nathan!"

The air stilled. Nathan's expression shifted—you could see the fight between wanting to throttle me and wanting to say something he couldn't unsay. He tossed the practice blade onto the mat and stalked toward me, close enough that I could count the pulse flicks in his neck, the shallow dents in the hollow above his collarbone. "Why can't you take anything serious, Sadie? What's your problem today?" he hissed, voice quiet but lethal.

"You," I snapped, unable to keep the word from tumbling out. "You're my problem. One day you're all teamwork and praise, and then you turn around and act like a jealous asshole."

He opened his mouth, but I barrelled on, hot with the fury of months that felt like years of being alternately underestimated and over-examined. "It's like you want me to fail. Or maybe you're just waiting for it, so you can say you told me so. You don't even make sense! One minute you're holding my hand and telling me I'm a 'force of nature,' and the next you're acting like I wrecked your life by existing in the same room. So which is it, Nathan? What the hell do you want from me?"

The words echoed in the empty gym, bouncing off the cinderblock walls and dying somewhere above the rubberized mats. Nathan just stood there, breathing hard enough I could feel the heat from his chest. For a moment I thought maybe he was going to yell back, but he didn't. He just stared at me—through me, even—and in the long, teeth-gritted silence, I realized I wanted him to answer more than I'd ever admit.

When his voice came, it was low. Not angry, but scraped raw at the edges. "I want you to survive this job. I want you not to die, or worse. Is that so fucking hard to understand?" He raked his hands through his hair, leaving it rumpled and spiked.

"Yes, it is when you treat me like a pariah. You always have." I respond, all of a sudden tired.

He was silent for a beat, and I watched the memory of that retreat flicker across his features. "You remember that week differently than I do," he said, jaw clenching, the vulnerable note chased quickly by disdain. "You have no idea what was going on."

Wait. He remembers me from the retreat? "I thought you didn't remember us meeting there?" I ask, unable to keep my curiosity at bay.

He looked at me, a new kind of tension bristling in the space between us. "That's what I said, yeah. Doesn't mean it's the truth." He licked his lips, and for once, I felt less like I was watching an enemy and more like I was standing next to someone who'd gotten lost on the same dark road and just now realized we were both still moving forward.

I tried to hold his stare but faltered, the room suddenly claustrophobic with old wounds. "Then why did you act like you'd never seen me before?" It came out quieter than I'd intended.

"Because, you were reserved, you stayed away, but I was curious as soon as I saw you." He says staring far off into the distance. "I made that joke about you doing parlor tricks because you unsettled me. I know that's not a good excuse, but it's the truth. I could tell you were more powerful than you were letting on. When you flipped me off, I knew I'd never forget the only girl who didn't fall for my bs." He let the silence sit, the confession hanging raw between us. "I messed up, okay?" Nathan said, voice a little hoarse. "I figured if I pretended you didn't matter, then maybe it wouldn't—" He stopped, jaw twitching, and gave a humorless laugh. "Forget it. Doesn't matter."

I stared, trying to make sense of this slivered, human version of Nathan Blackwood. "You keep doing that," I said, and was surprised to hear my own voice shaking. "Cutting off right when it's about to mean something."

He flinched like I'd hit him. "Because if it means something," he said, "then I have to admit I—" But he didn't finish. Instead, he turned, grabbed the practice sword off the mat, and jammed it back onto the rack with enough force to make the metal shudder.

"Ugh!" I said, stomping behind him, whining like a petulant child. "You are so annoying when you do that!"

He spun, fast, hand braced on the rack, eyes burning. "When I do what, Sadie? When I try to keep you from getting yourself killed? When I care more than I should?"

A long, hard silence. My heart wouldn't stop pounding. I was suddenly aware of every inch between us—intolerable, electric. I reached out, not sure if I was going to hit him, or hug him, or just maybe fall apart. "So, to sum up, this is about you being jealous?" I ask, trying and failing spectacularly at landing the joke. He looked like he could strangle me at that very moment but instead he just let out a sound that might have started as a growl and ended as a laugh, though there was zero humor in it. "Stop twisting things," he said. "This isn't about the stupid elves, or Tiffany, or whatever you think. This is about you and me being on the same goddamn team and…" He trailed off, eyeing the line of the gym mat as if it could tell him how to finish a sentence for once in his life.

I sighed, dragging a hand through my hair, suddenly bone-tired. "It always gets like this with us, doesn't it?" I said, softer now. "We build up, explode, then spend a week pretending it never happened." Nathan shrugged, but the fight was gone from his posture. "Yeah, well. It's easier than the alternative." I almost asked what the "alternative" was, but I didn't want to hear it. Or maybe I did, but only in the safety of a bar at midnight, not here, not in the blinding fluorescents of the Lux Bellator gym where every secret went to bounce off the walls like a cursed echo.

He turned away, started toward the showers, but hesitated at the door. "I'm proud of you. I know I don't say it enough." He glanced over his shoulder, the edge of a battered smile tracing his mouth. "Next training—let's try not to kill each other."

I snorted. "No promises." He left then, leaving a ghost of aftershave and ozone in his wake. I slumped down on a bench, head in my hands, and let the residual anger sputter out, leaving nothing behind but melancholy and a little curiosity. I replayed every second of the fight, every echo of the retreat, every flicker of… whatever sat underneath the surface between us. "Invincible, my ass," I muttered, and for a rare moment wondered what my life would look like if I let myself actually care.

The rest of the day passed in a cold haze. I did my rounds, filed the reports, attended the mandatory safety seminar where Hadeon delivered a half-hour PowerPoint on the dangers of fae glamour in office environments. (Key takeaway: the copier is not, in fact, self-replicating.) Kat texted me memes about demon-fighting, and Chloe left a box of extra-strength tiger balm on my desk with a sticky note: "For the next time Nathan gets under your skin. Which, let's be honest, is probably now" She wasn't wrong.

Sometime after five, I decided the only way to reset my brain was a walk. I left HQ, turned down the side streets that bled into the Park, and let the city swallow me. Summer had finally broken through the asphalt, and the air was thick with honeysuckle, rot, and the hot garbage cocktail that only Manhattan could conjure. The dusk flickered blue and gold through the trees, and every so often a kid would whiz by on a scooter, trailing laughter and sticky-sweet cloud of ice cream.

I found a stone bench near the old band shell and decided to sit, and people watch for a while. It wasn't long before I noticed a change in the atmosphere. Subtle at first but slowly thickening the telltale sign of demon aroma filled the area.

It started with a strange glimmer at the edge of the playground—like a mirage, a trick of the heat—but then it sharpened into a dark, prismatic ripple that no human else seemed to notice. I stiffened on the bench, hands clenched and pulse spiking, tracking the shimmer as it bled around a pair of seesaws and then pooled next to the checkerboard picnic tables.

This was how it always went. Sometimes they came quietly, like a fog rising out of dry gutters, but more often they came like this: shameless, bright-eyed, and hungry, testing the limits of what humans would refuse to see.

I waited for the thing to materialize—sometimes it took a minute, the veil lazy or stubborn—but a face soon bloomed out of the shimmer, thin and translucent as a soap bubble, wearing the shape of something halfway between a nineteen-fifties milkman and a cigarette ad. The demon was learning. It wore the uniform of everyman: white shirt, pressed slacks, the smile a waxy slot of teeth. It even rolled its sleeves to match the other joggers, blending in with the languor of the after-work crowd.

I watched it scan the park, its gaze sliding off the parents and nannies and phone-absorbed teens. Not a threat. Then its eyes landed on me, and every cell in my body braced.

It rolled its neck, as if shaking off a cramp, and strolled over—slow, casual, but with the kind of precision that drew lines between here and kill zone. These were the most dangerous demons of all. "Sadie Baker. Well, isn't this a treat?"

The demon's voice was like a radio stuck between stations, every word garnished with static and the faint shriek of metal on metal. The people around us didn't even notice. I flashed a wan smile and shrugged, as if being stalked in Central Park by a minor infernal was just another Tuesday.

"Nice disguise," I said, matching its tone as it sat next to me, one arm draped over the back of the bench.

"Thank you. I pride myself on my versatility." The demon's grin widened, stretching too far, revealing teeth that belonged in a bear trap. It studied my face with a gambler's focus, eyes shifting color between heartburn yellow and a sickly, highlighter green. "You're looking well. The city agrees with you."

"Cut to the chase," I said. "I'm off the clock. If you want to gloat, do it fast."

The demon's face softened with mock offense. "You wound me, Sadie. I'm here in a purely advisory capacity." It reached into a conjured breast pocket, pulling out a cigarette, then, perhaps in a gesture of solidarity, offered one to me.

I took it, more to keep my hands busy than because I actually wanted one. If the thing was going to try a sympathy play, I wasn't going to make it easy.

"Surprised you're not trying to drag me to hell or whatever," I said, "what with your boss sending dukes to knock on my door."

"Hell is overrated," the demon said, popping the cigarette in its mouth and lighting it with a flick of his wrist.

"So, you said you're here in an advisory position. Tell me why you're all after me." I ask, hoping I'll finally get some answers.

"That is quite the complex answer, my dear. But let's just say, you're angel blessed. Your power is unlike any witch of modern society. There are a few demons back in hell interested in taking the power for themselves, using it for the usual world domination plans." He said sounding bored.

"Angel blessed?" I ask, unfamiliar with the term.

"Yes, a rare gift bestowed upon you by a powerful angel, an archangel most likely." He says giving me a clinical once over. "You must have made quite the impression."

I'm so confused I'm legitimately at a loss for words.

The demon smirked, tapping ash onto the ground with a languid flick. "You must be special, Sadie. Most witches only get a spark—enough to light candles, shuffle a Tarot deck, maybe banish the odd poltergeist if they're lucky. But you? You're packing something old. Something big. And the right infernal, with the right leverage, would eat their way straight to the top of the food chain."

I shivered at the precision of his words. Something in me

wanted to recoil, to reject the idea that I was anything but another grunt, another survivor in the supernatural rat race.

"What do you want?" I asked, my voice dry as the heat off the pavement.

The demon's smile got smaller, more confidential. "Nothing, honestly. I'm not even supposed to be here. But I like seeing a witch in an existential crisis. It's… entertaining. The others, though?" He blew a smoke ring as I tried to swallow the boulder wedged in my throat. "Are you warning me?" "Think of it as a professional courtesy," it replied, the smile sliding off its face, replaced by a thin, brittle empathy. "Crossroads are always tricky, Sadie Baker. The first thing to go is the ground under your feet."

It uncrossed its legs, crushed the cigarette under its immaculate shoe, and in a shimmer of heat, vanished—leaving only the burnt twist of filter, and the sour taste of dread curling over my tongue.

For a moment, I just sat there, staring at the spot where the demon disappeared. Then I pulled out my phone, opening our team group text, typing out a quick recap of what just happened.

Just had a park bench heart-to-heart with a demon. Apparently, I'm "angel blessed." Also, everyone's still trying to eat my soul. Thoughts? Silas responded first, as always his response useless as ever: <3 <3 <3.

Kat responded next: "Angel blessed? Hell yeah. You know what that means, right? You're basically the Chosen One. Or a really hot target. Probably both."

A moment later, Hadeon chimed in: "That explains much. Will provide extra wards for the apartment." I wanted to laugh, but the lump in my throat had calcified into something jagged.

The minutes ticked by and nothing came from Nathan. Guess, my run-in with the demon was unimportant. He was probably too busy with Tiffany.

I trudged home, buzzed with a blend of anxiety and rage that only a personal visit from a demon could inspire.

Orion greeted me at the door, winding around my ankles and purring with the sort of smug satisfaction only a cat with a full food bowl can manage. I dragged myself to the kitchen, set down my phone, and ran the tap until the water came out cold. I drank straight from the faucet, hoping to flush the taste of sulfur and secondhand smoke from my mouth.

The apartment was quiet except for the soft hum of the city outside. I stood in the stillness, trying to sort the tangle in my head. Angel blessed. What the hell did that mean? Was Michael the archangel the demon hinted at, the one who "bestowed the rare gift" on me? If so, he'd done a damn poor job of prepping me for what that meant. I had half a mind to call him, to demand he tell me what he'd hidden all these years. But then I remembered Michael never answered, not unless he wanted to. He was like that: all benevolent mystery until it was inconvenient for him.

I flicked on the TV for background noise and scrolled through my messages, looking for a sign that the world, or at least my team, was still spinning. Nothing from Nathan. Why does that bother me so much? I thought about calling Kat, but she was probably knocking back tequila shots with Hadeon at the all-night billiards place by our building. Instead, I opened the browser and started searching every reference to "angel-blessed witches" I could find. Around midnight, I gave up. Still no response from Nathan, I tried to put his lack of reaction out of my mind. Clearly, I didn't matter to him.

I left the blue glow of my laptop burning on the coffee table and went to bed, bracing myself for a long, restless night. I almost made it to sleep before I heard a knock at the door—a soft, polite tap that clearly did not belong to Kat, or to anyone who'd ever lived in my building. My heart climbed into my throat. I padded to the door, every instinct on red alert, and peered through the peephole.

Nathan.

He stood in the hall, hands stuffed awkwardly in his pockets, tie loosened like he'd only just escaped some formal hell. A humid wave of embarrassment washed over me; I almost didn't open it.

But I did.

He looked up, caught my gaze, and for a second neither of us moved. Finally, he cleared his throat. "You didn't answer your phone," he said.

That was rich, coming from him. "Didn't hear it," I replied. "What's wrong?"

He hesitated, toeing the threadbare carpet. "I got your group text. About the demon."

I didn't know what to do with my hands. I crossed my arms and leaned against the jamb, forcing a smile I didn't feel. "Yeah. Angel blessed. It's all very Harry Potter, minus the fun and merchandise tie-ins." My voice was brittle with fatigue, but I wasn't about to show him how rattled I actually was.

His expression flickered, less the usual hard-edged mask and more a slow, worried thaw. "I should have come sooner. I'm sorry."

Knowing he was probably with Tiffany, I just gave a nonchalent shrug, trying to show it didn't bother me.

He looked past me, into the dim cave of my apartment, and said in a voice so low I almost didn't catch it, "Are you okay?"

I wanted to brush it off, to treat him like the strictly professional, strictly platonic team lead he so clearly wanted to be, but that wasn't the truth. I was tired and scared and the thing in the park had left a bruise deeper than any hit I'd taken in practice.

"Not really," I admitted, keeping my voice steady by sheer force of will.

Nathan nodded, as if he'd expected nothing less, and then, to my surprise, said, "Can I come in?" I stepped aside, and he moved past me, careful not to brush my arm—a small, deliberate movement that made my chest ache.

He surveyed the living room, its mess of books and laundry and semi-sentient cat, then hovered awkwardly on the threshold between the kitchen and main room. I watched him, trying to decipher which Nathan had shown up: the cold, surgical pro; the half-broken comrade from the basement; or the version who once, just once, looked at me like I was the only person left in the world worth saving. He drummed his fingers on the countertop, the old agitation spiraling back into his shoulders. Then he pushed away and turned to face me, sudden and close. "I know I'm not easy to work with," he started, voice low and rough. "And I know I've given you a thousand reasons to hate me." His gaze ticked down, then back up—this time, with a look I recognized from the gym, the one that meant he was about to say something he'd regret. "But I was worried when I saw your text. Terrified. I needed to make sure you were okay for myself."

"That was four and a half hours ago, Nathan." I say, a little irritated that it took him so long to see my message. Okay, a lot irritated.

"I get it, you're busy. I'm not your responsibility outside of work." I placate, backing away from dangerous territory.

I was halfway through sliding into a self-pity monologue when Nathan interrupted, his face tightening in frustration. "Baker, stop. You are my responsibility, on and off the field. That's the whole damn point—" He caught himself, eyes darting to where Orion glared with feline judgment from the top of the fridge. The words seemed to rock him, as if he'd only just realized what he'd said and how it sounded. He glanced away, then back, caught in a tug-of-war between running and staying.

I shrugged, the weight of it all heavier than I'd let myself admit until now. "It's fine. You don't have to sell it, to pretend like you care. You've never liked me, not at the retreat when we were teenagers and not now. I'm a big girl; I can handle it."

Nathan's whole face seemed to collapse, like I'd just delivered a punch square to the solar plexus of his self-image. "That's not true," he said hoarsely. "It was never true." He closed the space between us, every movement restless and too fast and then, suddenly, too careful, like I was something that could break if he got too close. "You don't know how hard it is for me to… I don't know. To not fuck this up." He shook his head, exhaling hard. "You remember how you said I was jealous?" He tried to laugh but couldn't find the sound. "I am jealous. I see you with everyone—Kat, the team, even the damn elves— and all I can think is why can't it ever be easy between me and you like that." He looks back at me, eyes tortured. "Please, Sadie. Help me out here, I'm struggling." I walk closer to him, slowly as if he is a wild animal I may spook. I don't know what possess me to do it, but I reach my arms up and around his neck, hugging him tight and burying my face in his shoulder. For the briefest moment, Nathan froze. Then everything in him uncoiled, and he wrapped his arms around my waist and held on like I was the only buoy in a storm. I could feel the tremor running through his frame, the tension of months— maybe years—without anyone to lean on. The kind of need you only recognize when the other person is close enough to hear your heartbeat misfire.

We stood like that for a long time, neither of us moving, not even when Orion yawned so hard I swear I heard his jaw crack. The city rumbled outside; in here, all I could hear was Nathan's measured breath and the faint, frantic thrum of my own pulse.

"I don't want to be scared for you all the time," Nathan said, chin brushing the crown of my head. "But I don't know how not to be. You get under my skin, Baker. It's… infuriating." He laughed, a real one this time, low and melted around the edges. "I want to protect you, but I also know I can't, not from everything."

"I'm not asking you to," I said, muffled by the cotton of his shirt. "I just want to know you're on my side." I tilted my head up.

"Always," he says, voice barely a whisper. I angle my face just enough to where our lips are but a breath away from one another. He wastes no more time, planting a sweet, gentle kiss to my lips that demanded nothing and offered everything.

The world didn't end. The lights didn't flicker, the angels didn't descend to shake their gold-tipped fingers at us. It was just Nathan, mouth warm and a little hesitant, letting me decide what happened next. So I kissed him back, not deep or desperate, just long enough to make it real.

When we eased apart, I could see he was already way too embarrassed. His cheeks pinked and his eyes darted away, "I really shouldn't have done that." He said, though he didn't sound like he regretted it. "I'm your boss, there are rules- I, I should go." He turned towards the door, a man in panic. I watched, slightly amused, slightly annoyed.

I let him get all the way to the threshold before calling out, "Nathan?" He paused, braced by the doorframe like he might try to pry the whole building open with his bare hands. "Yeah?" "Next time," I said, voice a little steadier, "you can just say you like me. Less messy than all this existential drama." He huffed out a laugh, the kind that comes from way down in the ribcage. He didn't turn around, but I heard it, and it was enough. When the door clicked shut behind him, I stood in the empty apartment, alone except for Orion and the electric aftertaste of the kiss.

It wasn't until three a.m. that I realized I'd never once considered how it might feel to really belong to someone, or to let someone belong to me. The world hadn't ended. Maybe, if I dared, it had just started.

19

Angel Blessed; Whatever That Means

By the next afternoon I was going crazy trying to understand what the demon meant by angel blessed? Is that why my magic was so powerful, why I could do things no other witch could? Also, if I was angel blessed, who was the angel that blessed me, and when? I sit at my computer typing in random search terms hoping to get a hit.

Nothing. Just occult fanfic and a handful of True Haunting podcasts pushing self-published e-books. Five clicks in and I find a spiral of conspiracy Reddit and a blog where a woman claimed she'd been "blessed" by an angel in the Target parking lot—she got a free donut, so who's judging.

After hours of fruitless searching, the only concrete thing I found was that the phrase "angel blessed" was largely the provenance of conspiracy blogs and the sort of paranormal websites with more animated gifs of spinning pentagrams than actual citations. According to one, angel-blessed witches were "walking lightning rods," magnets for supernatural weirdness and doom, but also occasionally able to bend reality if pushed to the edge. That sounded both promising and likely to get me murdered in spectacular fashion.

Phone in hand, I tried to trace back my earliest memories of magic—back to the muddy riverbank in Indiana where I swore I saw something trailing after me in the willow shadows, back to the sleepovers with Kat where I could make a candle flicker just by wanting it. Had Michael been somewhere in the margins the whole time? I don't think so. He's a powerful Nephilim, but they don't have archangel powers. I tried to remember when I'd first felt truly different—when I'd first suspected that maybe there was more to my "gift" than a family legacy and too much time in musty libraries. Maybe I'd always known, but you can't always see what you're running from until it runs you down.

Another thirty-seven minutes and twelve half-assed Google results later, I concluded the following: the phrase "angel blessed" was a bafflingly uneven mix of Christian parenting blogs, anime fanfiction, and one extremely questionable subreddit that I will never, ever visit again. Nothing solid about witches, or why a demon would care if one had an angel's cosmic golden stamp of approval.

I leaned back, cracked my knuckles, and cursed softly. The sunlight filtering through the window was New York golden, honeyed and heavy, but it did nothing to relieve the icepick frustration burrowing into my skull. I wanted answers and had exactly zero.

I could try Michael, but he would just ignore me, he's not exactly an open book and was more than likely to give me the run around. Out of options, I went to the one place a witch in search of forbidden, heretical, or slightly embarrassing grimoires could always count on: the Occult Archives in the Lux Bellator basement.

It was three levels below ground, a subterranean vault lined with rows of locked cages and rolling ladders that looked like they'd been borrowed from Hogwarts by way of Rikers Island. The air was always a dozen degrees colder than upstairs, the lighting a jaundiced pall cast by bulbs older than my parents' marriage. The only sign of life was today's archivist on duty, a spectral wisp of a woman named Tilda who oversaw the stacks like an underpaid ghost librarian. She arched one eyebrow as I scanned in.

"Back so soon, Baker? Didn't you take half the demonology section home last month?"

"I'm feeling nostalgic," I said, spreading my arms in a "what can you do?" gesture. "But this time, I'm looking for angelic cross-pollination. Anything on witches with… you know, extra features?"

Tilda's smile was a thin, sharp cut. "Try the left-hand shelf, past the cursed diaries and before you hit the lycanthropy newsletters." She went back to knitting something black and lacy that might have been a hat or a shroud. I trudged down the aisle, trailing my fingers over the cracked vellum and faded foil stamped spines. Most of the books had been rebound multiple times—stitched together from fragments of older texts, patched with handwritten margin notes in five or six different languages. If you wanted to know what humanity had learned about the supernatural in five thousand years, it was all here, dogeared and sullen, waiting for someone desperate enough to care.

It took about twenty minutes and several papercuts before I found a plausible lead: an anonymous codex with the jazzy title "Supernal Afflictions and Gifts of the Mortal Coil." The author must have been an academic with a flair for the dramatic, because every chapter opened with an epigraph in Latin and closed with a doomsday prophecy. There was an entire section devoted to "hybrids"—mortals who'd been touched, marked, or infused by an otherworldly being.

According to the index, the "angel-blessed" showed up in precisely two paragraphs, jammed between "Cambionic Manifestations" and "Cases of Spontaneous Stigmata." I squinted at the faded script, trying to stumble through the florid English:

"In the rarest circumstance, a witch or sorcerer of mundane birth may bear the luminous taint of angelic influence—by direct intervention, or by ancestry unrecorded. These Unwilling Vessels are marked by their fierce resistance to infernal corruption, but in equal measure suffer the attention of Hell and Heaven alike. It is the nature of such an individual to attract both the miraculous and the monstrous, and to walk the narrowest path between the two until the vessel… bursts."

Lovely.

I skimmed the rest, hoping for a cheat code, but it was just a laundry list of historical sad endings: witches drawn and quartered by Hell's finest, others who burned out in a blaze of glory that sometimes took a city block with them. No happy endings. But one footnote, jammed in the margin and underlined three times, caught my eye: "In several historical incidents, the marked individual was known to be haunted—often literally—by manifestations of their angelic patron. This presence offered not only protection, but sometimes drove the vessel toward fateful confrontation." I closed the book, heart rattling. Haunted by an angelic patron. Was that why, whenever my life went to hell, some invisible voice seemed to steer me out by the skin of my teeth? Or why, even now,

I sometimes swore I caught a glimpse of blinding light in the corner of my eye, gone the moment I turned? I signed out the tome and headed home, the whole thing taking three times as long because Kat waylaid me in the elevator, loaded with questions about my "romantic progress" with Nathan and whether I thought fae would ever invent a gluten-free beer that didn't taste like "troll sweat." I fielded her questions as best I could, then ghosted her excuse about a migraine and retreated to my apartment, where Orion greeted me by throwing up on my "Live Laugh Hex" doormat.

Perfect ending to a perfect day.

20

Tick Tock Trauma

The next few days were strange in the way that unspoken things change a whole city. Nathan and I tiptoed around each other, all brisk hellos and stiff nods during morning musters, but I caught him watching me across every crowded room, and once—just once—brushing my hand as we passed in the corridor and not letting go for a full two seconds longer than he had to. He never mentioned the kiss and neither did I.

But it pulsed between us, humming like a live wire, every time we were near enough to feel it. Kat and Chloe noticed in under a day, of course. Kat kept giving me this look, sly and conspiratorial, and Chloe started slipping "lovebirds" into every sentence with surgical precision. Even Silas, who was either an empath or just emotionally reckless, smiled every time he caught the two of us not quite making eye contact over the conference table.

Work didn't slow down. If anything, our team doubled its calls: vampires running credit card scams in Queens, a cabal of hedge-witches turning old ladies into obsidian garden statues along the Upper West Side, and the usual parade of poltergeists haunting the city's subway tunnels. "You'd think even the ghosts would want a vacation in summer," Kat groaned one night, peeling off her bulletproof vest and letting it thud to the floor of the locker room. "But no. They see us getting a rhythm, and they're all, 'RUIN IT.'"

Nathan was crisp in the field, all business, but in the moments between, I'd catch wind of the softer version I'd met in my living room. He started bringing coffee for the team, always remembering my order (black, two sugars, but not the fake stuff), and made a point of running drills with me instead of just barking instructions.

We got good. We got really good, moving like a pack, everyone knowing their lane and staying in it—except when the world flipped itself inside out, which happened more than once. A week after the demon's warning, Silas got a call—a simple exorcism at a Brooklyn antique store (owners complained of poltergeist activity, suspiciously aggressive dolls, and an old lady whose haunted rocking chair had taken to pelting visiting children with knitting needles)—I was already vibrating with anticipation. Since we were the only two in the office at the time, we took it.

"I love haunted antiques," Silas said, clapping his hands. "It's always the little things that try to kill you. Never furniture, never art. Always clocks, dolls, or, if we're lucky, a sentient chamber pot."

We climbed into the suv, cranking the AC and batting aside the stale, slightly-cilantro scent of leftover Taco Bell wrappers. Silas drove, as he always insisted, weaving recklessly through the side streets and giving the finger to anyone in a car with a bumper sticker. I read through the file: the owner, an ancient woman named Mrs. Laverne, claimed the poltergeist only targeted children and, in a whisper, admitted that her beloved grandfather clock had started "biting" people.

The store was a shoebox wedged between a vape shop and an abandoned laundromat, the interior lit by a haze of dust motes and the eerie glow of 1970s Christmas lights strung permanently along the rafters. The minute we walked in, a music box somewhere in the depths started playing a cracked, off-tempo waltz. Silas rolled his eyes. "Of course. Never a Sousa march, always some creepy child melody." He led the way, ducking past a shelf of porcelain dogs, and called out, "Mrs. Laverne?"

We heard a shuffle and a frustrated clatter from the rear. The woman herself emerged, hunched and shrunken, but with eyes like obsidian marbles set in a face that had spent a century frowning at everyone else's idea of progress. "About time," she snapped, waving a gnarled hand at the chaos around her. "It's gotten worse."

I surveyed the scene: tables overturned, a heap of mismatched clothing writhing as if alive, the faintest whiff of ozone layered over the decay of mothballs and carpet glue. "Could you describe the activity?" I asked, ducking as a toy plane dive-bombed over my head and embedded itself in the wall. Mrs. Laverne grunted. "Objects move. Lights flicker. Grandfather clock tries to eat anyone under five foot three. It's ruining my Yelp rating, and I will not die a one-star business." "Noted," said Silas, who was already scanning the room with his vampire vision for the epicenter of the disturbance.

The hair stood up on my arms. "Let's see the clock," I said. She cackled and led us to the back, where the grandfather clock loomed, stately and malignant, its pendulum swinging just out of time with the music box. The wood was pitted here and there with tiny, ragged holes—bite marks, if you squinted. Silas let out a low whistle, then licked one finger and touched the clock face. "Ow!" He jerked back, shaking a drop of blood off his finger. "Son of a—" The clock chimed in response, the note bell-clear and tinged with menace. Silas and I exchanged a look: this was no ordinary haunting. We made our circuit: circle the perimeter, clock any movement, ignore the mannequins unless they moved first (they always moved first). On the second lap, the temperature dropped fast enough that my breath fogged. "Classic poltergeist," I muttered. "We can finish this before lunch." I dug in my bag for a binding sachet, fingers numb and slow, and by the time I straightened up, Silas was already in the thick of it—backed into a corner by a swarm of china dolls, their jaws unhinging just wide enough to cracklingly chant: "TICK TOCK TICK TOCK." The grandfather clock started vibrating, its pendulum a blur. With a pop, the glass face shattered, and a gout of black mist exploded out, knitting itself into a shape of a human.

"Okay-" I said, adrenalin kicking up a notch. "That's new."

The mist congealed into a woman, her features flickering with static—sometimes the delicate bone structure of a Victorian cameo, other times a pinched, feral snarl. She hovered just above the ground, dress trailing smoke, eyes hollow but aware. Mrs. Laverne shrieked and dove behind a battered rolltop desk. Silas, finally in his element, squared up to the specter and drew a line with his boot on the warped linoleum.

"Poltergeist," he announced, "You are being evicted under the Greater New York Paranormal Code. Section Seven: No haunting outside designated hours unless pre-approved by the city council." He flashed a fanged grin. "You have sixty seconds to peaceably un-manifest before we get creative."

The ghost didn't answer, but the dolls all turned their heads with eerie precision, their necks creaking as their glass eyes swiveled towards me, each pair reflecting a cold, calculating gaze. The room was filled with their relentless chorus—"TICK TOCK TICK TOCK"—a sound so overpowering it seemed to vibrate through the very walls, causing the lights in the shop to flicker and spasm erratically.

My fingers trembled as I reached for the binding sachet and my athame, my voice barely a whisper as I muttered the containment incantation under my breath. The words flowed more smoothly now, a testament to either my practice or the urgent fear of being torn apart by these vengeful, animated timepieces. Once the protective circle was complete, Silas tossed me a vial of holy water. We exchanged a knowing glance—he would create the diversion; I would focus on the binding. Silas lunged forward, his eyes alight with an unholy enthusiasm, clearly relishing the chaos more than he should.

The spectral figure recoiled but instead of retreating, it launched itself at us. Silas absorbed the impact, rolling with the ghost's icy grasp as he quickly uttered a rough banishing spell, causing the dolls to shriek and collapse into lifeless heaps at our feet. I slashed the athame through the thick, tense air, igniting the sachet and scattering powdered salt through the swirling haze. The ghost let out a piercing shrill, flickering into a semi-corporeal state before rocketing towards me. The air around me was abruptly void, leaving my lips to crackle and my skin to prickle with static electricity.

I braced myself, the sharp, metallic taste of corroded batteries flooding my mouth, and completed the final line of the binding just as an arctic mist engulfed me from head to toe. My senses were obliterated; sight and sound vanished, leaving me trapped in a vortex of blinding, white-hot agony that seared through my veins like liquid ice. Somewhere, a world away, Silas's voice pierced the void, screaming my name with desperate intensity.

"Sadie! SADIE! Count to five!"

I forced myself to comply. Each number took an eternity, as time itself stretched and warped. By the time I reached "four," the entity within the clock convulsed violently. I clenched my jaw, summoning the memory of every time Michael had rescued me from chaos like this, and unleashed the raw, untamed magic. The subsequent explosion of light and sound was so overwhelming that consciousness slipped away, leaving me adrift in darkness for a fleeting moment.

When I came to, I was on my knees, surrounded by a snowdrift of shattered porcelain and a cloud of dissipating mist. Silas stood over me, holding out a hand. "You still alive?"

"My soul's attached, if that's what you mean," I croaked, letting him haul me to my feet. Every bone in my body hummed; the binding had leeched power from every cell. My vision kept doubling, then flashing black before resolving into the kaleidoscope antique shop. Mrs. Laverne poked her head out from behind the desk, eyes wide and wild. "Did you get it? Is it gone?" Silas dusted off his pants and flashed the old woman a rakish grin. "All clear, ma'am. You can resume commerce as usual. Might want to burn the clock, though." He nudged the grandfather clock with his boot; the pendulum hung dead, its ornate face now just aged brass and glass gone dull. The dolls, too, were inert—toppled on their sides, eyes empty. The malaise in the air was gone, replaced with a faint citrus of Silas's aftershave and the warm, calming smell of old books. I clung to the edge of a display case, steadying myself.

The adrenaline was dropping, leaving behind a migraine and a cold sweat. "Well, that was fun," I muttered, dragging a shaky hand through my hair. My arm stung. I looked down to see a line of red where a porcelain jaw had closed around my wrist and left a ring of tiny, serrated punctures. Silas spotted the blood and pressed a handkerchief into my palm, his voice uncharacteristically gentle. "Let me see." He dabbed at the bite, then shrugged. "Nothing a few stitches and a whiskey can't fix." I pressed the cloth to the wound, biting down on the urge

to whimper. Instead, I glared at the destroyed clock, still feeling the ghost's claws scraping at the inside of my skull. "Next time, someone else can take the store," I told Silas, but even as I tried for a snarky grin, my stomach rolled.

"Deal." Silas was already scoping the ruined shop for anything valuable, whether in a supernatural or purely mercenary sense. "You okay? You looked pretty out of it there."

"Just tired. Drained. Standard Tuesday."

He eyed me for a second too long, then nodded. "We'll file the report on the way. Then, you need to see the healer when we return to headquarters."

We limped out to the car, my hands shaking so badly I almost missed the ignition. I focused on the road, on the periphery of the Brooklyn bridge and the monotone flow of traffic, forcing myself not to think about the ghost or the demon's words or how, deep in my bones, power had started to feel less like a gift and more like a time bomb.

Back at headquarters, the healer on call—today it was a sweet, seventy-year-old witch named Rita—patched me up with a muttered blessing and a slightly alarming poultice that smelled like NyQuil and burnt sage. "It'll scar nicely, honey," she said, dabbing my wrist with a glowing cotton ball. "But you'll want to eat something heavy, stat. You pushed yourself harder than you should have, for your level." "Is there a magic word for carbs?" I joked, but my hands still shook as I reached for the protein bar Rita offered. Silas hovered outside the med bay, lurking like a guilty dog, but the moment I stepped into the hall, he lit up. "You're a goddamn rockstar, you know that?" He pulled a face, then added, "Sorry for almost getting you clocked to death." "Hazard of the trade," I said, and he laughed, the easy, unapologetic way that made everything seem a shade less bleak. We limped down to the locker room, where Kat and Hadeon were both sprawled on the ratty couch that passed for team seating. Kat was eating cold Chinese out of the box, her hair a catastrophe, while Hadeon—shocking no one—was grading the spectral density readings on a battered tablet. "You look like roadkill," Kat observed, mouth full. "Thanks," I said. "You too." "Poltergeist?" Hadeon asked, gaze flicking to my bandaged arm. "More ambitious than usual," Silas supplied. "It tried to drag her through the grandfather clock's inner workings. Sadie nailed it, though." Kat whistled, clearly impressed. "I'd have paid actual money to see you go twelve rounds with a haunted clock. See? This is why I said you'd be MVP." "Spare me," I groaned, but the validation felt better than painkillers. I collapsed next to her, wolfing down half her spring roll before she could stab me with a chopstick. "Anything new from the demon-watching front?" I asked, directing the question to Hadeon, who rarely missed a detail. He shook his head. "Nothing on the usual channels. But there's chatter about a gathering in Chinatown tomorrow night. Could be a lead." "Fantastic," I muttered, dragging my sleeve over my sweating brow. "I was worried our week would get boring." I collapsed against the back of the couch, letting the familiar drone of Hadeon's voice and the close, salty scent of Kat's takeout anchor me to the moment. It was easy, here, to forget that I was anything but another rookie on a scrappy team. Eventually someone mentioned drinks at The Cloak (our daily routine) to which we all agreed was much needed after a wild day of possessed clocks and an army of porcelain dolls.

21

Denial and Other Nightmares

As soon as we hit the bar, Chloe and Kat were already halfway to the dart board, while Hadeon lingered by the TV, glancing up at the muted news crawl about a mayoral bribery scandal that was, hilariously, being blamed on "malicious metaphysical influence." Silas got the first round, and I nursed a gin and tonic, eyeing the bottle of Advil behind the bar like it might be a better use of my next five dollars.

It was one of those nights where the city's mood leaned reckless: a tangle of undergrad kids, two tablefuls of vampiric financiers (they didn't drink, just bought and sold six-dollar shiraz by the case), and the usual barflies who knew better than to ask why our table kept laughing even when no one had said a word. For the first hour, I felt normal. Not powerful, not hunted, but just a girl at a bar with co-workers who could scrape her off the pavement if she needed it.

Kat—already two shots in—leaned sideways and whispered, "You never told me what's up with you and Blackwood." Her eyes glinted, equal parts mischief and concern. "You okay, or is this the start of a workplace romance cautionary tale?"

I shrugged, chewing the straw in my glass, and tried to come up with an answer that didn't sound pathetic. "We kissed. It was weird. I think it broke his brain."

Kat snorted so hard she inhaled her beer. "God, I love it," she said. "Just keep him off-balance."

I was about to make a quick retort when Nathan himself walked in, Tiffany attached to his arm like she had tentacles. My heart shuttered and I had to turn away to avoid showing the absolute meltdown happening on my face. I faked interest in the dart match, pretending I didn't care, pretending it didn't bother me that two nights ago we'd breathed the same air in my apartment and now he was right back to square one: perfect suit, perfect hair, perfect girl. Tiffany laughed at something he said and clung to him with the frenetic assurance of someone who'd never been told no. For all the world, they could have been the Rolex ad in a magazine for people who actually shopped in the back of Town Cars.

Kat followed my gaze and swore under her breath. "He's an idiot. You're a snack, and he's settling for brandless bran flakes."

I barked an unwilling laugh, but it didn't stick. "I don't care," I lied. "Let them be happy. She probably compliments his oversized ego."

"You okay?" Kat repeated, softer this time. I nodded, nose stinging, suddenly keenly aware of all the things I hadn't admitted, even to myself. "I don't know what I am," I said, watching Nathan scan the shelves behind the bar, not once looking at Tiffany as she rattled off a string of complaints about the wine list. "It's like we get close, and then he bolts. Like he's afraid I'm a trap." Kat snickered. "To be fair, you are a trap. You're the kind of girl who sets off every alarm in a guy's nervous system."

"Thanks?"

"That's a compliment," Kat insisted. "He's not over you, you know," she murmured. "Even I can see that, and I have the romantic intuition of a houseplant."

"Doesn't matter," I lie. "I'm over him." I avoid looking over there, pretending he doesn't exist. My team does their best to keep me in high spirits despite internal spiral.

But Nathan was everywhere, even when I wasn't looking. I could feel the gravity of his regard at the back of my neck, a secret orbit, a tide I couldn't wade out of. At some point, I realized my glass had been empty for ten minutes, but I was still rolling the straw between my teeth, distracted, waiting for something to happen or, more likely, not happen.

It was late into the night when I finally decided to detach myself from the group. Carefully, I gathered my belongings and slipped away quietly, not wanting to create any unnecessary commotion. As I turned the corner to navigate through a narrow side street, my eyes caught sight of a shadowy figure dressed entirely in black. A hood obscured their features, casting an ominous presence across the road. A frigid chill coursed through my veins as I instinctively reached for my phone, fingers poised to dial Kat or Silas for reassurance. With a quick glance back up, the mysterious figure had vanished into the night, as if swallowed by the night. Had it been a mere illusion conjured by my weary mind? Urgency propelled my steps as I hurried home, the encounter still lingering like a ghostly whisper in my thoughts.

That night was a relentless torment of fractured sleep and terrifying nightmares filled with shadowy figures and demonic pursuers. In one especially horrific vision, a man of haunting beauty emerged, his presence almost painful to behold. His long, ebony hair cascaded down to his broad shoulders, and his eyes pierced through the darkness with sharp, cunning intent. But it was the massive, black wings unfurling behind him in a menacing arc that screamed danger. A fallen angel. His lethal smile cut through the dream, freezing my very blood as he whispered a chilling promise to see me soon.

I bolted up right covered in sweat. That one felt too intense. Too real. It was nearly impossible to sleep after that, the nightmares tentacles working their way through my brain even after I'd forced myself awake. I lay shivering in the blue-black dark, heart hammering like it was trying to break out of my chest. The words—"I'll see you soon"—throbbed in my head until they lost all meaning, just a coil of sound and dread. I spent the next two hours in a liminal state: too tired to get up, too wired to sleep, every muscle coiled tight as a tripwire.

When I finally got up in the morning, my body felt as if it had been marinated overnight in graveyard dirt and shaken dry with a paint mixer. Orion, my furry emotional support demon, eyed me with an intensity that suggested he was either worried I'd stopped breathing or plotting his next assault on the cereal shelf. I took my time getting ready, moving slow so as not to rattle loose what little energy I had left.

The city was already boiling by nine a.m., the sky a dull lid pressing the stench of hot dog carts and exhaust onto the pavement. Headquarters was a wall of glass and steel that looked as out of place in Brooklyn as a jewel in a tooth. The team was already gathered—Kat perched on the back of the couch, jeans torn and hair spiked in every direction; Chloe and Silas playing a wordless game of chess with bottle caps and balled-up napkins; Hadeon scanning the news feeds on his phone, lips drawn tight with whatever he'd found.

Nathan was nowhere to be seen, something about using a vacation day. Good, I need a day without the complication that is Nathan hanging over my head. I made a beeline for the coffee, slammed two mugs back-to-back, and then, grabbed my gear to go.

By lunchtime, we'd already put out two supernatural brush-fires: a banshee loose in a Morningside Heights dorm, and a magic-maddened iguana rampaging through the petting zoo in Prospect Park (the iguana was, in fact, someone's ex-boyfriend, which made the de-cursing that much more awkward). I got back to HQ still shaking bits of iguana tail off my jacket.

22

A Prince, a Dress, and a Ghost in My Heart

The rest of the team was out. The silence was unfamiliar, and I relished it, gulping coffee and scrolling through last night's incident reports in my office. At some point, I must have nodded off, because I woke to the shrill ring of my office phone, with my face mashed into the sticky linoleum, a line of drool connecting me to a half-eaten cinnamon roll.

"Baker," I answer, attempting to get my bearing's. "Sadie? Hello, it's Prince Rothilion. I hope it is okay to contact you?" His ethereal yet regal voice coming through the speaker.

"Roth, hi!" I say a bit surprised to hear from the handsome elf. "Absolutely, fine. How are you?"

There was a pause, as if Rothilion was recalibrating how to speak to a human female in the context of a casual phone call and not a treaty negotiation. "I am well, thank you. I hear you have been rather heroic lately—banishing a demon Duke, subduing a poltergeist, and assorted other acts of valor." I could practically hear the smile in his voice. "You are making the rest of us look lazy."

I almost corrected him—it was more like 'getting by on the skin of my teeth and the goodwill of my teammates'—but he sounded so delighted I couldn't bring myself to ruin it. "Just doing my job," I said, which sounded pathetic even to me, so I added, "and attracting supernatural rage like a one-woman lightning rod. Seriously, is there a curse for that?"

He laughed. The sound was like glass bells, and for a second I remembered the way every head in the bar had turned when he walked in last time. "If there is, I assure you it is a rare gift. Which is why I was calling…" He hesitated, then the silk in his voice coiled a little tighter. "I wondered if you might join me for dinner. Nothing official—just a meal. I promise to keep the political discourse to dessert."

I blinked. "Like, dinner-dinner?" I said, because I am the aristocrat of smooth conversationalists.

"If that is the correct term," he answered, and now there was a flicker of nervousness—real, not calculated. "I would enjoy your company. You have a such an enchanting aura."

My cheeks burn with a fierce blush at the compliment, my mind a whirlwind of indecision. On one hand, Roth is handsome, kind, and regal in his elven grace. Yet, my heart stubbornly clings to Nathan, tangled in a web of emotions I can't ignore. But Nathan is still entwined with Tiffany, and he has drawn a firm line between us, citing our professional ties as an insurmountable barrier. A small, defiant smile creeps onto my lips as I realize that an exhilarating night out with Roth might just be the escape I desperately crave. "I'm in," I said, "but you're picking the place." Roth sounded genuinely pleased. "Texting you the address. 7 o'clock? Dress as you please, though I must confess, I hope for 'enchanting' rather than 'tactical.'" I stifled a laugh and barely resisted the urge to say, "You just want to watch me fumble with cutlery." Instead, I promised to meet him there, then hung up and stared at the phone as if it were a live grenade. It wasn't a date. Not really. Roth was a prince, with secrets tattooed behind his eyes and a smile that suggested half of his compliments were engineered for maximum effect. But the way he'd said, "I would enjoy your company"—it made the flakes of my heart that still clung to Nathan flinch, then fizzle with what might be relief. Or, more likely, preemptive regret. Kat's head appeared around the office door, her eyeliner already halfway melted off in the humidity. "You look like you just got asked to prom by a supermodel." "I have a dinner with Roth," I said, voice too casual. "It's not a big deal." Kat's eyebrows hit her hairline. "Are you kidding? It's a huge deal!

It's your first date night of the summer! You have to let me help you get ready." Within 30 minutes, we were back at my apartment, half her makeup bag and a travel-sized can of hair glitter, which she insisted on using liberally. "You know, for the drama," she explained, painting cat-eyeliner wings on me so aggressive they could have flown me to the moon. I endured the beautification ritual with a fatalistic calm, letting her nix my battered jeans for the one black dress I owned that didn't smell like sorrow or fabric softner. "You look hot," Kat said, giving me a once-over with hands on her hips. "If Nathan sees you, he'll combust." I didn't mention that the last thing I wanted was for Nathan to see me. Or that maybe, deep in some traitorous gland, I did.

I checked the mirror before I left and barely recognized myself: the hair smooth and shining, the dress clinging in the right places, the eyes huge and haunted, the way they always were. Orion blinked at me from the couch as if to say, "So this is your final form?" I ignored him, grabbed my bag, and headed into the heat-thick dusk.

The place Roth picked was on the Lower East Side, a restaurant that looked like a pawn shop from outside—no sign, just a brass knob and a crooked neon "OPEN" hum—but inside it was a riot of light and color: scarlet banquettes, walls papered in sepia photographs of lost cities, and tables set with cutlery gleaming dangerously.

I spotted Roth leaning casually against the restaurant's arched doorway, lantern light catching the sharp line of his jaw and illuminating his easy, confident smile. When the hostess led us to a secluded corner booth draped in burgundy velvet, I felt the muscles in my shoulders unclench for the first time all evening. Roth's presence was like a warm breeze—witty, charming, and genuinely curious about my day-to-day life. By the time we slid into our seats, the sting of Nathan's rejection had faded to a distant ache.

The room smelled of fresh basil, roasting garlic, and simmering tomato sauce. Soft golden bulbs hovered over each table, casting intimate pools of light on crisp white linens. As Roth handed me the menu, he launched into one amusing tale after another about the absurdities of elven court life.

"Picture this," he said, grinning as he replayed the memory in his mind. "I'm standing before an ancient elven dignitary who won't stop lecturing me on the precise angle at which you're supposed to shake an acorn before you store it. The whole recital lasted ten minutes. I swear, I nearly bit through my tongue to keep a straight face."

A laugh slipped out of me, light and genuine. "I guess royal protocol isn't all it's cracked up to be."

He leaned forward, eyes dancing with mischief. "Oh, the

perks are nice—silken robes, endless banquets—but between you and me, humans are infinitely more entertaining. You never follow any predictable script."

As we sampled bruschetta and sipped velvety Chianti, I found myself enjoying the easy rhythm of our conversation. Yet beneath every smile, my thoughts fluttered back to Nathan's apologetic eyes and the unanswered questions I'd left hanging between us.

When Roth offered to walk me back to my apartment, the night air felt cool against my flushed cheeks. Under the glow of streetlamps, I turned to him. "Thank you for a wonderful evening, Roth. You've been so understanding."

His smile softened, and for a moment his usual sparkle dimmed to something almost tender. "The pleasure was mine, Sadie. Tell me—does your heart belong to someone else?"

Heat rushed through me. I hesitated, staring at the cobblestones. "I…it's complicated."

He nodded gently, as if he'd expected this answer all along. "Matters of the heart usually are. But I hope we can still be friends."

"I'd like that," I whispered, touched by the warmth in his voice.

We said our goodbyes, promising to meet again soon, and as I turned away I felt a familiar weight settle in my chest. Why couldn't I muster more than friendship for Roth? Why did Nathan's face haunt every quiet moment? I realized I had to look inside myself and untangle these messy emotions.

Before I went inside, I glanced around at surroundings. Shadowy storefronts and silent sidewalks seemed to echo my melancholy. Even the brisk wind felt colder, carrying the faint scent of leftover pasta sauce and damp pavement.

When I finally reached my front steps, Mr. Orion padded out of the darkness, his Orion twitching. Normally he'd greet me with a jubilant meow and wind his body around my ankles. Tonight, though, he glided past without so much as a glance. His aloof departure stung more than I expected. Ouch, indeed.

23

Runes, Regret, and Reactions

I slip into the office just after dawn's pale light floods the lobby, my shoulders heavy with the prospect of another day filled with rejection, tangled emotions, and lurking insecurities. The hum of hushed conversations and the tap-tap of keyboards greets me, a chorus of normalcy I'm not in the mood for. Everyone—faces pressed to screens, backs turned to me—suddenly swivels when Kat's sharp voice pierces the quiet.

"Sadie, girl, you must have really captivated Roth on your date last night—he just sent you a massive gift box. It's waiting on your desk."

It's as if gravity shifts; the curious gazes igniting a flush up my neck. I can't bear to meet Nathan's eyes—my cheeks redden at the imagined heat of his glare drilling into my skull. But Kat's triumphant sparkle gives her away: she's well aware of the scene she's created.

My heart thumps as I navigate towards my office. There, atop the pristine wood desk, sits a package so substantial it seems unreal—a glossy black gift box crowned with an emerald-green satin bow. My fingers tremble as I untie the ribbon and peel back crisp wrapping paper, revealing beneath it a jade-green cloak folded like a sleeping creature. Its fabric gleams with a subtle iridescence, and a hood arches into an elegant point—an unmistakable sign of elven craftsmanship.

This isn't merely a garment; it's a warrior's mantle, woven from spun moonlight and secrecy, steeped in elven lore. To my knowledge, no one outside their realm has ever been granted such an heirloom. My breath catches as I unfold it, tracing the embroidery: delicate runes and swirling vines stitched with silver thread.

Nestled in tissue paper is a small parchment note, ink smudged at the edges as if touched by kind hands. My pulse quickens as I read Roth's looping script:

"Sadie,

Thank you for the delightful evening we shared. It's rare to find friendship untainted by politics. I offer you this cloak as a token of our bond. May it guard you against every foe that threatens our realms.

Your friend,

Roth."

A hush falls over me as warmth floods my chest, chasing away the chill of rejection that's shadowed me for weeks. If only my heart could sort itself out so easily. Why can't I feel the same flutter for the handsome Roth instead of Nathan—so smug with his perfect good looks. I glance up to find Kat watching, her jaw dropped and eyes shining with envy.

"Oh my God," she breathes, stepping closer until the ribbon brushes her fingertips. "Sadie, do you realize what you're holding?"

I press a hand to my throat, still stunned. "Yes. It's an elven warrior cloak. Stories say they're crafted with magic strong enough to deflect arrows and dark spells."

Kat's eyebrows soar. "They're sacred heirlooms among the elves. They never give them to outsiders—much less gift one on a whim." She reaches out reverently, brushing a finger over the silver-threaded runes that trace the hem. "You're literally holding a part of their history."

I lift the cloak slowly, marveling at how the fabric pulses with a life of its own, cool to the touch yet humming with power. The intricate vine-like patterns twine across the surface, each stitch glowing faintly as if stirred by my heartbeat.

Kat's voice drops to a whisper: "And Roth—he just… sent you this because he enjoyed a dinner with you?"

I hold up the note again, the parchment murmuring in my hand. "He said it was a token of friendship." The words feel like a gift in themselves, bright and hopeful.

Kat glances between me and the cloak, awe transforming her features. "Sadie, you've made an impression he'll never forget." She exhales, her excitement contagious. "I'm so jealous."

For the first time today, I find myself smiling—cradling a piece of legend in my arms and letting myself believe that maybe, just maybe, I've found a place among friendlier realms.

Kat's hands hovered over the cloak, as if she were afraid to touch it—like it might evaporate, or bite. "What are you going to do?" she whispered. I shrugged. "Wear it, I guess?" The minute the words left my mouth, Kat's face broke into a wicked grin. "Try it on," she urged, already gathering my hair back in a quick twist to help me slip it over my shoulders. The material settled against my skin with a weightless, silken coolness. For a second the office, the city, the noise—all of it went flat and soundless, and I could hear my pulse ticking like a metronome in my ears. The hood, when I pulled it up, dimmed the lights to a blue-green underwater hush, and the silver runes along the seams flared, then faded, then seemed to breathe with each inhale I took.

"Babe," Kat said. "You look like a literal comic book hero. Like, Vampire Hunter Sadie. Or a Tolkien witch, but actually hot." I snort, as she spins me toward the window's reflection. I looked like myself. Only… lit from within, masked in shadow. The cloak didn't make me feel powerful, or hidden. It made me feel… untouchable.

Silas peeks his head in and freezes. For once, the sarcastic vampire who has something to say about everything, cannot form words.

"I'm not saying you could seduce an entire coven of Southern Baptists with that look, but I am saying you might need to sign some kind of ethics waiver before wearing it in public," he managed, then looked at Kat. "Where do you even buy something like that—Roth's private tailor?"

Kat, conspiratorial, plucked a tiny tag from the neck seam. "Not even. Inscribed. This is custom. With your name, Sadie." She turned the fabric to show a line of silver glyphs stitched just under the collar.

My pulse flickered, just a beat of raw animal panic before the pride kicked in. I tried to brush it off—"the elves have a thing for embroidery"—but I caught Silas's sidelong look and had the sense not to finish the thought. He understood. Maybe better than I did.

Silas eyed the drape of the cloak, then dropped his voice: "Don't ever let Blackwood see you in that. He'll combust on the spot." "Maybe I want him to combust," I said, and the words felt lighter than I expected. Truer, too. Just then, Nathan barged in, face a mask of storm clouds and anger.

His gaze drifted over Silas, then Kat, then finally hit me, and if I could have harnessed the voltage in that one look, I could have lit up all of midtown for a week. He went absolutely still, the color draining from his cheeks, and for a second I thought he might actually be struck dumb. But this was Nathan. He never stayed speechless for long.

"Where did you get that?" he said, his voice two octaves lower than usual—dangerous, even for him.

I shook my head, a lock of hair slipping loose from the hood and catching a filament of morning sunlight. "Roth sent it as a present," I said, struggling not to enjoy the way the words made his jaw clench. "It's an elven warrior cloak. Apparently, they're hard to find."

"Hard to find? They don't exist outside of Faewild archives," Nathan said, moving into the office so fast that Silas actually took a step back. He reached out, not quite touching, just hovering his palm over the edge as if I were radioactive. "That's insane. What did you do, save his life?"

"Actually, I just went to dinner with him." I flashed a smile at Kat, who bit her lip to keep from cackling. "He said he enjoyed my company."

Silas, sensing the upcoming drama, grabbed Kat and yanked her out of the office, closing the door behind him as he went. He didn't want to give us privacy, he's way too nosy for that. Besides, he's a vampire he could hear from two floors down if he tried hard enough. No, he wanted to give the illusion of privacy. As soon as the door shut behind them, I made a big show of admiring the cloak before sitting down at my desk to play on my phone ignoring the angry inferno in front of me.

"Take it off," Nathan said, and there was a crack in his voice that startled even him.

"What?" I didn't look up from the phone. It buzzed with a spam text, a fake IRS scam, so I deleted it and waited for him to repeat himself.

He let out a raw, strangled sound, half laugh and half warning. "The cloak, Baker. Take it off. "

"Hashtag, no." I said, still refusing to give him the satisfaction of looking up. "It was a gift from someone who sees me as a true friend and enjoys spending time with me. I'm sorry it bothers you.— Actually, I'm not."

Nathan's hands braced on either side of my monitor, caging me in. His blue eyes bore down, sharp as surgical steel. "You don't know what you're playing with," he hissed.

I smiled up, sweet and guileless. "Are you talking about you or the prince? I gotta tell you Nathan, jealousy is unbecoming of you."

"Sadie, do whatever," he says in that tone he used when we first met. "Date every supe in Manhattan for all I care."

"Thank you for the permission." I say pleasantly which

causes him to only grow angrier.

He actually slammed his fist on the desk this time—not hard enough to crack the wood, because this was Lux Bellator and the furniture was literal indestructible-grade, but loud enough to rattle the pencil cup onto the floor. "Fine," Nathan growled, stepping back, arms crossed so tight I could practically hear the tension in his jacket sleeves. "If you want to show up every day looking like a billboard for cross-realm fraternization, go for it. Just don't come crying to me when it backfires." "Oh, you're such a saint worried about my emotional baggage." I wasn't even sure which layer of sarcasm I was on anymore, but I could feel my cheeks prickling. "Maybe, worry about yourself."

He laughed, a short, breathless, furious thing, as he leaned in close to me. "And what exactly do you mean by that, Baker?"

I took my time answering, because I wanted to get it right. I wanted to slice, not just sting. "I mean you're the one who started this. You're the one who waltzed into my apartment in the middle of the night making me think I was more than just a blip on your radar, then spent the next three days pretending it never happened. You're the king of emotional backfire, so don't pretend you're above it." I hated the tremor in my throat on the last few words, but I powered through.

Nathan stared, jaw set, fingers curled so tight his knuckles blanched. For a moment I thought he might finally say the thing I'd wanted to hear since I was sixteen, but instead he just pulled in a long, raw breath and let it out through his teeth. "That's not fair, Sadie. I—we can't date. We are teammates." His voice cracked. He shook his head, like he could exorcise the feeling out of his skull if he just moved hard enough.

I set down the phone, folded my hands precisely in front

of me, and said, "Okay, that's fine. But, you don't get to be jealous." I braced for the retort, but what I got instead was a silence so total it sucked all the air out of the office.

After what felt like forever, he finally spoke. "I just wanted to make sure you were happy." Another silence—this one softer and a little bit broken. "If Roth makes you happy, good. If anyone does, good. I just—" He closed his eyes, the muscles in his jaw working overtime, and then, with a shudder that seemed to squeeze all the fight out of him, he turned for the door.

I rise, catching his sleeve before he got more than two steps. The fabric twitched under my hand, and for a split second, I thought he might shake me off, but he didn't. He just stood there, shoulders squared, the line of his back as rigid as a brick wall.

"Nathan," I said, "Roth is my friend. Nothing more. The cloak could save my life in the many battles I face, I'm honored to have received it."

His posture softened, just enough that I could see the tension draining out of the sinew between his shoulder blades. "You don't owe me an explanation," he said, voice pitched so low it was almost a growl. "But you—"

I let go, folding my arms like a shield, and waited him out.

"You could have said no," he finished, but the edge was gone. What remained was almost worrying, a hollow disappointment that made me want to set fire to the office just to put him back to rights again.

I didn't dignify that with an answer. I just shrugged, a little, and muttered, "It's not always about you, Blackwood." Then, feeling a weird courage, I added: "But you're allowed to be jealous. As long as you don't make a habit of it."

He turned, and for the first time all day, I saw the real him—the one who had shown up in my apartment, the one who held me like I was breakable and precious all at once. He opened his mouth, closed it, then opened the door, stepping back into the hall with a look that said, Maybe, just maybe, he'd call a truce.

And then he was gone, off to wherever workaholic Nephilim go to brood about their own emotional ineptitude.

I shut the door and slouched back in my chair, staring at the cloak in wonder. I wanted to wear it forever, to let its otherworldly quiet bleach out every ugly thing in my mind. But more than that, I wanted to feel what it meant to be chosen—not just as a tool or a pawn or a threat or a project, but as an equal. A friend, a partner—hell, even a favorite. The runes glimmered under my fingers, catching the late-morning sun, and as I traced the stitched lines, I realized I was smiling.

The day passed in a strange, soft glow. No crisis. No demon lord. Just backlogs and Kat popping into my office every twenty minutes with some manufactured excuse—did I have a stapler, did I want half of her bagel, could she "just, like, hold" the cloak for a second because she wanted to "feel the vibe." By the end of the shift, she'd tried it on four separate times, and the last go-round she nearly made off with it before I chased her down.

When I finally left, the city was in its golden hour—all the buildings edged in fire, the sidewalks fizzing with the last good humor of a Thursday. After hanging my cloak in the closet, I take a moment to refill Orion's bowl with fresh water and food, watching my furry companion as he eagerly dives into his meal. With a sigh, I grab a granola bar from the pantry, its wrapper crinkling softly in my hand. The kitchen's gentle, warm light bathes the room, casting a cozy ambiance. I pick up my phone and scroll through the contacts until Roth's name appears. My thumb hovers over the screen for a moment as I take a deep breath, steeling myself before pressing the dial button. The phone rings a few times, the sound echoing slightly in the quiet room, before Roth's rich, melodious voice fills the air.

"Sadie, what a delightful surprise," Roth greets warmly, his words like a comforting embrace. "I take it you received my gift?"

"I did," I reply, my voice tinged with awe at the memory of the unexpected present. "Roth, it's incredible. I can't believe you gave me something so precious."

I can almost hear the smile stretching across his face as he replies, "I'm glad you like it. I thought it fitting for a warrior of your caliber. And," he adds with a playful lilt, "I may have heard through the grapevine that you could use a bit of cheering up."

A soft laugh escapes me, filling the room with a lighter air. "Let me guess - Kat?"

"Your friend is quite perceptive," Roth chuckles, the sound deep and genuine. "And concerned for you. She may have mentioned some… workplace tensions."

I sigh, my fingers brushing over the cloak's soft, luxurious fabric, its texture comforting against my skin. "It's complicated. But this gift… it really means a lot, Roth. Thank you."

"You're very welcome, Sadie," he responds warmly, sincerity woven into every word. "I meant what I said in the note. Your friendship is valuable to me, and I want you to be protected in your dangerous line of work."

We continue to chat for a few more minutes, our conversation weaving a tapestry of warmth and camaraderie. By the time I hang up, the room seems brighter, and I feel lighter than I have in days. Roth's kindness and the incredible gift have lifted my spirits considerably, leaving me with a renewed sense of hope and gratitude.

24

Bowling, Beer, and Beheading

The next day went by in a rapid secession of minor supernatural disturbances and mountains of paperwork. By that evening, I meet up with Kat, Chloe, Silas, Hadeon, and Nathan at a bowling alley to relax after a monotonous week. The tension between Nathan and me is at an all-time high, so we mostly steer clear of each other.

The alley's neon gloom bounces off the lacquered lanes, turning even the cheapest beer into something resplendent. Kat and Chloe immediately commandeer a table and crash into mutual shit talk. Hadeon perches at the scoring computer, entering everyone's names in gothic type—he insists it's on theme—while Silas hovers, the king of low-stakes menacing, alternating between swiping pizza and making lewd jokes about bowling balls.

Nathan lingers at the edges, phone glued to his hand, eyes periodically flicking up to check if anyone's noticed his disengagement. I notice, of course. Every time. But I pretend to care more about the rented shoes than his proximity. I try to ignore him and that little voice in my head that keeps mocking me with the knowledge that he's probably texting Tiffany right now and that he probably feels nothing about the invisible line we drew between ourselves.

We start our first game. I'm up last in the rotation, which seems to amuse Kat to no end. "Save the best for last, right?" she smirks, hurling her ball so hard it ricochets between bumpers, takes out three pins, and scares a toddler two lanes over. Chloe's a close second, rolling with the feral grace of someone who grew up brawling in abandoned gymnasiums. Hadeon approaches his turn like a chess puzzle, lining up the shot three times and then ghosting the ball straight down the center, a division of pins so mathematically precise I want to clap. Nathan's turn is a whole demonstration in over analyzation and talent.

I line up for my first roll, the ball heavy and unwieldy in my hand. Kat offers a cat call that turns every head in the place; I answer with a middle finger and send the ball careening down the gutter. Perfect.

The night is a comic strip of awkward micro-interactions. I accidentally brush the back of Nathan's hand when we reach for the cheese fries at the same time; he jerks back and knocks over an entire tray of diet sodas. Hadeon drops casual, barbed observations about how the human psyche can be unsettled for weeks by a single unresolved emotional incident ("Not that any of you mortals would understand such torment," he deadpans, eyes flicking to me and then to Nathan). Chloe and Kat try to set me up with the lone bartender who, even after five minutes of relentless banter, only knows me as "the girl who can't bowl for shit." I toast to that. By game three, the rest of the team is comfortably buzzed and I'm starting to believe maybe I'll survive the evening with only secondhand embarrassment.

I wrestle with the growing wave of irritation, trying to suppress it, yet it swells uncontrollably. I can't help but wonder, what does she have that I don't? But then again, maybe I'm overthinking it. Perhaps there's more to this than I can see, or more than likely, I'm just not good enough in his eyes.

"Hey guys, sorry, but I gotta run." Nathan's voice slices through my spiraling thoughts like a cold knife. "I'll see you all Monday." My heart plummets into the abyss, but I'll be damned if I let the agony stain my facade. I muster a quick, detached wave in his direction, donning a mask of indifference as my insides twist.

I bowled a strike on my next turn, out of sheer spite. Kat and Silas mobbed me with hugs, whooping like I'd just cured rabies, but even their cackling celebration couldn't shake the memory of Nathan slipping through the lobby doors, face carved out of stone.

By 10 PM, I've had enough bowling and more than enough pretending that I'm okay. As I am waiting for my ride, the shadows around start to appear darker somehow. I sensed the tell-tale sign of dark magic, and my drunken fogged brain instantly began to clear as adrenaline kicked in. I reached into my bag an pulled out my new cloak from Roth, realizing I'm going to need every advantage I could get as the smell of sulfur hit my nostrils. A demon was nearby.

I carefully pulled my cloak over my shoulders, ensuring it covered every inch of my body. My back pressed against the cold brick wall of the bowling alley as I tried to melt into the shadows, becoming one with the darkness that surrounded me.

My heart thundered in my chest as I cautiously surveyed the dimly lit street, straining my eyes for any sign of the demon lurking in the night.

The putrid stench of sulfur crept closer, and my heart pounded in my chest as I strained to see through the dimly lit street.

The shadows seemed to writhe and twist unnaturally, almost taunting me with their unholy energy.

I reached into my pocket, pulling out my phone. First, I called Kat. Nothing. Then Silas, Chloe, and finally Hadeon. No answer. Shit. What were they doing? I didn't want to, but I was out of options. I tried Nathan, straight to voicemail. Perfect. I frantically type out an SOS message on our group chat, hoping someone sees it soon.

The demon chose that moment to materialize, folding out of the shadow cast by a streetlight, its silhouette human for a heartbeat before the façade slipped.

The demon fully manifested, its red eyes gleaming as it surveyed the area. It was tall and gaunt, with elongated limbs and wickedly sharp claws. Not a type I recognized immediately, which made it all the more dangerous.

The demon was massive, easily seven feet tall with curved horns, an upper-level demon no doubt. It was very rare to see one of those in this dimension.

The demon stepped out of the alley, its eyes locking onto me. A cruel smile spread across its grotesque face, revealing rows of razor-sharp teeth.

"Well, well," it rumbled, its voice like gravel. "What do we have here? Sadie Baker. I hear the boss is looking for you."

Why won't Hell leave me alone?

I steeled myself, pushing down the fear threatening to overwhelm me. This was bad. I was alone, tipsy, and facing an upper-level demon with minimal weapons. But I couldn't let it roam free in the city.

"Sorry to disappoint," I called out, doing my best to keep my voice steady despite the adrenaline coursing through me, "but I'm not much for playing." The demon's chuckle resonated through the shadows, a sound reminiscent of bones grinding together in a macabre symphony. "Spirited little thing, aren't you? I'm going to enjoy breaking you." Its voice dripped with malice. "No, thank you," I replied, my heart pounding like a war drum. "Oh, but I insist." It lunged forward with a speed that defied nature, its razor-sharp claws slicing through the air where I had been standing just a heartbeat before.

Thank God for Elven cloaks and their magical properties, I thought, feeling the cloak's enchantment shimmer around me like a protective aura. I rolled to the side, the ground rough beneath me, and came up in a crouch, a throwing knife poised in my grip. I let it fly with precision, aiming for the demon's eye, the blade slicing through the air like a silver streak. The knife struck true, embedding itself in its target, but the demon merely snarled, its expression a mask of fury as it plucked the knife out with a growl, the metal glistening with dark ichor.

Before I could regain my footing, he was upon me again. I swiftly dodged and rolled across the gritty pavement as my phone began to ring, its shrill tone slicing through the chaotic night. Oh, so now they wanted to talk. Weaving through the labyrinthine streets of Lower Manhattan in a surreal game of cat and mouse, I answered my phone, panting heavily.

"Yes?" I wheezed, struggling to divide my attention between

the relentless pursuit and the conversation.

It was Silas. "Sadie, are you okay? What's going on?"

"Oh, I'm just dandy. Working on my cardio. How are you?" I replied with feigned cheerfulness, trying to steady my breath as my heart thundered from the exertion.

Before he could respond, a deep, guttural growl tore through the air, emanating from the massive demon looming behind me. Its leathery wings quivered with anticipation, and its eyes burned a malevolent red, casting an eerie glow around the darkened alley.

"Sadie, what the hell was that?" Silas demanded, his voice laced with alarm.

"Oh, you know," I shrugged nonchalantly, wiping the sweat from my brow, even though he couldn't see me. "Just your average upper-level demon. We ran into each other and decided to play a little game of tag." My words dripped with sarcasm, masking the adrenaline-fueled tension of the moment.

In reality, this demon was anything but ordinary. Towering over me, its immense muscular frame rippled with an intimidating display of inhuman strength. Yet, despite the terror clawing at my insides, I couldn't let my friend know just how petrified I truly was.

"He is currently it," I grinned, feigning a bravado that I did not feel.

The demon's razor-sharp claws scraped menacingly across the metal of a nearby car, sending a shower of sparks cascading through the air. Instinctively, I ducked behind the vehicle for cover as the acrid smell of burning rubber and sulfur invaded my senses, churning my stomach with a wave of nausea and unease.

"Anyway," I continued, trying to sound casual while remembering I was on the phone, "nothing I can't handle. But if you're not busy, maybe send some backup? It gets boring after a while with just two players."

Silas erupted with a string of curses on the other end of the line. "Shit. Where are you?"

Glancing around frantically, I tried to get my bearings as I sprinted down the dark, deserted street. Flickering streetlamps cast shadows on the buildings, their dim glow barely cutting through the soul-sucking darkness.

"Um, corner of… ack!" I shrieked, diving out of the way of a scorched-earth blast of hellfire. My heart pounded so hard I could swear it was trying to escape my chest. "Corner of West 4th and Jones!"

"I'm on my way, I'll alert the others," Silas said urgently. "Just… try not to die. I don't have time for a funeral this week."

"Working on it," I muttered as I hung up.

I whirled to face the demon, wringing every last drop of arcane oomph from my half-functioning, slightly buzzed brain. The creature stalked closer, claws carving angry gouges in the pavement like a pissed-off parking attendant.

"Clever little witch," the demon snarled, its eyes blazing with fury.

"But your party tricks won't keep you alive long."

It reared back, hellfire coalescing between its talons. I tossed up a half-assed magical barrier. The fireball hit, the shield exploded like my dignity after karaoke night, and I rocketed backward into a parked car with enough force to set off every airbag on two blocks.

Pain bloomed across my body as I crumpled to the ground. The demon's maniacal laughter echoed in my ears. Smooth move, I thought, scrambling to my feet.

I yanked a throwing knife from my boot and closed my eyes concentrating on its blade while picturing a lethal longsword. Transformative magic is not my strong suit. With my luck I'll end up with a balloon animal or something equally as ridiculous, but it's worth a shot. My only shot really. To my astonishment, within seconds, I'm holding a brilliant sword, sharp and deadly, ready to filet a demon.

Fueled by rage—mostly at Nathan—I charged.

It propelled me forward as I struck the demon with deadly precision. I don't know who this girl was, as I dodged and lunged, like the elite fighter I always dreamed I could be.

The sword felt absurdly balanced in my hand, humming with deadly intent. The demon's smug grin faltered, its eyes widening, as if sensing the shift in the air.

"What's this?" it growled. "The little witch has some bite after all."

I ignored it, lunged with surprising speed, and let the blade do the talking. It sliced through tough hide, black ichor spraying like the worst tattoo ever. The wound sizzled on the pavement. The demon stumbled, shock painting its face. Bloody hell, it did not see that coming.

"Impossible," it snarled, backing away slightly. "No mortal should wield such power."

I grinned fiercely, twirling the sword with newfound confidence. "Guess I'm full of surprises."

The demon's shock quickly turned to rage. It lunged at me with renewed fury, claws slashing through the air. I parried its attacks with my magical blade, each clash sending sparks flying. The sword seemed to guide my movements, making me faster and more precise than I'd ever been before.

The demon became frantic in its movements, but I pressed on. Like a warrior of myths, I was everywhere all at once. It seemed we were locked in battle for hours, though it was probably just a few minutes, when he made his fatal mistake. He faked left, but went right, trying to swipe me with his deadly claws. But I saw it before he did it, like an out of body experience, and was prepared. I brought my sword up, slicing through his neck with ease, watching his head fall to the ground and roll away from his body. Eww.

I took a deep breath and looked up into the shocked faces of my teammates who had arrived just in time to see my demon decapitation, a tableau so metal it probably scorched itself directly into their memories forever. Kat's jaw hung open so wide a passing moth could've set up residence in there. Silas, was shocked silent, which was its own kind of miracle. Chloe whooped, loud as an airhorn, and Hadeon just stood there with one silvery brow arched, a curl of admiration—or maybe respect, or maybe just fear—etched onto his face.

"Well shit," Kat finally managed, inching closer as black ichor fizzed hungrily along the curb. "Did you just... is that guy dead? Like, capital D Dead?"

"His head's off, so... yeah." I tried to wipe at my chin, but the ichor had gotten everywhere, spangled up and down my cloak, the Elven runes pulsing faintly as they repelled the worst of it. My hair probably looked like a crime scene photo. "That was gross, by the way. I'd recommend not looking directly at it unless you're into nightmares."

Silas sidled up, peering at the demon's severed head like a kid with a new bug in a jar. "Sadie, that was sick. Literal and figurative." He turned to Hadeon. "That's two decapitations this month. I say we get her a little sticker chart."

Chloe, always ready with a towel or an inappropriate joke, handed me a package of Lemon Scented Wet Wipes. "You were like a warrior out there, Sadie." He voice awed.

I hadn't noticed Nathan standing over to the side, he'd been so quiet and still. But when I looked up through my ichor-spattered hair, he was there, framed by the neon halo of the nearby bar and the sticky black arterial spray pooling beneath the demon's corpse. His expression was unreadable, the muscles of his jaw slack, then tight, then slack again, like he couldn't decide which emotion deserved to break through first: horror, awe, or something else entirely.

He took a half-step toward me, stopped, then came all the way over, slow and careful. I realized I was shaking—either from the fight or because I was about to get reamed out for violating seventeen different safety protocols. Instead, Nathan reached out and, with infinite gentleness, brushed a clot of blood from my cheekbone. His hand hovered there, not quite touching, like he was trying to memorize the shape of my face without breaking the spell.

"I told you to be careful," he said, and his voice was all rough edges, barely holding together.

I snorted, wincing a little as the adrenaline drained and the pain set in. "That was careful. Careful and also very, very awesome."

Kat whooped, then Silas shoved her aside to clap me on the back, nearly sending me sprawling. "She's right. That was next-level. Like, you keep this up, we're gonna get stuck on media duty with the amount of cleanup you're creating." Silas gestured at the demon head, which, even in death, twitched like a thing not quite convinced about its own mortality. "Dibs on the horns!" Chloe cackled, then immediately set about sawing one off with a pocketknife she'd definitely stolen from supply.

Nathan ignored the circus, eyes locked on mine. "Where did you learn to do that?" he said, so quietly I almost didn't catch it over Kat and Chloe's running commentary about how hard it was to get demon blood out of suede.

I shrugged, even though every muscle in my back was singing. "I don't know. It just… came to me." I wiped the blade on my now-ruined jeans and tried not to wobble. He just stared at me for several long moments before boss mode kicked in. "Silas," Nathan barked. "Contact the cleanup crew, have them out here stat." He then turned to Kat and Hadeon. "Go handle the civilians, make sure they stay out of the scene." "Chloe," he continued. "Guard the scene. I'm taking Sadie home." He gently grabbed my wrist, directing me in the general direction of my apartment with a grip that told me the conversation wasn't over.

25

I'm Fine (She Lied)

We didn't speak for the first five blocks. The city was fever-bright around us, sirens bouncing off glass, the Friday pulse swarming louder than either of us could talk over. Nathan kept his hand on my wrist, thumb pressed to the inside where my pulse hammered, as if he needed physical proof that I was still alive.

When we reached my building, he didn't let go right away. Instead, he held on, watching as I tried to key the front door with hands that trembled just enough to fumble. Only when we'd climbed all three flights to my landing did either of us breathe, and even then, it was a shaky truce.

I stopped at my door, blood drying down my left sleeve, and turned to face him. "You look like you're about to throw up," I said, trying to break the tension. My voice was half an octave higher than usual.

"You scared the shit out of me," Nathan answered. For once, he didn't bother with the ice or the sarcasm. He looked exhausted, the more-human-than-not version, and for the first time I wondered how many years he'd been holding himself together with pure willpower and caffeine.

"I'm fine. You forget I have nine lives. It's like a union thing for witches in this city." I tried to smile, but it snagged somewhere on the way out.

He didn't laugh. "You're not fine. You fought an upper-level demon alone. You should be dead." His hand lifted, hovered at my cheek, hesitant. "Sadie, you could have died. You get that, right? Whatever that demon was, it was sent for you. And whoever sent it knows what you are." His words tasted like midnight panic. I looked at the floor, at the battered tip of my left boot, then back up.

"Yeah," I admitted quietly. "Getting that vibe." I get my apartment door unlocked as I stumble inside, Nathan reluctantly following. I dropped the cloak on a chair, shucked my blood-soaked outer layer, and collapsed onto the couch. Nathan stood awkwardly in the middle of the room, caught between flight and the gravitational pull of the couch.

"I can patch myself up," I said, my voice somehow steady despite the night's events. "Thank you for helping me get home."

He ignored that, kneeling in front of me, grasping a kitchen towel, and starting to dab at my arm. It stung more than I let on, but I didn't complain. The weird thing was: I liked it. The careful way his fingers held the edge of the cloth. How he examined my wounds like they were a puzzle he needed to solve. When he finished, he looked up, intense-blue eyes searching my face.

"I'm sorry," he said. "For leaving-for everything."

Words hovered on the tip of my tongue, but they wouldn't come out. The silence between us felt dense, like it could crush us both, yet somehow it didn't. Part of me wanted to tell him it was okay because maybe it was. But another part wasn't so sure. He was with Tiffany, not me, and that was a truth I struggled to accept. "No need to apologize," I finally managed to say. "You leaving early had nothing to do with the demon attack. They've been after me since I got to New York. It is what it is." But even as I spoke, I wasn't sure if I believed it myself.

Nathan pressed a hand to his brow, as if holding in all the things he wasn't supposed to say. "I know that. I just—" He stopped, fingers splayed, then dropped the towel on my thigh and sat back on his heels, legs folded under him like a kid in Sunday school. "I shouldn't have missed your call," he said, quieter now. "You were in trouble, and I wasn't there—." The defeat in his voice sends a sadness coursing through me.

"You were busy, I don't expect you to be at my beck and call." I say, taking the high road when all I want to be is a brat.

"That's not how I see it," he said. "You're my team. You always will be." There was more there, an unspoken confession sharper than any ward or weapon. It hung in the air between us, a live wire threatening to snap. I wanted to reach out, to touch his face or take his hand or just break the damn spell, but my fingers curled tight around the couch cushion instead. "I'm okay," I said again, softer. "I'm not leaving any time soon." I tried for a smile, and this time, it didn't snag. "Plus, I have a magic cloak." He gave me a look. "That thing's going to make you a target," he warned, but there was a tilt to his mouth that meant he wasn't really scolding me. "You should wear it anyway. You're..." He stopped, exhaled, and shook his head. "Never mind." I let the silence spool out, waiting for him to finish. When he didn't, I nudged, "What? I'm what, exactly?" He hesitated, then, as if he was pulling a splinter from his own ribcage: "You're the best thing we've got." He stood up, paced the living room once, twice, then leaned in the doorway, watching me with an intensity that made my skin prickle. "I know I act like a jerk. I know I push too hard. It's because I—" Again, the words tripped on the way out. "I don't want anything to happen to you." He grabs his phone, searching for- something. "I'm going to have someone here at all times to guard you. The demon attacks are increasing; they clearly want you for your angel blessed talents."

"Wait, you're assigning me a bodyguard?" I said, my voice pitched between outrage and awe. "Like, a supernatural babysitter?" Nathan was all business again, as if the last two minutes had been erased and replaced with crisp protocol. "It's not a punishment. It's protection. I can't be here all the time." Of course not, he has *Tiffany*. "And after tonight… we can't risk it. Not with what you're carrying." I bristled at the word. "I'm not carrying anything. I'm just me." He looked at me like I'd missed the point, but didn't argue. "Humor me, Baker." He thumbed a few contacts in his phone and fired off a text, then holstered it with a finality that meant I wouldn't get out of this by debating him. I didn't have the energy, anyway. My right arm felt like it was filled with glass, and the memory of the demon's voice gnawed at the edge of my mind. Nathan stood in the doorway, tense, as if he were waiting for an aftershock. "I'll send someone up to spell your windows and front door tonight," he said. "If you sleep, keep the cloak near. You earned it." "I don't need someone to come and spell anything. Go back to your girlfriend, I'm good." I was so close to be mature. I spin and head towards my bedroom, not even pretending to care if he can find his own way out.

The front door slammed, rattling the frame. I got as far as

the end of the bed, tugging off my boots with one hand, before a sharp, unbidden sob cut through the static of exhaustion. I pressed my forehead to my knee. The room spun gently, like a centrifuge separating every molecule of want from every hard pellet of pain.

Orion leapt onto the bed, sniffed the dried ichor at my sleeve, and then kneaded a persistent paw into my thigh until the ragged breathing settled. I'd never felt more like a little kid, and less like the warrior Nathan thought I'd become. A shudder started in my chest and worked all the way out to my fingers, which still gripped the hilt of a steak knife I'd brought in from the kitchen out of habit, like it would make a difference against the next thing that wanted me dead.

26

Rise of the Jaded Knight

I woke up at dawn, sweat-wet and tangled in the blanket, but alive. Outside, the city was a bruised peach, sunlight spilling over the rooflines. I was feeling every bit of last night's adventure. My body ached, my head was pounding, and I had about a million missed calls and texts from my teammates. I ignored them all as I dragged myself out of bed and into the shower.

As the hot water soothed my aching muscles, I replayed the events of the night before. The fight with Nathan, the demon attack, the magical sword, the other fight with Nathan… it all felt like some bizarre dream. But the bruises blooming across my skin were very real reminders.

Before long, I'm at headquarters even though it's a Saturday thanks to my party with the demon last night. I'm ready to dive into the chaos. But as I stroll in, I realize there's a slight snag: all eyes are glued to me, and a couple of cameras are capturing my every move.

Kat beelines toward me, her face a cocktail of concern and awe. "Sadie, everyone's buzzing about it. You're a hero! The media's calling you the Jaded Knight. Both the humans and the supernatural ones!"

I wrinkle my nose at the moniker. "Why?" I ask. I mean, really? That's a stupid name. Of course, I'd end up with a name that sounds like a medieval stripper.

"Because of your cloak silly. It's the color and because a couple of the witnesses said you looked like a woman jaded. Add to that someone, I don't know who, let it slip about you and Nathan."

I frown at that.

Why do these things always happen to me? And, why couldn't I have gotten a cooler nickname? I've never in my life heard of something so ridiculous. I liked the knight part but, we need to work on that name though.

I shook my head, trying to process this new information. "The Jaded Knight? That's… something."

Kat grinned. "I think it's cool. Very mysterious and badass."

Before I could respond, Stephen, our division chief, stuck his head out of his office like a curious meerkat. "Sadie, can I have a word?" he asked, sounding like he was about to deliver either a compliment or a pink slip.

I shot a nervous glance at Kat, who gave me a thumbs-up and a wink that said, "Good luck, soldier," and then followed Stephen into his office. To my surprise, Nathan was already there, looking as if he'd just been told his internet history was about to be publicly released.

Stephen motioned for me to sit down. "Sadie, I've heard some rather extraordinary reports about last night's little adventure. I need to hear your side of the story."

I took a deep breath and launched into the tale, from the initial demon sighting to the epic showdown that made the last season finale of any TV show look like a kid's birthday party. Stephen listened with eyebrows climbing so high they were practically in orbit.

When I finally wrapped up, Stephen exhaled like he'd been holding his breath since the dawn of time. "Well, Sadie, I'm impressed. We knew you were a valuable member of our organization, but with the media buzz and FanFare your demon battle has stirred up, you're now the new face of the organization."

I sat there, processing his words like an outdated computer trying to run a new software. Media buzz? FanFare? Was I destined to be stuck with that ridiculous Jaded Knight moniker?

"Sadie, are you okay?" Stephen's voice interrupted my internal meltdown. "You look...alarmed?"

"I hate the title. The Jaded Knight thing. It's stupid," I said, grimacing like I'd just bitten into a lemon.

He met my gaze, eyes twinkling with mischief. "I'm sorry to say, I think it's probably going to stick. The paranormal tabloids and the human world news alike are all over it."

Great, just great. I sighed, accepting my fate as the reluctant hero with a cringe-worthy nickname. "Alright, I guess I'll have to get used to it. Is that all, sir?"

"Not quite," he replied, his tone shifting to something more serious. "We need to do a press conference; everyone wants to hear from the Jaded Knight."

Fantastic. Just what I needed—a public debut as the world's most reluctant celebrity.

I forced a smile, nodded, and promised I'd try not to swear too much on live television. Nathan—silent the entire time—stood to leave, but Stephen stopped him. "Stay, Nathan. We need a unified front." He turned to me, softer now. "You're not in this alone, Sadie. If you need anything—protection, resources, time—ask. The media can be bloodthirsty. We don't want you eaten alive."

I mustered another shaky smile and ducked out, straight into the gauntlet of stares, questions, and cellphone flashes. Kat grabbed my arm, steering me like a toddler with a loaded diaper. "Don't worry," she whispered, "after sixty seconds you'll be numb to the whole thing. Pretend you're promoting a miracle skin cream for daytime TV." She mashed my hair into something that almost looked intentional and shoved a tube of lipstick in my hand, daring me to use it.

The press conference was set for noon, an hour of purgatory away. I spent it in the break room, cycling through every possible question I could be asked and every possible way to say "I was just doing my job, please stop calling me a knight." Chloe hovered in the doorway, updating me on the social media pulse ("You're trending!" "People are debating your species!" "Some guy proposed via DM!"). Hadeon offered to run a subtle fae glamour to smooth out the circles under my eyes. Normally I would have said no, but today I nodded and let him work the spell, feeling the tension in my skin dissolve into something almost pleasant, the emotional equivalent of a silk robe after weeks in a burlap sack.

At 11:58, a handler from HR hustled me to the conference room, where the agency's logo hung as a banner backdrop in sharp, authoritative blue. There was a sea of microphones— human media, paranormal blogs, indie podcasts with skulls and pentagrams for logos, even a couple of elven reporters who looked bored and faintly judgmental. Nathan hovered just out of frame, stone-faced and silent.

When it was time for me to speak, I walked up to the podium with my palms sweating and my heart jackhammering so hard I thought I'd vibrate the mic off its stand. The room was a murmuring blur; somewhere, a phone trilled with the ring tone from Scream, and no one even paused.

Stephen delivered his prepared statement and then opened it up to questions. It felt like a dam broke as everyone started screaming my name at once. I felt like a deer in the headlights, but I stepped up to the podium, my heart racing as I faced the sea of eager reporters. The flashing cameras and clamor of voices were overwhelming, but I took a deep breath, channeling the confidence that had helped me defeat the demon.

"Ms. Baker," one reporter hollered over the chatter, "can you tell us more about your battle with the upper-level demon? How did you manage to defeat such a powerful creature on your own?"

I paused, choosing my words like a cat burglar picking a lock.

"It was definitely a wild ride. I leaned heavily on my training, my magical mojo, and a healthy dose of quick thinking. Plus, the team at Lux Bellator has been my rock, prepping me for these kinds of hellish encounters."

Another reporter jumped in.

"Rumor has it you wielded a magical sword in the fight. Is that true?"

I nodded, deciding honesty would save me from a bigger headache later. "Yep, I did wield a magical sword. Think of it as a regular dagger with a magical energy drink—gave me the extra oomph I needed to send the demon packing."

"Ms. Baker!" a reporter in the front row shouted. "What's it like being called 'The Jaded Knight' after your kickass heroics last night?"

I swallowed a groan at the nickname. "I'm just glad I was able to protect the city," I replied diplomatically. "The name was… unexpected."

"Who inspired your jaded vibe?" another reporter piped up.

I felt my face heat up like a toaster oven on overdrive at that personal dig. The room suddenly went quiet, with everyone's eyes glued to me like they were watching a soap opera. I could see Nathan stiffen out of the corner of my eye.

"I'm afraid there's no juicy story there, just a rumor," I stated, trying to keep my tone as even as a yoga instructor's. "My main gig is protecting the city and doing my job like a pro."

The reporter, not one to back down, prodded further. "But come on, surely some deep, steamy emotions fueled your new and improved powers?"

A wave of frustration hit me like a bad hangover. "These aren't new tricks, folks. I've been in magical boot camp my whole life, which is why I could put that demon in its place. As for the emotional saga, I have no idea who cooked up that fairy tale, but it's just rumor, really." The questions kept coming, but I started to relax into it, shifting from deer-in-headlights to slightly-irritated alley cat. By the time the elven blog correspondent asked about the cloak—whether it was a sign of imminent interspecies alliances—I actually laughed. "The cloak's a one-off," I said. "Gift from a friend. No treaties signed, no armies amassed. Unless you count me and my cat as an army. In which case, yes. We are invading Brooklyn." There were a few more rounds of blather—about safety protocols, about the threat of "supernatural escalation," about whether I planned to run for office (I laughed so hard

I almost snorted). And then it was done. I was officially the Jaded Knight, bane of upper-level demons and darling of clickbait headlines everywhere. I had survived the press conference, and if I never saw another microphone again, it would be too soon.

As I staggered offstage, Kat and Chloe gave me a standing ovation from the hallway, while Hadeon (already back at his computer) emailed a list of memes featuring my unfortunate new nickname. "I'll print t-shirts if you want," he wrote. "For the brand." I ducked into my office and collapsed into the spinning chair. All that public speaking had left my mouth dry and my brain leaking from my left ear.

I sat there, letting the silence stretch, until a soft knock tapped at the door. It opened a crack, and Nathan's face appeared in the gap. For the first time in weeks, he looked less like he was bearing the sins of humanity and more like, well, a guy who'd just seen his ex's face plastered all over the city. "Is it safe?" he asked, tone soft enough that it might have been mistaken for concern.

I rolled my eyes, but couldn't keep the corners of my mouth from twitching. "Only if you promise not to call me 'Jaded Knight.' Or make a big deal about this morning." He stepped inside and closed the door, hands tucked in the pockets of his slacks. "You were great up there," he said, and for a second, he looked almost bashful. "I mean it." Coming from him, those words weighed more than all the bouquets and congratulatory emails in the world. I shrugged, picking at a scab of glitter stuck to my wrist from Kat's 'emergency war paint.' "It's not exactly what I signed up for," I admitted, voice low, "but… it could be worse." Nathan drifted to the edge of my desk, gaze flicking to the sunlit band of cloak on the back of my chair.

"Sadie, I know things are weird between us. I know I've messed up a lot when it comes to you, but I want you to know I care. You have become a part of the team." He said, his voice steady with conviction. "And a friend." He adds so softly I barely hear him. While his words are kind, they break me all the same. My feelings for Nathan aren't relegated to the friendzone, but that is all he is offering.

I nodded—what else could I do? I tamped the hurt down so deep it vibrated through my bones, and I forced a small, brave smile. "Thanks, Nathan. That means a lot." And it did. Even if it also kind of sucked. He moved to the doorway, hands flexing at his sides like he was fighting to keep them in his pockets. "Do you… want to grab lunch?" he finally asked. "Or, we could hang here. Whatever you want, Jaded Knight." He tried for a joke, but it came out tired and raw. I could have lied, told him I had meetings or a stakeout or an existential crisis to attend to. Instead: "Lunch sounds good." Maybe if I said it out loud, if we ate a sandwich like normal people and didn't mention the tension between us, it would all be okay.

27

One Truth, Then War

We grabbed sandwiches from the food cart downstairs and ate on the fire escape, perched above the humming city. We sat in silence, both lost in our own thoughts, swinging our feet and occasionally flicking balled-up napkins at eachother. At some point, Nathan reached over and brushed a stray bit of lettuce from my cheek with a thumb that lingered too long for "just friends," then immediately looked away as if the sun was suddenly fascinating. "You know how I told you I remembered you at the retreat?" He asked.

I pause, not expecting him to bring this up, but curious what he had to say.

"Yeah?" I say coming out more like a question.

His mouth twisted into a quirky half-smile, half-grimace. "I meant it when I said our interaction stuck with me. You were the only one in that place who didn't try to butter me up. While other girls were practically throwing themselves at me, you stood there rolling your eyes like I was some cheesy magic show."

His voice carried a hint of awe as he reminisced. "I spotted

228

you right away, thought you were the most stunning girl I'd ever laid eyes on, but you seemed less interested in me than in watching paint dry. I eventually cracked that joke about parlor tricks, trying to get under your skin. You flipped me the bird and blew me off. I couldn't get you out of my mind. Then, as fate would have its laugh, you end up on my team years later, and, well, you know how that story goes." I sit there, floored by his revelation. I had no clue that he was just as affected as I was that day. To cut the tension, I toss out a joke. "I'm sure that must've put a dent in your overinflated ego."

"More like a crater," he laughed, the sound soft and self-effacing, almost sweet. "Honestly, you ruined me for every woman that came after. None of them had your… attitude."

"You mean, my emotional baggage," I shot back, but this time it was an olive branch, not a barb.

He looked at me sidelong, blue eyes crinkling. "That too. I've never been good at admitting when something matters to me." He nudged my foot with his. "You're not easy to get over, Baker. It'd be easier if you were."

I tried to play it cool, but my heart rattled inside its ribcage. We ate in companionable silence for a while, the city's energy a swirling halo around us. Down on the street, a delivery guy wrestled a hand truck over the curb, cursing under his breath. Somewhere in the next building, a saxophonist warmed up, wheezing out the same crooked scale again and again. The world continued to spin, oblivious.

Nathan finished his sandwich and gazed straight ahead. "I know I'm not supposed to say this, but I wish things were different." He pinched the bridge of his nose. "I wish I could go back to the first night. Do it right. Tell you what I was thinking instead of hiding behind all that… protocol."

I was at a loss for what to do with that bombshell. My mind was screaming to probe deeper into his relationship with Tiffany. They might not have been officially dating, but she was constantly orbiting him, a planet drawn by an unspoken gravitational pull. The harsh truth, however, was that it didn't matter. Nathan was ironclad when it came to rules, and the rules were absolute: teammates couldn't date, no exceptions.

I mustered the last of my composure, folding the sandwich wrapper into a perfect square. "It's fine, Nathan. Honestly. I don't need a do-over. I just want to know that you'll have my back, whatever happens." I tried like hell to give the words the finality they deserved, but he saw through it—he always did.

His lips parted, searching for a reply, but he closed them and nodded instead, as if that was all he deserved. We watched the city in silence, each of us bracing for whatever fresh hell the universe was bound to serve up next.

The quiet lasted until Kat texted: Emergency. Conference room. Now.

We slid down the fire escape and darted through the side entrance, Nathan trailing half a pace behind me. The entire team was already there, fanned out around the longest table in the Lux Bellator arsenal. Chloe bounced on her heels, Silas looked deadly serious (a bad sign), and Hadeon had his laptop open, displaying a shaky video still.

A demon. Many demons. "Alright, everyone knows their roles." Nathan's commanding voice booms. We will handle containment and evacuation of any civilians still inside. Remember, these are upper-level demons we're dealing with. Stay alert and watch each other's backs at all times. Baker, you're shadowing me. No arguments."

I didn't argue. Not this time. Kat flashed me a thumbs-up

and flipped her hair, cocky as a rockstar. Chloe snapped her gum and loaded a tranquilizer gun with rounds that, if half the rumors were true, could drop a rhino at twenty paces. Hadeon muttered under his breath, scrolling through arcane sigils on his screen, as if the only thing separating us from doomsday was one well-timed copy-paste.

28

The Fight Before the Fall

We geared up, holstering weapons and re-checking charms and comms. The elevator ride down was three floors and forty seconds of pure, collective dread.

"We're going in loud?" Silas asked, just to be difficult.

"No," Nathan said, adjusting his earpiece. "We go in smart, we go in tight. If anyone gets isolated, call out once and fall back. This thing has already killed two of ours. We're not losing anyone tonight."

The words hung heavy in the car as we barreled through the dusk toward the Lower East Side warehouse. It was just starting to rain, a thin scum of water slicking the windshield, turning the world outside into a smeared watercolor of brake lights and neon. I pressed my forehead to the glass, counting the seconds between lightning and thunder, pretending it was a countdown to something cleaner than what waited ahead.

Inside the warehouse, the air was thick with the copper tang of blood and the colder, sweeter burn of sulfur. Four bodies on the loading dock, each flayed in a way that said "message" as much as "murder." The city's finest had already cordoned

232

off the block, but it was clear nobody really wanted a piece of this scene. That was what they had us for.

We fanned out, sliding between crates and stacked barrels, Nathan on point and me close behind, his eyes a pale phosphor in the gloom. The team moved like a single organism: Chloe and Kat circling the perimeter, Silas and Hadeon hanging back as rear guards. Silas with a loaded crossbow that looked like it had been dragged straight from the set of a B-movie vampire flick but was, in fact, the real deal.

Up ahead, fire flickered in a holding bay—a bonfire built entirely from packing pallets and what looked, distressingly, like the legs of a mannequin. Please be a mannequin. The heat rising off it was wrong, not the clunky assault of regular flames but a dense, vibrating pressure that made your molars ache. In the retreating darkness behind it, I saw the outlines: one tall, angular thing with horns like a spiral staircase, one shorter but broader, bunched with the kind of muscle you only saw on nightmares and Renaissance statues. Demons. More than one. We circled the fire, closing the gap with the slow, practiced menace of people who'd been through this dance before but still felt the cold bite of its music. Nathan's hand found my shoulder, squeezing once—don't move until I do—and then he slipped forward, cat-quiet, into the ring of smoky light. The demons saw him instantly. "Nephilim," the tall one hissed, voice peeling the words open like a can of battery acid. "Come to play, or just to watch?" "Neither," Nathan said. "We're here for the bodies. You can leave now and keep yours, or we do it the hard way." The second demon laughed, a sound like pipes bursting in a frozen house. "She's the one," it said, its gaze flicking past Nathan and straight to me. The force of it almost made me stumble. "The angel-blessed. My Lord will be pleased." I could feel it, a kind of psychic static crawling up my arms—the awareness that the fire wasn't here to burn, it was for show, and what mattered was all the shadows it created.

The first demon lunged, jaws dislocating with a crack, and Nathan launched into motion, faster than I'd ever seen him—sword erupting in blue fire, arcing up in a vertical slash to parry the horns before they could gut him. The clang sent white sparks chewing up my vision. I dove left, blood singing in my ears, rolling behind the maze of crates and drawing a runed chalk from my belt.

The fight was sound and blur, echo and heat. Chloe harried the second demon around the perimeter, peppering it with tranquilizer darts, each of which sparked and fizzed as they hit. She remained human for now, but I know her wolfy side was ready to play. Silas was to her right using his crossbow to mow down demons. Hadeon was attempting a bit of fae magic while Kat, in her lion form was a flurry of jaws and claws.

I stuck close to Nathan as he requested.

Things went sideways, fast. The lead demon realized it had a limited window before the odds evened up, and with one monstrous bellow, swept its tail through a row of barrels, sending them flying. I braced, ducked, and felt two hundred pounds of aluminum drum graze my shoulder blade, the pain a red flare through my whole left side.

The distraction was enough. The second demon, still pursued by Chloe, doubled back and powered straight through the fray, arms outstretched for me. Nathan shouted, a split-second warning, but I barely heard it—there was just the sickening lurch of being yanked off my feet, claws closing around my ribs like a bear trap, the world going blurry and then impossibly bright as the demon hurled us both straight through a sheet of plastic into the chained-off sub-basement.

We hit the concrete with a meaty thud, and for a second I saw stars. The demon was on me in a heartbeat, claws at my throat, jaws already drooling that same black ichor. It was smiling, if you could call something with no lips and too many teeth that. Its words were a wet rasp, hotter than the blood trickling down from my scalp.

"You're coming with us," it said. "Alive or—"

I didn't wait for the finish. I jammed my thumb into its eye, shoving back with every ounce of leverage the gym and Nathan's training had hammered in.

It screamed, lurching back, but I rolled with the motion, landed a kick to the hardest part of its knee. Something gave— a cartilage pop—and it staggered, cursing in a language that burned my ears. I scrambled upright, drawing the emergency salt capsule from my boot. The demon, either too hungry or too stupid to check itself, came for me again. I cracked the capsule in my hand, salt splattering everywhere; its skin hissed, peeled back, and for one glorious moment, it was blind and leaking.

I ran.

There was no plan, but my feet carried me through the maze of half-lit corridors, the only light a flicker of emergency strobes and the low hell-glow that trailed every step I took. I could hear more demons, their voices multiplying, converging. I ducked into a side room, slammed the door, and pressed my back to the chipped concrete as the demon's howls echoed closer.

Then—silence. That special, pre-impact hush that warned

you something worse was coming.

A fist punched through the drywall next to my head, claws missing my ear by a hair. Plaster exploded in my face, grit filling my mouth, and I bit back a scream. Another hand. Then, the outline of a face in the gap—teeth, eyes, the writhing tangle of alien hunger.

I ran for the opposite wall, shoulder-checking the filing cabinet that waited in the corner.

It toppled beautifully, slamming into the demon's midsection and pinning it for the split second I needed. I vaulted over the desk, slipped in a puddle of my own blood, and crashed through the exit door into the main sub-basement. There were more voices now—some human, some not—and feet pounding the stairwell above.

Nathan's voice cut through the noise: "Sadie! Where—"

"Down here!" I shrieked, ducking another set of claws as the demon wrenched itself free, now limping but even more determined.

Nathan barreled in with the full incandescent violence of his angelic blood, sword burning so hot it seemed to swallow the shadows instead of make more. He didn't hesitate, not for a beat. The blade went straight through the demon's side, blue fire cauterizing the wound even as it split the torso nearly in half. The thing went down, not dead but howling and writhing, and Nathan spun it one more quarter-turn before driving the hilt square into its forehead.

"Move," he said, tone clipped and terrifyingly calm. His eyes raked over me just long enough to make sure I was in one piece, then he wrapped my left arm over his shoulders and bodily dragged us back towards the stairs.

The warehouse sounded like a slaughterhouse now, screams and gunshots and the guttural chuff of demons in freefall. Kat met us at the bottom of the steps, fur matted with gore, one ear torn nearly in half but eyes wild and alive. "Two more up top," she shouted. "Chloe

is almost out of darts." She gnashed at a demon's ankle as it thundered past, refusing to let go even as it tried to kick her off. Nathan kept us moving, pushing me up the stairs in front of him like a pawn he was determined not to lose. We burst out onto the main floor just as Chloe dropped the magazine on her tranquilizer gun and went for her backup—two wicked little knives, one in each fist. She flashed me a bloody grin. "Last stand, babe," she hollered, and together we ducked behind a splintered crate as the lead demon shrugged off three crossbow bolts and bore down on us with the dreamy patience of a nightmare that knew it could take its time.

"Plan?" I gasped, struggling as blood poured into my eye, bright and slick like liquid fire. Kat had maneuvered around, fiercely grappling with the demon's legs; Hadeon uttered an incantation, each syllable vibrating the air with the ominous potential of an explosion if he finished in time. Nathan locked eyes with me, his gaze wild and blue, searing like a blast furnace. "Hold the line," he commanded, urgency dripping from his voice. "We've got seconds for a banishment. If we falter—" His sentence was violently interrupted by a colossal demon, its razor-sharp horns scraping against the ceiling as it launched a lethal attack at him. "You cannot stop what is coming!" it roared, its voice a thunderous quake that shook the very foundations of the building, sending shivers tearing through our spines.

"What's coming?" I shouted, desperately deflecting a crushing blow from another demon. "Who's coming?"

Suddenly, the ground beneath us convulsed violently. The demon we battled froze, a malicious grin stretching across its grotesque face. "It begins," it growled, its voice like the grinding of stone. "The gate opens. He comes."

That doesn't sound good.

29

The Gate Between Worlds

The ground beneath our feet continued to rumble, cracks spreading across the concrete floor. A deafening roar filled the air, drowning out all other sounds. "We need to get out of here!" Nathan shouted over the noise, grabbing me around my waist, pulling me along with him. "The whole building's coming down!"

I could barely hear him, the cacophony was so all-consuming. But I followed, trusting only in the hard, calloused feel of his hand and the desperate certainty in his voice.

We sprinted up the stairs, weaving through debris and the bodies of the wounded—some demon, some human, some too mangled to tell. Ahead, Chloe and Kat had formed the kind of barricade you only see in movies: a wall of gutted vending machines, scavenged rebar, and, somewhere in the wreckage, a Caution: Wet Floor sign that seemed wildly insufficient. Kat, in full beast mode, was all muscle and teeth, jaws snapping through the air between us and the surging horde. Chloe, bloodied but still on her feet, swung a steel bat in perfect, ugly arcs, each blow landing with sickening, satisfying thuds.

Behind us, the warehouse buckled. Support beams screamed as the ground fissured wider, a black-purple light seeping up from below like some anti-sunrise. For a moment, the demons stopped fighting. They just stood, backs to us, heads bowed, waiting for whatever was coming up through those cracks. I felt it in the pressure of the air, the way your bones know a storm before your brain does.

A rumble, then a shriek. The world went sideways. The warehouse roof peeled back, a trick of pressure and magic, opening like the top of a sardine can. A cyclone of shadow spewed upward, shot through with runes and hellfire. Time slowed around the vortex or maybe it was a portal? Voices stretched and wind battered us flat to the tarmac, until the city itself seemed to draw one long, terrified breath.

The center of the cyclone pulsed, then spat a figure onto the broken cement. Not a demon—at least, not any kind I'd seen before in real life. He was beautiful, almost human: seven feet tall, a muscular build, cheekbones made for GQ, and black wings that stretched out behind him in a macabre display. This was the fallen angel from my nightmare. I'm pretty sure this is also the 'he' who wanted me for my angel blessed powers.

He landed with a seismic crack, his bare feet shattering the pavement. For a moment, he simply stood there, wings furled, head bowed, the light caught in the blue-black silk of his hair. Then he looked up at us, and I saw that his eyes were not the empty pits of a demon's but obsidian glass, deep and greedy, rimmed in gold. He smiled—a real, dazzling, straight-to-the-marrow smile. For a flicker, I almost forgot we were running for our lives.

"She is here," he said, and his voice was the last few elegant notes of the band before the Titanic sank into the water. He looked straight at me, through Kat and Chloe and the wall of vending machines, through the rebar, through whatever petty glamour I might have conjured to make myself small. "Hello, Sadie."

My mouth went dry. I felt, for the first time, the living weight of the cloak on my shoulders—how it trembled, how the runes along the seams prickled against my collarbone. The fallen angel took a few lazy steps forward, as if to a lover, not a war. The demons dropped to their knees in his wake. "You are as lovely as I had hoped," he said, tilting his head just so.

The sight of him made the back of my jaw ache with terror, and some darker, more embarrassing curiosity. Every cell in me screamed to run, but it was like being caught in the gravity of a black hole—one wrong move and I'd be nothing but memory.

Nathan pulled me back, one arm crushing around my waist. His other hand fumbled for his sword, never breaking eye contact with the angel. The blade flickered with a pale blue light, not nearly as bright or wild as before. I could feel the fear in his grip, could taste it on the air, pungent as cordite.

"What do you want?" Nathan managed, his voice flat—like the question was tactical, not existential. The fallen angel did not flinch; in fact, he looked delighted. "Nephilim, you must be Blackwood. They said you would be trouble." His eyes flicked to the sword, then to Nathan's hand still tight around my arm. "But she isn't yours to keep," he crooned, and for a moment—for a heartbeat—his gaze bored so deep I felt my own soul skitter sideways, looking for somewhere softer to hide.

I barely noticed Hadeon and Silas flanking from the shadows, or the subtle shift as Kat and Chloe braced to pounce if the world ended, which it basically already had. The angel looked up at the ruined ceiling, then back at me, a genuine sadness in the cant of his shoulders. "You are tired, Sadie. Why do you run? You know already that this is what you were made for." The words, meant to comfort, landed like coffin nails. I tried to summon a snarky rejoinder, but my tongue was glued in place. "I don't know what you want," was all I could manage, and I hated how scared I sounded. The angel's smile grew softer, almost paternal. "I want what we all want," he said. "To come home and your power is going to get me there."

"You're not taking her," Nathan said through clenched teeth. He planted himself in front of me, sword raised, all knight-in-shining-armor from the old stories. The fallen angel gave him an indulgent smile. "You are brave, Nephilim. Predictable, but brave."

He fixed his gaze on me once more, utterly disregarding the sword aimed at his chest, and in that fleeting moment, a cold, unwavering certainty washed over me—he could kill Nathan with nothing more than a thought if he could leave that circle he was in. Something tells me he is bound to that circle. Thank God for small miracles. Just then, a blinding explosion erupted behind the fallen angel, yanking his focus away for a split second. Nathan didn't hesitate; he seized my hand with a desperate urgency, and we bolted, hearts pounding with the weight of impending doom.

We crashed through a fire door, down a concrete stairwell, and out into the rain-choked night. Headlights swept over us from every angle—cops, first responders, at least two news vans already on the scene. Nathan didn't let go, not even when we were clear of the building and could have blended into the panicked crowd. He pulled me under the dark lip of a delivery truck and pressed me hard against the cold metal, his chest heaving, water pouring from his hair and nose and chin. He looked alive, more than I'd ever seen him, even if half that life was terror. "Someone report." Came Nathan's urgent whisper. "We're okay." Chloe said, breaths coming out ragged. "Silas, Kat, Hadeon, and I are about a block away from the warehouse. It appears the fallen cannot leave the area. Perhaps he is bound to the location and that's why he needs Sadie?" She mused.

"Or he's playing with us," Silas said, voice more wired than usual. Nathan nodded, jaw set. "Get yourselves safe. Do not engage. I'll regroup with you at the fallback." He clicked off the comm and sagged, still bracing me against the truck like I might take off if he loosened his grip. The downpour drummed on the metal, washing away the blood and sweat from my face until I could almost imagine it was just rain, and not the world's worst day. I coughed, shivering. "You can let go. I'm not going anywhere." "I know," he said, but didn't move. His hand slid up to my jaw, thumb gentle at my temple, and for a second it was like we were floating, pressed together in the hush left after a car crash, the city's chaos on mute. "You okay?" he asked, his voice shredded down to its real shape. "No," I answered, "but I like that you asked." He started to say something else—a confession or a curse, I'll never know because his phone started to ring.

He let it ring, eyes flaring up to the rain-sick sky in a gesture of pure, miserable comedy. Only when it stuttered into silence did he speak. "It's not her, you know. Tiffany is—" He fumbled for a word, found none, left a chasm where the proper noun should be. "She's just-"

"I don't care." I say, voice as hard as a stone surface. "Really.

Date her or don't, it's none of my business."

But he shook his head, like if he could just get these last words right, something would change. "I care, Sadie." There was a desperation in it, some rope fiber in his throat pulling tight. "I care so much I can't think half the time. Would it help if I told you that there is nothing serious between Tiffany and me. We go out sometimes, but we are not together."

"No, Nathan, it would not." I say confused as to how this makes him sound better. "You are using Tiffany, while playing hot and cold with me. Also, you've said it yourself, we can't be together because we are on the same team."

"I'm not using Tiffany." He responds, voice tinged in irritation. "We agreed to keep things casual. She knows there's someone else. Someone I would give my life for."

"Well, as messed up as that sounds, Nathan." I explain. "We need to get out of here before we dig any deeper into your romantic shortcomings."

He almost smiled, but didn't, just let his head fall back against the van and exhaled rainwater and regret. "Point taken." He straightened, eyes hardening to battlefield blue. "Let's get out of here."

We peeled off the side of the truck, circled through the crowd (which, by then, had thickened with every species of bystander and gawker and journalist in the city), and made our way east toward the fallback: a coin-operated laundromat that doubled as a secure comms hub for Lux Bellator. Inside, Kat was already human again, her arm wrapped in a bloody dish towel, and Silas had commandeered some sewing needles for some kind of impromptu field surgery on Hadeon's thigh. The only real daylight came from a row of flickering overhead fluorescents and the endless, hypnotic spin of the dryers. I'd never been happier for the smell of detergent in my life.

Nathan ran point, checking all the exits and windows. Then he turned to the rest of us, every muscle in his jaw set to 'Don't Interrupt Me.' "That was a fallen angel," he said, no preamble, no comfort. "He's hunting Sadie. He'll escalate until he gets her. I need honest answers: did anyone else see or hear something—anything—he did that could give us a weakness?"

Heads shook, one by one. Even Kat, who usually could be counted on for a snide remark, just pressed her lips together and stared at the floor.

Nathan leaned against a dryer, face in his hands. He looked more tired than angry now, like the weight of inevitability had finally cracked through. I leaned into him, not sure if he or I needed the hug more.

He blinked, and then folded me closer, using one hand to cradle the back of my head like he was working out how much longer it would be until I shattered. The fluorescent lights stuttered overhead, the world shrinking down to the bones and heat of his body and the faint reek of sweat and cheap soap. For a long minute, neither of us spoke; it was almost like sleep comforting and familiar.

The spell broke when Chloe, voice echoing in the cinderblock echo chamber, said, "So, what do we do now? Wait for him to knock again, or…?"

Nathan straightened, releasing me slow, and his face was bleak but clear. "It appears as though he has not fully manifested in this realm. Something is holding him back. Our number one priority is getting Sadie to Stephen to see what he wants to do next."

It was dusk when we reached the Lux Bellator tower, the lights on every floor blazing like a manic Christmas tree.

Stephen was waiting for us in the lobby, flanked by two security guards and an assistant with the permanently startled look of someone who had once been abducted by a poltergeist and never fully recovered. "You're late," Stephen said, but there was a catch in his voice that made me think maybe he'd doubted we'd come back at all.

We took the elevator up to the top floor, the executive suite reserved for moments like this. Stephen, was already waiting for us.

"First," Stephen began, "the fact that the Fallen have made open contact changes the game." He looked at me in a way that made even the inside of my skin itch. "Sadie has always had unique abilities. We now have confirmation that the other side sees her as a — linchpin, for lack of a better word."

I braced, waiting for the new assignment that would either get me killed or promoted in the next forty-eight hours.

"Your mission," said Stephen, "is to keep the Fallen from making direct contact with Sadie again. Your secondary mission is to find out what their endgame is. If the rumors of a gate opening are true, we need to identify the location and seal it before they finish whatever ritual they've started."

He turned to Nathan. "Blackwood, as usual you're lead on this. Choose your team and your tools. Pull in outside help if needed—this isn't a 'solve it in-house' job anymore."

Nathan nodded, eyes flicking sidelong to me and then back to Stephen. "Understood. We'll need a warlock. Preferably one willing to take risks, not just tinker with candle magic."

Stephen nodded. "I'll get someone in here immediately. Everyone but Sadie, you're dismissed." My heart sank as the rest of the team filed out, leaving me blinking in the chill vacuum of executive air conditioning. I forced myself not to fidget; the last thing I needed was to look like a kid called to the principal's office, even as every nerve in me screamed to run for the stairs.

30

The Other Side of Always

Stephen regarded me for a long, unreadable beat, fingers drumming a low, arrhythmic pattern against the glass surface of his desk. "I won't waste your time," he said, finally. "This is bigger than you, or me, or any one of us. You know that, yes?" His voice was gentle, almost fatherly, which unnerved me more than a week's worth of demon attacks.

I nodded, fighting the urge to fixate on the grid of security screens that loomed behind him, each flickering ominously with the chaotic aftermath we'd left at the warehouse. His voice cut through the tension like a knife. "What I need from you now isn't just compliance. I need your trust." The word trust reverberated through the room, dense and intentional. "You're going to feel isolated. Targeted. Maybe even betrayed. That's exactly this fallen's- Azazel if our intel is correct-plan. Divide and conquer. Throw you off your game." He leaned forward, his glasses reflecting the harsh light, turning his eyes into unreadable voids. "Sadie, I've scrutinized your file. I know you've got the grit to handle this. But things are spiraling into peril, danger closing in on you and your team. It seems Azazel is restricted in movement, leading me to one precarious option. It's far from perfect, but it's all we've got. I want to extract you from New York, relocate you to a smaller Lux Bellator site where you can vanish from prying eyes and lurking demons. Disappear off the grid for a while."

The words hung in the air, echoing.

I tried not to show anything—fear, relief, the strange pang of knowing some part of me wanted to stay, to see how close I could get to the sun before my wings melted. "When?" I asked, the word crisp and businesslike.

"Tonight," Stephen said. "As soon as possible."

"Do I get a say in the matter?" I asked, almost idly, trying to gauge if this was truly a last resort or just the best play for HQ's insurance premiums.

Stephen tilted his head. "You can say no. I won't force you. But if you stay, the collateral damage will escalate. Azazel is fixated, he needs your power to make a full comeback on earth. And his methods… well. We've both seen what he's willing to do. I want you alive, Sadie. Preferably in one piece."

I looked down at my own hands, remembering how the sword felt in them, how the running felt, how Nathan felt when he said he cared. Alive, sure. In one piece? Harder to picture.

"Where are you sending me?" I asked.

He forced a strained, taut smile onto his lips. "Relax, it's not Outer Mongolia if that's what's gnawing at you. It's Chicago— still a sprawling, bustling market, teeming with supernatural law enforcement demands. You'll be camouflaged in the open, operating under a fabricated identity while we concoct an elaborate narrative for your sudden vanishing act here in Manhattan.

Yeah, but no Kat, no team. No, Nathan. I want to refuse, but Stephen is right, I'm putting my team and others in grave danger by sticking around New York.

It's not a death sentence, just an exile. I agreed, because I'm not a monster, and because the look in Stephen's eyes told me it was already decided anyway. He handed me a burner phone, a fake driver's license with my own face and an absurdly Midwestern name ("Samantha Wexler, really?") and an envelope sealed in red wax. "Your go-kit is downstairs. The car will take you directly to the airport—after making a stop at your apartment to gather your things. Tonight at sunset, you're officially off the map." "Can I—" I started, then bit it off, realizing I wasn't sure what I was even asking for. "Can I say goodbye to my team?" Stephen hesitated, then: "Quickly. And make it subtle. No dramatic farewells: the walls have ears." I took my envelope, my new name, and the sudden weightlessness of imminent flight, and walked out of the office feeling less like a pawn and more like a piece someone had just sacrificed for the endgame. Downstairs, the bullpen was deserted. The only sign of life was a flicker from Kat's desk lamp, and the faint echo of Silas's playlist from the break room. I slipped past both, not trusting myself to hold it together if I saw any of them.

I creep down to the lobby, hiding in the shadows as though they can hide me from whatever lay ahead. Just as I reach the doors, Kat's voice calls out behind me. "Sadie, wait up!" I turn to see my whole team, Kat, Hadeon, Chloe, Silas, and Nathan at the top of the escalator, standing in an uneven row like a firing squad or maybe—in some dark, sweet way—a family. Kat was first down the steps, her wild hair shining even in the sodium lobby light, and she grabbed me hard, arms locked so tight it was almost a tackle. "What happened with Stephen?" She asked with a hint of worry in her voice. "I'm having to go underground for a bit. And before you ask, I can't say where." Kat's jaw dropped, all impulse and fight, like she might actually try to storm the admin suite and claw the answers straight out of an executive. "Don't you dare pull a lone wolf, Baker—" "It's not a choice," I said, surprising myself with how calm I sounded. "Orders. They're moving me off the board until things cool down." I smiled for her, for all of them. "It's not a forever thing. Just a— relocation." For a moment, nobody spoke. Not even Silas, who usually managed to find a one-liner for every fresh trauma. It was Chloe who broke the silence, her voice wobbling with something so raw it made my own throat sting. "You're not coming back, are you?" I managed a shrug. "If I'm lucky, I'll get reassigned here when this shitshow burns out. If not, well—" The idea of living in Chicago and fighting were-mobs in the Midwest, felt so abstract that even my anxieties couldn't get a grip on it.

I kept my head down, unwilling to glance at Nathan yet, in case the composite of his face—concern, regret, an uncoiling of all the words he'd never say—somehow undid the shape of my dignity. Silas offered a lopsided salute, and Hadeon did that little nod that might have meant respect or just an aversion to hugging in public. Kat squeezed my forearm until I wondered if she'd draw blood. "You better call," she threatened. "Every damn day. Or I'll find you and murder you for real." Chloe was the last to step forward, her eyes wet but her voice dry as tinder. "We'll keep the home fire burning for you." The way she said it, I almost believed it wasn't goodbye, just a holding pattern, a comma and not a full stop.

And then there was Nathan.

He waited till the others dispersed, pretending to check their phones or pick at the grout in the marble lobby floor. Even now, the gravity between us yanked at my ribs and throat, but I rooted my feet and met his gaze straight on. He looked every inch the war hero: shirt stained with some mix of rain and demon blood, jaw set as if by a team of surgeons. He didn't speak, but the silence between us was already a conversation, loaded with edits and revisions and things we'd both deleted for each other's sake.

He reached out, almost tentative, his fingers wrapping around mine. "You don't have to do this," he said, voice low and rough. I blinked, hard, refusing to let the moment dissolve into tears. "Yeah, I do. Everyone is in more danger because of me."

"At least tell me where you are going," he begged. The composed man I am used to was nowhere to be seen as Nathan was almost frantic. Tears filled my eyes as I told him, "I'm not supposed to tell anyone, but I will try to stay in touch."

He tipped his forehead to mine in a gesture so gentle the pain of it was almost holy. When he stepped back, his smile was crooked and thin, but real. "See you on the other side, Baker."

I closed my eyes, pulse hammering, and said, "Watch your back, Nephilim."

He smiled. It was a small, sad smile, "Always."

I turned, made it two steps and then turned back. "Hey Nathan?" I called causing him to lookup. I launched myself into his arms for one last, desperate hug and for a moment, I thought I might splinter under the force of it. His chin found the curve of my shoulder, his hands flared against my ribs—one ink-smudged, the thumb worrying at my jacket seam—and

I felt him breathe me in, like if he committed me to memory at the molecular level, it would be enough to hold. He didn't say anything. He just held on, like he wasn't sure when he'd get to do it again, and maybe neither of us would have bet on the odds.

I broke first. Not for lack of trying. He let me go with a shudder, and when I looked up it was like we'd rehearsed this in a thousand other lifetimes: the same broken smile, the same unsaid apology, the same hope colliding against the far wall of sense and circumstance. I didn't look back after that. I walked straight out into the neon New York dusk, blinking hard, pulse a wild, stuttering thing. The taxi was waiting at the curb, just where Stephen said it would be.

31

The Last Look Back

My apartment was exactly as I'd left it: boots still drying on the radiator, three text notifications from Kat unanswered, Orion burrowed in the laundry and nursing a vendetta against my newly hemorrhaging absence. The suitcase I'd never really unpacked came out from under the bed, followed by the crumpled black dress from the Roth dinner, the ruined jeans, the elven cloak, and three chargers for burner phones past and present. I debated packing the framed picture of Kat and me from her disastrous birthday party but left it on the counter where I could see it, just for now.

I gathered Orion into his battered carrier and stood in the middle of the living room, surveying the strata of my old life—coffee rings on the table, business cards jammed into a shot glass, the battered armchair that still smelled faintly of Silas's aftershave. Maybe if I closed my eyes, I could convince myself I was about to meet Kat for drinks, or trade barbs with Chloe over cold pizza, or even walk out into the hallway and bump into Nathan on his way to some other disaster.

But the city outside was different now, humming with a new,

predatory quiet. I double checked the windows, left the keys on the counter with a note for the next unlucky tenant, and walked out without looking back.

The car was waiting at the curb, a nondescript sedan manned by a driver whose eyes never quite met mine. "Airport?" he asked, already shifting into gear. "Yeah," I said, and watched the city unreel in reverse: the corner deli with the hand-lettered sign (OPEN 24/7—or until we get murdered!), the subway entrance pulsing with regret and old gum, the tired scaffolding clinging to brick like the city's own scab. It all looked the same, but I'd become the ghost. At JFK, the driver handed off a slim envelope of cash and my "official" travel docs, then gave me a nod of such practiced indifference that I almost thanked him for it. I wheeled my suitcase to the check-in, shouldered Orion' grumbling crate, and did the whole civilian charade in a fugue so deep I barely remembered my own name, fake or otherwise. The terminal food court was full of people pretending not to cry over plastic trays. I found a table by the window, unzipped the carrier, and let Orion squirm free onto my lap. He kneaded my thigh mercilessly, purring loud enough I had to nudge him to keep it down. "New city, new rules, buddy," I whispered, giving his chin a scratch. "Try not to get us noticed before we hit the baggage claim." He blinked, unimpressed. I watched the slow progress of the clouds dragging their purple bellies across the skyline, watching for any announced sign of apocalypse, or at least a glimmer of 'You made the right choice.' There wasn't one. There was only the dull ache of abandonment, and the odd, sour taste of freedom. When my flight finally boarded, I handed over my ticket, breezed through the gate, and fell into the last window seat, staring out at the fading sun.

As I stepped onto the plane, a whirlwind of emotions churned violently inside me. Excitement crackled for the new adventure ahead like an electrifying current, yet sadness clawed at my heart as I left my team behind. A persistent, gnawing ache throbbed in my chest, one I desperately struggled to ignore. Pressing my head against the cold window, I forced myself to rest as the plane began its slow, steady taxi. My gaze was fixated on the iconic New York skyline, a city where I had transformed beyond recognition—growing into a seasoned agent, forging unbreakable bonds, confronting unimaginable perils. I had fallen deeply in love, only to be thrust into a life-or-death escape.

A heavy lump rose in my throat as the plane roared to life, lifting off the ground, the sprawling cityscape shrinking beneath us. This was no longer a dream; it was a stark reality—I was leaving New York, leaving Nathan, maybe forever behind. But as we soared to 10,000 feet, a crushing weight began to crumble from my shoulders. My friends would be infinitely safer, spared from the tempest that followed in my wake.

Thank You for Reading

Thank you so much for reading *The Jaded Knight.* This story has been a labor of love for the past few years, and it means the world to me that you've joined me on this journey.

If you'd like access to exclusive extras—like bonus chapters, monthly gift card giveaways (yes, I bribe my readers with gift cards—no shame), behind-the-scenes content, and more—be sure to join my reader newsletter here.

Come for the freebies, stay for the shenanigans.

About the Author

While for her fictional tales she goes by her pen name, Eliza Nevius, you may know her by her real name, Erin Egnatz. When she isn't chasing ghosts, wrangling college students, or decoding ancient ruins, she's spinning tales that blend romance, fiction, and sometimes a touch of the paranormal. A published author, seasoned ghost hunter, and professor of history, archaeology, and English, she is also the creator of *Hauntings Around America*—a platform dedicated to all things eerie and unexplained. Armed with a BA from Central State University and an MEd from the American College of Education, she has been featured in *Newsweek*, Fox Chicago, WAVE TV, Fox Cincinnati, NBC Seattle, and beyond. She lives somewhere between chaos and caffeine with her husband, three kids, two dogs, four cats, and one incredibly judgmental bearded dragon.

You can connect with me on:

🌐 https://www.phantompublishing.com
🐦 https://x.com/PhantomPubllc
📘 https://www.facebook.com/alexa.phillips.16503
🔗 https://www.elizanevius.com

Subscribe to my newsletter:

✉️ https://phantompublishing.com/newsletter

Also by Eliza Nevius

The Burning Vow (Book 2 in The Lux Bellator Series)

Hiding in plain sight was a risky plan.

After a devastating confrontation with the fallen angel Azazel, Sadie is forced to vanish from New York under a fake identity, exiled to the shadows of Lux Bellator's Chicago branch. With her magic on lockdown and enemies closing in, Sadie walks a razor's edge between duty and self-destruction—all while pretending to be someone she's not.

Back in New York, her old team isn't handling her absence well. Nathan, the Nephilim commander who never quite said what he meant, risks everything to find her. Kat, Chloe, Silas, and Hadeon are uncovering forbidden rituals and ancient relics that point to a single solution: The Burning Vow—an angelic bond powerful enough to protect Sadie and sever Azazel's grip on the human realm. But the vow comes with a cost...

When the veil between worlds thins and a final, cataclysmic ritual is set in motion, Sadie must choose between saving the people she loves and unleashing a force that could unmake her.

Heart-pounding, magical, and laced with a slow-burn romance that scorches, The Burning Vow is a fierce continuation of the Lux Bellator series—where loyalty is tested, love is forged in fire, and the only way out... is through the flames.

Professionally Unprofessional (Book 1 in The Strategically Chaotic Series)

A Romantic Comedy

Lexie Phillips has a bestselling novel, a thriving start-up publishing house, and a closet full of sarcastic T-shirts—but not a clue how to share office space with the six-foot-tall finance bro next door who looks like he was raised by spreadsheets and arrogance.

After years of working out of coffee shops and converted garages, Lexie and her best friend Maci finally land their dream office in a sleek downtown Chicago high-rise. Bound Books Publishing is on the rise, the paint is barely dry, and success finally seems within reach.

Enter Ben Maddox: brooding, brilliant, and built like every bad decision Lexie's ever made. His financial firm occupies the space across the hall, and from the moment they meet, it's clear they're oil and water—with a side of combustible chemistry. He's precision and pressed collars. She's coffee stains and chaos. He thinks her "business" is cute. She thinks his face would look better with a book thrown at it.

Ben is precision in motion—until his firm needs him to impress a new client who values family men and flashy lifestyles. That's where Lexie comes in, his smart-mouthed neighbor and brand-new fake fiancé. Their fake engagement is supposed to be strictly business. No feelings. No drama. Definitely no flirting.

But when late-night strategy sessions turn into stolen glances and tequila-fueled confessions lead to lakeside kisses, things start feeling a little too real. Add one rockstar memoir, a random escape to Vegas, and a confession that rocks them to their core and all of a sudden being "professionally unprofessional" might be the smartest move either of them has ever made.

Fake dating was never meant to feel this good… or get this complicated.

Full of laugh-out-loud moments, sharp banter, and slow-burn heat, Professionally Unprofessional is a love letter to ambition, found family, and the kind of romance that shows up when you least expect it… usually wearing a tie.

If you loved The Hating Game and Beach Read, get ready to fall for the sarcastic slow burn of Professionally Unprofessional.

Professionally Unraveled (Book 2 in The Strategically Chaotic Series)

The other side of the chaos, control, and completely unplanned love story.

Benjamin Maddox has everything under control—his firm, his future, and his finely tailored life. As the youngest partner at one of Chicago's most prestigious financial firms, Ben lives by one rule: feelings complicate the bottom line. But all that control unravels the moment Lexie Phillips stumbles into his office building with a chaotic energy and a mouth that doesn't know when to quit.

Their fake engagement was supposed to be strategic. A polished illusion to help land a multimillion-dollar client. But the longer Ben plays the role of Lexie's fiancé, the more the lines blur—and the harder it becomes to remember where the performance ends and the truth begins.

From awkward elevator run-ins to tequila-fueled confessions, Ben is forced to confront the emotions he's spent a lifetime avoiding. Lexie challenges his every instinct—and makes him want more than just professional success. She makes him want her.

But when secrets, exes, and Lexie's fear of vulnerability collide with Ben's own emotional blind spots, their carefully built façade comes crashing down. To win her back, Ben will have to risk the one thing he's never risked before—his heart.

Told entirely from Ben's perspective as it dives into the mind of the man behind the suit, exposing the insecurities, passion, and quiet longing beneath his polished surface. Get ready to fall in love with Ben Maddox all over again.

Note: This is a companion novella to Professionally Unprofessional from Ben's Point of View.

Strategically Inappropriate (Book 3 in The Strategically Chaotic Series)

Maci has a plan for everything—except maybe her own love life. As the co-founder of Bound Books Publishing, she's used to controlling chaos, not starring in it. But after an alcohol fueled one-night stand with her friend Eli occurs, that chaos she has been trying to avoid hits her head on. Now, everything is messy. Crossing that line has made things awkward. Add to that the emotional crisis that is her best friend, Lexie, and Maci's life has turned into one big ball of drama.

Eli doesn't do relationships, emotions, or spontaneous anything, but Maci seems to be the exception to his rules. He thought they could keep things casual—until his ex resurfaces, his family starts pushing for a reconciliation, and Maci starts dodging him like he's contagious. Suddenly, he's not so sure detachment is working out.

When Lexie and Ben rope them into helping plan their wedding, the romantic tension between Maci and Eli goes from simmer to full-on inferno. Between rogue glitter explosions, cake disasters, and tipsy grandmas, the line between friends and lovers is not just blurred—it's basically a smoldering crater.

Now Maci has to decide: is she brave enough to break her own rules for a chance at something real?

And can Eli finally open his carefully guarded heart—before he loses the one person who makes him want to?

Because love? It's never part of the plan... but sometimes it's exactly what you need.